I0699628

Sacred Ponds

by

R B Koester

Bronze Press

All incidents and dialogue, and all characters with the exception of some
historical figures, are products of the author's imagination and are not to be
construed as real. Where real-life historical figures, institutions, or parties
appear, the situations, incidents, and dialogues concerning those persons,
institutions, or parties are entirely fictional and are not intended to depict
actual events or to change the entirely fictional nature of the work. In all
other respects, any resemblance to actual persons or parties, living or dead,
events, or locales is entirely coincidental.

Published by Bronze Press, LLC
www.bronzepress.com

Library of Congress Control Number: 2025909982
ISBN: 979-8-9914155-4-5

Acknowledgments

I would like to thank Pamela Kelley for her initial review of my writing, Anthony Mangano for his insights and support as my invaluable writing coach and editor, Maya Myers for her honest and thoughtful reviews and assistance with editing, Matthew Ricciardi for proofreading, and my family for encouraging my writing.

To Jen, Lauren, and Audrey

Sacred Ponds

Part I

Marmoutier Abbey

Carolingian Empire, circa 800 AD

1. The Abbey

In a clearing near the front of the abbey gate, Pierre waved.

"Pass the ball," he yelled at Jean. He was open, and any pass from the outfield to the midfield would score a point. The boys were playing Phaininda, a game originating in Rome that they had made their own by adopting a rule that the ball had to be passed at least twice within a team before one could score. It made it more of a team sport.

Reluctantly, Jean complied. "Go ahead, try your luck, Pierre," Jean yelled as he passed the ball. Pierre caught it, but was blocked and could not get it to the midfield. Instead, three of the players from the opposing team pushed him violently out of the field. It took three of them, given that Pierre was tall and muscular, but they managed.

"Don't ask for it if you are not free," Jean whispered as Pierre stumbled into the bushes at the edge of the dark forest that overshadowed the abbey and obscured both the sun and the view of Tours, the town in the valley below.

"He always does this," Jean said to the other three boys on their team. "Head of the team, but not part of it." The other boys nodded, adjusting their robes to shelter from the cold autumn air.

All the novice monks looked the same in their robes, but they were not. Jean was privileged, the son of a nobleman. In the Carolingian Empire, there were only about one hundred such noblemen, and they held absolute power, interacting directly with Charlemagne. Jean, however, did not care for status. He had persuaded his parents to let him have an education, at least for a few years, something they would come to regret.

Pierre represented the opposite end of the spectrum, and he knew it. He was an orphan with no family connections that he was willing to discuss. He yearned to be like Jean, or even better, like Jean's brother, who was being groomed to take over his father's position—an ambition different from Jean's that consumed him.

Despite their differences, they had become friends; at fifteen, they were the two oldest novices. What they had in common, above all, was a healthy disrespect for the older monks, though for different reasons. Pierre thought they were too reverent of each other and Rome, while Jean thought they were too restrained and should lead a fuller life.

When Pierre returned, it seemed that no one was waiting for him; instead, the boys were squinting into the setting sun, watching as a wagon pulled up the muddy road that led to the abbey. Two oxen drew the wagon, and its wooden wheels squealed as they rolled over rocks in the road. The beasts were struggling up the hill to the abbey.

"It must be him," Jean said as he started to run toward the abbey, leaving the other boys behind. They had been awaiting the arrival of Alcuin of York, the scholar recently assigned to lead the abbey. Jean wanted to be the first to tell Father Lucas, an older monk with whom he did special science projects after school.

"We think we're the best school in the empire, but he won't be satisfied with that," Pierre said to the other novices as they watched Jean run towards the abbey. Jean was surprisingly fast for his short, skinny body.

"There will be changes," Pierre said emphatically, trying to make eye contact. The other young monks looked down and nodded emotionlessly. They were intimidated by Pierre. He was not only older than them, but his piercing blue eyes seemed always to threaten confrontation.

The boys let their shoulders hang. They did not understand who Alcuin of York was or what ambitions he might have for the abbey. They were disappointed that the game had come to an end.

Jean was out of breath when he reached Father Lucas' study. "He is here!" he said in a high-pitched voice, trying to be dramatic.

"Who is here?" Father Lucas asked. Father Lucas was a quiet, contemplative man who preferred thought over action and refused to participate in Jean's excitement.

"Alcuin of York! I wonder what he's brought with him." Jean said, having caught his breath.

"Don't get your hopes up," Father Lucas said quietly. "Whatever it is, it won't be scientific books," Father Lucas continued, rising to join Jean. He was tall and towered over Jean. "Everyone is afraid of science—blasphemy, blasphemy."

Father Lucas and Jean left the study and walked across the barren courtyard toward the church, the only light and airy indoor space in the abbey. Everywhere else was dark, damp, and smelled of mold. The earthiness of the abbey resulted from the infrequent cleaning the monks gave it.

The monastery bell, a piece of pride for the abbey, rang six times as Father Lucas and Jean crossed the courtyard. It was time for Mass. In the courtyard, they walked by Alcuin of York and monks greeting him. Alcuin looked up in the direction of the bell as it rang. "I have brought six books with me," he said. "The one by Bede should go to whoever made the clock."

Jean turned to Father Lucas and raised his eyebrows. Father Lucas gave the slightest nod, but Jean could see the smile playing behind his eyes, for he had made the clock. Bede was one of the most respected English monks and biblical scholars at the time and was also known for his work on calendars. Any book of his was sure to be a treasure.

2. Alcuin's Sermon

"Jesus drew near and said to them, 'I have been given all authority in heaven and on earth. Go, then, to all peoples everywhere and make them my disciples. Baptize them in the name of the Father, the Son, and the Holy Spirit, and teach them to obey everything I have commanded you!" Alcuin had chosen the reading from Matthew 28 for the Mass he was officiating in honor of his arrival.

"The New Testament is clear. Convert everyone. No one can be left behind. When we recite the Nicene Creed, we proclaim one holy, catholic, and apostolic Church. One Catholic Church. Catholic from the Greek 'katholikos' meaning 'universal' and 'whole' or 'all-embracing.' Four hundred years ago, a council of bishops established the creed we recite in every Mass. Soon, we will have more councils to proclaim the right and only faith."

The words reverberated inside the high stone structure of the church as though they were the word of God—the echo amplified by the church being devoid of decorations except for a large cross, a simple altar, and wooden benches, all made of the same dark oak from the forest around the abbey. There was nothing to capture the imagination.

Pierre was the only novice who was paying attention. He watched the older monks' reverence. They were awestruck by Alcuin, and it dawned on him that religious knowledge equaled power.

Jean, meanwhile, was thinking about the wagon that had brought Alcuin. The wheels and axles fascinated him. One wheel on a wagon meant it would tip over; two wheels would make it hard to unload; three wheels would make it hard to turn. Four wheels made sense. Jean smiled. It was all a little silly, but he liked entertaining himself this way, particularly during boring sermons.

Alcuin proceeded to the communion part of the Mass, the sharing of the bread, the Eucharist, which mirrored Jesus' last supper before his crucifixion.

"Our unity with Christ is affirmed in the Eucharist, in which we share the body of Jesus Christ. As John 6:53–56 tells us, unless you eat the flesh of the Son of Man and drink his blood, you do not have life within you."

Pierre never understood this part: the actual body of Christ, his blood. Why? If all we eat comes from God, it might make sense, but Pierre knew it was meant to be more literal about the actual presence of God during communion. He rolled his eyes, but no one saw.

Of course, Pierre was not alone. No one in the monastery truly understood it. But what was worse was that they did not care. Marmoutier Abbey had the foremost academic reputation in the Carolingian Empire, but this was based solely on knowledge of doctrine, rather than understanding the underlying reasons behind it. No one ever asked for reasons and preferred the "mysteries of faith."

"Mysteries should not create power," Pierre told Jean at one point. Jean was the only one he would trust with such thoughts. Jean, however, shrugged it off. Science, not power, interested him.

After Mass, the brotherhood moved to the dining hall for dinner. The room was half the size of the church but had a vaulted ceiling, a fireplace, and tables with chairs that were more comfortable than the benches in the church. In the back of the room was a door to the kitchen, which was always open, allowing the sounds and smells of food preparation to permeate the room. It pushed back the usual smell of mold.

The dining hall was always busy with monks catching up. It was the only place where everyone relaxed. However, today was different. Alcuin's presence added formality. The monks chose seats according to seniority, with only the most senior monks seated near Alcuin. However, Pierre broke ranks. He did not select Alcuin's table, but one near it filled with middle-aged monks so he could listen to the newcomer's conversation. Pierre did not respect the intrigue of the brotherhood, but he wanted to learn from it. Over the noise, he unfortunately could only make out parts.

"An enlightened homily," one of the monks said to Alcuin with an unusual formality in his voice.

Another senior monk was more daring and asked what they were all wondering: "We are so far from York. How did you come to be appointed to head our abbey?"

"I met Charlemagne outside of Rome…" Alcuin started answering, smiling, happy to be able to boast. "The Lombard King Desiderius had once again tried to take over the papacy. He laid siege to Rome, but Pope Hadrian held him off by threatening to excommunicate any soldier who entered the city." Alcuin chuckled slyly. "It was enlightened. It gave Charlemagne enough time to come to Rome to rescue him. Our holy father is smart."

Alcuin straightened in his chair and continued as the senior monks stole glances at each other. They did not like his boasting.

"At the same time, I was asked to come to Rome by King Elfwald of York, who wanted me to persuade Pope Hadrian to name York an archbishopric. He felt that I could impress the holy father with all our religious and academic work. Little could the king have known that when I got to Rome, I'd find the holy father far more concerned with survival than academics. Anyway, I met Charlemagne just outside of Rome."

"So Charlemagne asked to see you?" the senior monk asked, flattering Alcuin.

"Indeed. Apparently, unlike Pope Hadrian, Charlemagne is intrigued by my work." Alcuin continued. "Do you know that he started our meeting by discussing the decision at the Council of Nicaea that Jesus is one with God and not his adopted son? What a peculiar topic for him to raise."

Alcuin did not share his skepticism about Charlemagne's interests and intentions. Charlemagne was widely known to be a ruthless conqueror. Clans he defeated were required to convert to Christianity on the spot or die. He had been particularly brutal with the Saxons, demanding not only their conversion but also destroying their sacred shrine, the shrine of Irminsul. When a Saxon tribe later attacked a Carolingian settlement and killed two dozen nobles, Charlemagne orchestrated a revenge execution of 4,500 Saxons, earning his nickname: Butcher of the Saxons. Alcuin did not believe that such a ruler was interested in the niceties of religious doctrine. He suspected Charlemagne had an ulterior motive but had not yet figured out what it might be.

"Charlemagne asked me to become a scholar at his court in Aachen," Alcuin continued proudly. "I am to head up the school where his children study, the Urbs Regale. Naturally, I told him I was a monk and an academic, so he agreed that I could reside here at Marmoutier Abbey when I am not at court."

"The Urbs Regale? Isn't that just a military school?"

"Currently, yes, but I intend to expand its curriculum."

Alcuin felt he had justified his appointment, but the senior monks wasted no time huddling when supper ended. They left to meet in the back of the church. It was a private space. One just had to speak quietly to avoid the walls amplifying what one said.

Pierre imagined they were upset. The monks grew up together and were a close-knit group. They had even avoided having a head monk by anything but title. They preferred a council of elders who grew up together. Even Father Lucas was part of that group despite the monks being scared of his scientific endeavors.

The idea that a complete outsider would lead the abbey did not sit well with the brotherhood. They also did not like the respect Alcuin coveted.

"He seems rather pompous," one of the senior monks said as they commiserated in the back of the church.

"I hate the idea of someone who has the ear of Charlemagne being at the abbey," another added.

3. Schooling

Pierre and Jean woke the next morning to the abbey bell calling everyone to morning Mass. Morning Mass was short and to the point. Homilies were kept to a minimum. Everyone wanted to get on with the day. For the pupils, that meant lessons in the dining hall.

On their way there, Pierre and Jean stopped in front of the small room that served as the library, though its complete collection contained only a dozen books covering religious topics. Abbeys would exchange books and copy them to add to their collections. Alcuin's books were already proudly displayed and were sure to be copied soon.

Father George stood behind a desk, examining a book, and proudly nodded when he noticed Pierre. Father George was one of the younger monks at the abbey. He had a constant smile and the rare talent of knowing Latin, Greek, and Hebrew. Pierre, too, was gifted at languages and assisted him after lessons.

"There they are," Pierre whispered to Jean as Father George grinned. Father George enjoyed Pierre and Jean being "brothers at arms," as he liked to joke.

"Yes, except one of the books will be given to Father Lucas," Jean said as they walked on.

Jean elbowed Pierre. "Oh, it must be killing you that I know something you don't about what is happening at the abbey." It was true; Pierre was usually well-informed, and Jean was not.

"I don't care," Pierre said, but he did, and Jean knew it. Pierre always wanted to be informed because he was secretly trying to devise a plan to leave the abbey. Only the sons of parents who paid for their education were allowed to leave the abbey. Jean was, but Pierre, as an orphan, was not. Pierre had this insatiable desire to succeed, to prove himself, away from the abbey. It was a way to fight his ever-present feeling that wherever he was, he did not belong.

Jean was still smiling as they entered the dining hall for their lesson. Pierre gave him a stern look when he noticed. He was not amused.

"You take things too seriously," Jean said and shrugged his shoulders as they found their seats.

The first lesson involved the scriptures. Father George led it. He usually arrived late, but was particularly late that day. It was hard for him to tear himself away from the new books he received.

"Pierre, you read the first passage," he said as he made his way to the front of the room. Lessons involved someone reading a Bible passage from the morning Mass in Latin and translating it. Father George liked to ask Pierre to read since he did not want to call on him to translate. Pierre enjoyed showing off his proficiency in languages.

One of the other students stumbled through the translation with the occasional help from the class. Everyone was happy when he was done.

No discussion about the passage's meaning followed; the class simply went on to another passage.

This method taught them the scriptures, Latin, and camaraderie. When Father Lucas took over the class, he was told it was how it had always been done.

The second lesson involved math. Tabulation of numbers was essential for administering the abbey and its vast holdings. Every monk was expected to learn rudimentary math. Jean excelled at math and frequently assisted other students in solving problems alongside the instructor. The instructor allowed it because he needed the help and because Jean's humorous and easygoing approach to math made the otherwise dry subject fun. Jean genuinely liked the subject matter.

That day, however, Jean was distracted. He kept thinking about the book that Father Lucas was sure to receive. Alcuin had said it had to do with the clock. The clock Father Lucas had invented was an interesting device made up of two bowls. He'd drilled a small hole in the first bowl and recorded how much water dripped into the second bowl between two sunrises. Then, he put twenty-four small marks into the second bowl, one for each hour. Every day, the top bowl was filled with an exact amount of water, and one of the novices would ring the bell whenever the water reached a mark in the second bowl. Jean wanted to know why Alcuin would wish for the maker of that clock to have the Bede book. Could this finally be their first scientific book?

Jean and Pierre each left the math lesson quickly and without talking. Each was preoccupied with what the new books might have brought for them.

Pierre went straight to the library to see Father George, who shouted "Catholic!" when Pierre entered. Father George's constant smile was rooted in seeing the humor in many things. Pierre smiled even though he did not appreciate the humor. Still, he gladly responded, "Universal!" Pierre remembered the linguistic lesson from Alcuin's homily. Father George quickly wrote "καθολικός" on a piece of parchment. Pierre looked at it and said, "κατά" means "about" and "ὅλος" means "whole," so catholic is about the whole or "universal."

"Your Greek is coming along well."

Father George usually spent the first half hour with Pierre teaching him Latin or Greek and the remaining two hours translating texts while Pierre sat beside him, trying to find words that Father George did not know. The abbey had two copies of the same book, one in Latin and one in Greek. Pierre could help Father George decipher unfamiliar words by finding the same words in both books. It was tedious and slow, but it worked, and it resulted in Pierre learning Greek.

"Did you see the senior monks at the evening Mass? They were in awe of Alcuin," Pierre commented.

"In this day and age, you get ahead by knowing the Bible," Father George said, raising his eyebrows.

"He will change things, won't he?"

Father George nodded and insisted that they start their work.

When Jean finally arrived at Father Lucas' quarters at the far side of the abbey, he found him hard at work reviewing the Bede book. When he was young, Father Lucas had been allowed to travel to study texts on mathematics, geometry, and astronomy. The notes from those trips were the only scientific documents the abbey had. One book would be a tremendous addition.

"Do you know what this book is mainly about?" Father Lucas said without looking up, and before Jean could make funny observations about the goings-on.

"What?"

"How to determine the day Easter Sunday falls on."

Traditionally, Easter was determined to fall on the Sunday after Passover. The Council of Nicaea decided that the determination of Easter should be independent of the Jewish calendar. The Jewish calendar had sometimes resulted in Easter falling before the spring equinox, which was deemed inappropriate.

"Finally, a book for us, and it's about fixing a religious date." Father Lucas said, slightly outraged. "It figures."

"Oh." Jean slumped.

"I've read enough." Father Lucas put the book aside, took a piece of parchment, and smiled at Jean. "Now, look at this. One of the monks traveling with Alcuin taught me how to multiply Roman numerals."

Jean drew nearer. The concept of multiplication was familiar to them, but they had always accomplished it through addition. If they needed to multiply a number by five, they added it five times.

Father Lucas drew a line on the parchment. "You create two columns. In one column, you write the first number, and then you successively divide that number by two, discarding the remainder until you end up with one. In the other column, you write the other number and successively multiply it by two until you reach the row where you ended the first column. Then, you eliminate all the rows where the number in the first column is even. Lastly, you add up all the remaining numbers in the right column. The sum of all the numbers in the right column equals the product of the two numbers."

Father Lucas went through an example. He showed that V times XXI equaled CV.

"No! You think this works?" Jean said, incredulous but beaming with enthusiasm.

Father Lucas and Jean abandoned the usual formalities between a novice and an older senior monk when they worked together. They were too excited about whatever they were working on. Theirs was a brotherhood of scientists.

They tried several examples. Each time, it worked. Then, they tried to determine a pattern. Why was it that one eliminated all the rows with even numbers? There had to be a reason for this, but they could not figure it out.

Finally, Father Lucas carefully but with some disrespect picked up the Bede book. He put it in front of Jean and said, "The book fixes Easter as being on the Sunday following the full moon that falls on or after the spring equinox. We can use the clock to determine the spring equinox when the sun rises and sets in twelve hours. From there, it is easy to figure out the day of the next full moon and the Sunday after that. We can anticipate the equinox by measuring the change in daytime and projecting when it will be twelve hours."

Jean hunched over the book, already studying it.

Father Lucas then stood up and took on a more serious posture. With his tall body towering over Jean, he patted Jean's shoulder. "I am going to see Alcuin. He will be excited to hear that we can determine Easter Sunday for the empire here at the abbey. In the meantime, you should study the book."

Jean shared Father Lucas' disappointment about the Bede book and did not listen to him. As soon as Father Lucas left, he went back to roman-numeral multiplication. He wanted to figure out why the new method worked. Why was it that one eliminated every second row? Or was it every row with an even number? He got a little frustrated because he couldn't remember. He played around frantically with some numbers to reconstruct what Father Lucas taught him. Relief only came when the abbey bell rang twelve times, indicating time for the midday meal.

Unlike dinner, which immediately followed Mass, the midday meal began with a prayer, followed by announcements. The meal usually consisted of a bland stew of barley, wheat, or rye. The only hope for vegetables was at dinner. Meat was reserved for special occasions such as festivals.

The announcement that day was about Alcuin's arrival, although it was hardly news. Alcuin was asked to say a few words.

"I have been asked by Charlemagne to teach at the Urbs Regale. We will expand the curriculum there, and I have agreed with the senior monks to do the same here. The Marmoutier curriculum will be expanded to include music and grammar. I am happy to announce that we have developed a motto for this school: *Studium, incite, et docere*. Study, learn, and teach."

Jean smiled at Pierre upon hearing this, and Pierre smiled back. They both lost respect at a young age for the little pretenses the church created for itself, or the petty sayings or ceremonies they fretted over. Of course, they did not admit this to anyone.

When all the pupils met in front of the abbey after the meal, the students commiserated over the potential changes. It finally dawned on them that they would have to devote more time to their studies.

"I told you," Pierre said, darting his eyes amongst the novices.

"It is not all bad," Jean responded, smiling hesitantly. "Alcuin brought books, including one that shows us how to determine which day Easter Sunday falls on."

Pierre raised his eyebrows. He wished that Jean had a better sense of situations.

As Pierre suspected, Jean was immediately beaten down by one of the other boys. "Who cares which day Easter Sunday falls on?" Everyone laughed.

Jean's father's status did not impress his fellow novices. They considered him too studious and had little respect for what he was doing with Father Lucas. Jean regretted having gotten carried away and lowered his head. He was relieved when the novices left to play hide-and-seek in the woods. Pierre and Jean never played. Pierre, for some reason, did not like playing the game.

Hide and seek consisted of dividing into two teams. One was dubbed the Carolingian team, with a boy playing one of Charlemagne's generals, and the other was dubbed the Saxon team, with one of the boys playing the Saxon leader Widukind. The Saxon team hid in a forested area near the abbey, and the Carolingian team marched into the forest carrying sticks as swords. It was a boyish reenactment of what was happening in the real world, except that Saxons sometimes remained undiscovered.

4. Aachen

Alcuin left Marmoutier Abbey for Aachen a week after arriving. Not long after that, a man named Sigewulf came to the abbey. Alcuin sent him. Sigewulf had the physique of a soldier, not a priest. In Aachen, it was well known that he did Alcuin's dirty work. When he arrived, he immediately demanded to speak with Father George.

"I need your book on iconography, the one by John of Damascus," Sigewulf ordered without introducing himself. Father George was in shock. It was a much-valued book, a centerpiece of the library.

Charlemagne had charged Alcuin with finding arguments against the Second Council of Nicaea. The current religious dispute in Christendom was about the veneration of icons. In the Eastern Catholic church of the Byzantine Empire, paintings of Christ and the Saints were venerated as part of religious services. This practice had never been part of the Western or Carolingian Catholic church. Then, in 754 AD, at the Council of Hieria, the Byzantine emperor outlawed the practice in consultation with over three hundred bishops. Icons were destroyed in Byzantine churches with such a vengeance that the churches ended up looking defaced. It was an affront to art and maybe even to God.

Charlemagne supported it because it caused a rift between the Byzantines and the pope. Then, much to his dismay, the decision was reversed at the Second Council of Nicaea just a few years before Charlemagne met Alcuin. It was part of a reconciliation of the pope and the Byzantine emperor that Charlemagne could not accept. The Byzantine Empire in the East and the Arab Umayyad caliphate to the south were the only parts of mainland Europe that Charlemagne did not control. Any reconciliation between the pope and the Byzantine Empire was unacceptable. It was not about religious niceties.

"And we need an expert translator," Sigewulf continued, in a demanding tone. "I heard Pierre, your assistant, is the best. What can you tell me about him?" Sigewulf bellowed at Father George. It was a terrible way to approach someone who always saw the good in people.

"He came to us from an orphanage," Father George replied slowly, "where they decided he was gifted. His caretakers at the orphanage suspect he knows where he is from, but he refuses to talk about it. He is ambitious, and yes, he is our best translator."

"I will take him with me," Sigewulf said flatly.

Father George, for once, was not smiling. He felt Pierre should have something to say about this and minded losing his most promising novice. He was also repulsed by Sigewulf's approach and body odor, which he was sure was not purely the result of his long travels.

If Pierre had something to say about it, he would have been more than supportive. He was thrilled to learn he would leave the abbey for Aachen. It was the way out he had hoped for.

Pierre never imagined he'd be leaving to research the veneration of icons, but the task mattered far less than the location. The court of Charlemagne was the center of power.

"I knew I would leave here one day," he proudly told Jean after he was told.

"I wish I could go," Jean replied, slumping his shoulders. "The Urbs Regale is hiring some well-regarded scholars. It would be great to be around them." It was one of the few times Jean had been jealous of Pierre or depressed, for that matter.

"Who knows? They may lose interest in icon worship. I may be back soon," Pierre said, trying to console his friend.

"We should be able to write," Jean said, trying to see some positive in the situation.

"When Alcuin travels back and forth between Aachen and Marmoutier, we can give letters to whoever is traveling with him. Let me know how you are doing and what you are learning, especially if you hear of any scientific discoveries."

"I will," Pierre agreed. He was still beside himself in terms of the opportunity he was given.

Jean then raised his eyebrows and smiled. "Oh, and good luck with Sigewulf. He will be fun to be around."

"Yes, a bit scary," Pierre said, smiling.

When Jean saw Father Lucas next, Jean continued to bemoan Pierre's good fortune. "We never make any scientific discoveries here. I wish I could go to Aachen."

"I told you, nothing of scientific importance is produced there—all the new scholars at the Urbs Regale focus on is literature and religion. The little science they teach, they recite. If they are lucky, they pick up some of the things being discovered in the Arab world, in places like Baghdad."

Sigewulf and Pierre set out the next day. The trip would take them about ten days—four to Paris, a city of less than forty thousand, and another six from Paris to Aachen. They only had one horse, so Pierre had to walk.

Sigewulf led the way. Occasionally, he would stop and wait for Pierre to catch up. The road to Aachen was sparsely traveled and dangerous. Saxon clans had been settled in the area to integrate them into Carolingian society, and they often organized small gangs to rob travelers. Initially, they passed through fields and saw some peasants; however, once they entered the forest, they were alone, but for a few older women collecting wood.

Pierre started falling seriously behind, and Sigewulf gave up stopping for him. Instead, he rode on and waited for him where they would rest for a meal. After more than an hour, Sigewulf began to worry. Pierre had not caught up. What if he had decided he did not want to go to Aachen, or worse, he'd run into Saxons? Sigewulf was responsible for delivering Pierre safely to Aachen and remounted his horse to look for the boy. He found Pierre talking to one of the women in the forest. When Sigewulf approached, she quickly disappeared.

"She was begging for money," Pierre explained with a shrug.

"From a novice monk?" Sigewulf thundered back. "From now on, we will ride together."

This plan made them faster, but it did not save them time. With two riders, the horse could cover less distance before being exhausted. Fortunately for Pierre, it allowed him to ask Sigewulf some questions.

"Can you tell me about the Urbs Regale? What is it like?" Pierre asked enthusiastically.

"You may be disappointed. There is no building for it. It is just the name they give to a group of scholars who write religious texts and teach Charlemagne's children."

"No building?"

"They gather in Charlemagne's palace, such as it is. Please don't get your hopes up; it is not that impressive. It has two stories. There is a throne room on the second floor. It is surrounded by buildings for the monks who administer the empire, mostly for tax collection and the raising of armies. The only impressive building is the Palatine Chapel."

"I have heard of it. I can't wait to see it."

"Everyone has heard of it," Sigewulf scoffed. "What have you heard?"

"Well," said Pierre, "it is octagonal, two stories high, made out of stone, and modeled after a church in Ravenna that Charlemagne visited."

"Indeed, but the interesting part is the interior. It is unlike anything I have seen. There is a sixteen-sided covered passage around the central cloister with a gallery on the second floor where Charlemagne's throne is. The entire interior is decorated with marble of all colors and bronze railings and ornaments. There is even a set of marble columns that was a gift from Pope Hadrian. It is the most amazing place." Sigewulf got a little carried away just then. It surprised Pierre. Sigewulf was Alcuin's enforcer and played the role well. Could he have such an appreciation for architecture?

"The church is connected to the palace by a palisade, which signifies how connected the church is to the empire," Sigewulf said with sarcasm, self-conscious about being too enthusiastic about the chapel. He looked over his shoulder at Pierre with a grin for emphasis.

"Do you know the teachings of Augustine?"

"Of course. We have studied his Confessions." Pierre responded. He wondered why Sigewulf would bring him up. Then, Pierre continued: "I remember he describes that when he was young, he stole fruit from a neighbor's tree, not because he was hungry, but because he enjoyed what was not right. He believes that humans have it in their nature to do wrong. Once they choose to sin, their will becomes permanently corrupted." Pierre was proud that he remembered.

"Yes, that is right," Sigewulf said. "I have seen enough bad people in my life to believe that. But that is not why I mentioned him. He also wrote something called City of God. In it, he draws a line between the church as a collection of believers known only to God and the institutional body of the church established on earth to proclaim salvation and administer the sacraments."

"Is he saying that the institution of the church could have non-believers?"

"Yes, keep that in mind in Aachen," Sigewulf concluded.

5. The Bad Book

Stewing over his lack of access to scientific advances, Jean walked down the hill from the abbey toward Tours, where his family lived. His despair heightened after Pierre left.

He reminisced as he looked at Tours lying below. It was a small town in a valley between two rivers, surrounded by fields and beautiful forests. The town was always bustling with energy. There were people from all walks of life - farmers, merchants, builders, etc. People who were, for the most part, enjoying life. Jean liked interacting with them, hearing their stories, and joking around. It was part of his easygoing nature, which he had inherited from his father and would have made him a good leader.

Jean looked at the dilapidated fortifications as he crossed a wooden bridge over one of the rivers that ran by the town and smiled. He remembered his father telling him that fortifications were unnecessary since the town had become part of the Carolingian Empire, an empire that no one would dare attack.

Jean had chosen to leave the town behind to study. His mother had to use all her wits to persuade his father to allow it. She wanted Jean to pursue what he wanted since his older brother was to take over from Jean's father. Jean's father did not understand the excitement of an education but reluctantly agreed. Of course, recently, Jean agreed with him more. He had learned most of what monks were allowed to learn.

Jean's family's large house stood in the center of town. It was larger than the other houses, mainly because it had an impressive throne room, where Jean's father met his subjects. Jean had not been in the room in a while and was looking at a large crucifix on one of the walls when his brother walked in.

"Mother had it installed to appease the church. I assume you don't object, Brother Jean," Luc, Jean's brother, joked as he walked up to Jean to embrace him, "Or is that not your title yet?"

"You are still the only one who can call me that." Jean laughed and hugged Luc. They slapped each other on the back. "What is new here, aside from the crucifix?"

They caught up. Luc had much to report about the empire and family. Jean noticed that Luc had gained confidence since he last saw him. He was growing into his role.

"And how are things with you?" Luc asked.

Jean told him about Father Lucas and how much he respected him. He told him about Pierre and the position he got in Aachen. Eventually, he confessed that he had exhausted what he could learn at the abbey, which frustrated him.

"I am not surprised," Luc said. "The abbey is afraid of science."

"We don't even have a single scientific book. The abbey won't provide any funds for it."

Luc tried to persuade Jean to return to Tours, but Jean had not given up yet. After a brief pause, he looked Luc straight in the eyes with an assertiveness and determination that surprised Luc. With a quiet but forceful voice, he then said what he had come to see Luc about:

"One of the merchants who comes to the monastery has an old book by Philoponus called *On the Creation of the World*. It critiques Aristotle's text on physics. It contains theories on what causes objects to move."

"Why don't you ask the abbey if you can copy it then?" Luc asked.

"They won't allow it. Philoponus was a Byzantine. In another book, he argues against the eternity of the world. Pagans used it against our theory of creation. The church declared Philoponus a heretic a hundred years after his death. Can you believe that?"

"And?" said Luc. "Seems clear. Not a good book—or at least not a good author."

"Well, I want to buy the book. It is my only chance to learn something new. I need some money," Jean responded.

"You are crazy. You could get into a lot of trouble," Luc said. "It can't be worth the risk. I mean—why do objects move?"

Luc again tried to persuade Jean to come back to Tours.

"There is always a role for you here, and if something happens to me..."

"You don't understand; it is important to me. I want to read that book," Jean responded.

After much pleading from Jean, Luc got up and left the room. He always felt guilty about being the "chosen one at court" and wanted to help Jean. He also did not like how upset Jean seemed to be. It was not like him.

Luc returned with a pouch with coins and placed it in Jean's hands.

"You can decide your fate, Jean. We owe you that. But be sensible! I don't think it is a good idea," Luc said, wanting to empower Jean.

Luc emulated their mother when she lobbied for Jean to pursue his dream of an education. Luc felt letting Jean chart his life was more important than avoiding harm. Jean appreciated that. He hugged his brother and returned to the abbey, but with the nagging feeling that he was about to do something truly dangerous for the first time in his life.

6. Theoduff

When Sigewulf and Pierre arrived in Aachen, Pierre was surprised by how small and dirty the city was. Charlemagne's empire spanned most of the continent, but his capital did not look like the seat of such a vast empire. The city's center mainly consisted of small makeshift wooden buildings, and dreadful slums surrounded it. Poorly clad children begged in streets that reeked of animal and human feces. Pierre could not believe the misery he was seeing or the overwhelming stench. There were no significant buildings except for the palace and the Palatine Chapel. Even the fortifications were sparse.

"Charlemagne's parents had a hunting lodge here," Sigewulf said in response to Pierre's bewildered expression. He was trying to be more matter-of-fact than when he had gotten carried away about the Palatine Chapel. "The fields surrounding the city have good soil and are well-drained. The sulfur springs here go back to Celtic times. Charlemagne believes in their healing qualities. Otherwise, there is no reason for the city to be here."

Sigewulf carefully guided the horse through the muddy streets.

"The Palatine Chapel does not disappoint," Pierre said as they passed it.

Guards in colorful uniforms flanked its entry port, and people in their finest clothes passed solemnly through the doors. Given the chapel's surroundings, that grandeur seemed contrived to Pierre. He complimented the chapel only to please Sigewulf.

"There is a mosaic inside with elders laying down their crowns for Christ—for Christ, not for the pope," Sigewulf said. He turned around on the horse and looked back at Pierre as he had before to emphasize a point.

They found shelter in a monastery not far from the palace. Alcuin's assistant, Theoduff, met them there. Theoduff was a small man with a nervous disposition that seemed to be driven by a high intellect. He could not stand still the entire time they met, pacing while speaking.

"We need to impress Charlemagne. I have written a text. I need these papers translated," Theoduff said, wasting no time. He nervously handed a sheaf to Pierre. "I'll need this back in two days. Charlemagne may ask to see me. He has little to do when he's not in battle. Unlike the Romans, he has no senate to contend with at home." Then he put on a sarcastic smile. "There are benefits to being an absolute ruler." He looked at Pierre to see his reaction. Pierre decided not to react. He was not sure what was appropriate.

"But he does worry about church matters," Theoduff continued. "Get this done as fast as possible in case he wants to see us."

"Wait until you see the chaos that is Charlemagne's family," Sigewulf interjected with his usual sardonic tone. "His first wife, Desiderata, was the daughter of Desiderius, the very king he defeated in Rome. The pope, of course, annulled that marriage. Since then, he's had three wives, two acknowledged concubines, and ten daughters. And the sons, of course."

Theoduff bristled at Sigewulf's disrespect, but he did not interrupt.

"All of his daughters are still at the palace. He doesn't want to give away any part of his empire as a dowry, and there are no rulers left with whom diplomatic marriages might make sense. He has defeated them all."

Pierre placed the papers Theoduff had given him on a table and asked respectfully, "Could that really happen? Could I go with you to the palace?"

"Perhaps. As Sigewulf so irreverently points out, the palace is not particularly formal, but you'll be going nowhere until you get these done," Theoduff said.

Theoduff then attempted to size up Pierre again. He asked Pierre about his translation experience and commitment to hard work. When he was satisfied, he briefly smiled at Pierre and left.

Pierre could not help but wonder what the most powerful man on earth might be like. It was exciting to think that he might see the man who controlled most of Europe, including, arguably, the pope. He had a reputation for being ruthless and having a tumultuous family life, but there seemed to be something religious about him. Was it all about his power, as Sigewulf would probably describe it, or was there some higher power, even from Charlemagne?

Pierre wasted no time and completed his translations in record time. Then, as Theoduff had forecasted, Charlemagne commanded them to come to the palace. Pierre got the distinct feeling that Theoduff wanted him to come along in case there were any disagreements about the documents he had translated. He was sure to be blamed.

In the hallways, they passed many women and children, as Sigewulf had said, until they were finally ushered into a room where Alcuin and some of his scholarly monks sat behind a large wooden table. They all looked up from where they were seated and stared at them with steely eyes, reflecting resentment. It was the most unwelcoming welcome Pierre ever witnessed.

"Congratulations on your instruction book," Theoduff told Alcuin to break the silence. "Using a dialogue between two pupils to teach Latin grammar is a novel idea."

"Why are you here?" Alcuin asked. He was not interested in flattery from Theoduff.

"I am presenting some findings on the Second Council of Nicaea," Theoduff responded. "It has been an honor to assist you in this."

Pierre felt certain this statement carried a whiff of sarcasm.

Alcuin looked at what Theoduff was carrying and stretched out his hands. "May I see? I was not aware you finished it."

"Not finished, just a draft. Not a final presentation; otherwise, I would have—"

"Libri Carolini?" Alcuin interrupted. "Interesting title. That should leave no doubt as to where your allegiances stand. I don't have to open it to know what it says." He handed the book back. At that moment, the chamberlain entered to usher Theoduff and Pierre away, leaving Alcuin behind. Pierre was sure he could feel Alcuin's stare from behind as they were allowed to see the emperor, while Alcuin had to remain behind.

When they entered Charlemagne's office, they found him studying maps over a large desk. There were no greetings, no introductions. Theoduff and Pierre stood waiting for Charlemagne to address them.

Pierre thought Charlemagne looked nothing like the man on the coins circulating in the empire. He was over six feet tall and muscular. Pierre was tall, as was Sigewulf, but Charlemagne had them all beat in stature. For a moment, Pierre wondered why he did not dwarf the horse he was riding on coins. Maybe Charlemagne had an unusually large horse? He had never seen such a large, imposing man.

"Tell me where you are with your work," Charlemagne finally said in a slightly high-pitched voice that surprised Pierre a little.

"Done. I am finished. This outlines all the arguments against icon worship." Theoduff proudly held up his book for Charlemagne to see.

"Good," Charlemagne said briefly, looking at its cover. "Now, I want you to organize a council of theologians in Aachen to debate its conclusions. Invite all of the candidates whose opinion you care for." Pierre thought that was an interesting choice of words.

Charlemagne continued, "I want it to happen within the next two months." Then he waved his left arm to dismiss Theoduff, who, together with Pierre, bowed as they left the room.

It was a quick and abrupt meeting, but Theoduff seemed pleased. He presented his work as completed despite telling Alcuin it was a draft. Pierre noted that. Such were the ways of the court, he supposed. It worked. Charlemagne empowered Theoduff.

When leaving, Theoduff hurried through the room where Alcuin stood without saying anything. Alcuin would find out soon enough. Pierre could not help but look at Alcuin, afraid that Alcuin might now consider him Theoduff's ally. Was he already making enemies at court?

Hundreds of bishops arrived in Aachen for the synod organized by Theoduff. While there was some debate, eventually, the synod agreed with Theoduff's findings. Icon worship, as practiced by the Byzantines, was not consistent with the teachings of the Bible. Charlemagne was delighted.

With the synod over, Pierre found time to write a letter to Jean:

Jean,

I hope things are going well for you. Sigewulf turned out to be agreeable. He is quite sarcastic about the church. You would like him.

Aachen is interesting. Every life in the city revolves around pleasing Charlemagne. I got to see him briefly when he asked Theoduff to organize a synod of bishops. I've gotten to know many influential people, and I believe I am starting to be part of this— learning the ways of politics, if nothing else.

Have you heard the rumor that Alcuin might be retiring to Marmoutier Abbey and Theoduff might take over the Urbs Regale? I hope it is true. If it is, I will move up with Theoduff.

I hope you are making progress at the abbey. There is no science to report about here.

Please let me know how things are going.

Pierre

When Jean read the letter, he crumpled it out of frustration. How the tables had turned: Pierre was out in the world, pursuing his dream even though there appeared to be some risks. He, on the other hand, was stuck at the abbey.

That day, Jean decided to contact the merchant who had the book by Philoponus. It was not easy. He made excuses to go to Tours and got the word out that he was looking for the merchant. After several weeks, the merchant appeared at the abbey. The monks wondered who he was but assumed it concerned Jean's family businesses. Jean went into the forest with him and bought the book with the money Luc gave him.

Over the following weeks, Jean read the book secretly in his room - cringing every time he turned a page. Nobody had read the book, and its crisp pages made a crackling sound when he turned them. Jean was sure this could only be heard if one listened closely at the door to his room, but he took no chances and turned the pages carefully.

As he read, Jean's intellectual curiosity came alive again. He was fascinated by the endless concepts. The book was unlike anything he had been allowed to read before. Father Lucas noticed how joyful Jean became. Something in his life propelled him, but Father Lucas did not know what it was and did not ask.

When Jean finished reading the book, it created a vacuum in his life. His existence threatened to revert to the mundaneness that had driven him to buy the book. Jean wanted to explore the ideas and work with them. That was the only way to perpetuate his thinking.

At one of his study sessions with Father Lucas, Jean could not help but bring it up.

"A while back, I bought a book," he confessed.

Father Lucas' inquisitive eyes went wide with excitement. He was surprised; he knew Jean could find the means, and they wanted a scientific text, but he did not expect Jean to buy one by himself. He was full of anticipation.

Jean smiled. "Don't ask me how I got it, but I did. It is the seminal work by Philoponus on Aristotle's theories on moving objects."

He brought the book from under his robe and tried to hand it to Father Lucas, whose excitement quickly changed to horror and disbelief.

Jean, not noticing, continued, "Philoponus's observations are quite interesting. I was thinking we could—"

"How could you, Jean?" Father Lucas interrupted Jean and shook his head. "I can't believe you would do such a thing. I am afraid we have to report this. Let's hope begging for forgiveness is enough."

"What? Why?"

"Philoponus was a Byzantine heretic. You know that. He believed that the Trinity of God consisted of three gods instead of one with three aspects." Father Lucas said, still in disbelief.

"Yes, but this book is not about that; it is about the movement of an object stemming from the energy imparted to it by its mover, energy that depletes as the object moves. It refutes Aristotle's theory of dynamics."

Father Lucas would not entertain this.

"You put every one of us, the entire abbey, in danger by having such a book. Did you think of that?"

Jean slumped in disbelief. Father Lucas ripped the book from Jean with unusual violence to make a point.

"You stay here until I return." Father Lucas then said, leaving to see the senior monks. Jean waited.

Father Lucas wasted no time and asked the senior monks to gather in the church. Such a gathering was rare. Nothing much happened at the abbey, and having it in the church was particularly unusual. The monks sensed its importance and repressed the usual banter, teasing, and chuckling about their foibles. Even the nicknames they had for each other were abandoned, and everyone greeted each other more formally.

Father Lucas then stood before them and explained what had happened matter-of-factly and quietly. Occasionally, he would pause to ensure no one had entered the church and was listening in.

"He has heretical thoughts," one of the monks exclaimed.

"Yes, he has heretical thoughts," Father Lucas agreed. "But maybe his thoughts about Aristotle's theories we should not judge so quickly," he said in a soft, conciliatory way. He made a point to piously stare at the crucifix that loomed large in the church. He could not say it, but he hoped the monks would think of how quickly Christ was judged. Father Lucas was hoping the monks would emulate Christ's forgiveness.

It did not work. The monks debated the subject for a while.

"There are limits to what is allowed. We all have given up a lot to be here," one of the monks commented.

It was true. They had all agreed to live by the rules; it was the only concession for an otherwise relatively comfortable life in the empire.

"We understand what you are saying, Father Lucas, but you must agree we have to report this," another monk insisted.

"We can't do that to Jean," a monk objected. "He is one of us, and he is young."

"He could get into a lot of trouble," another agreed.

"Yes, but we could all get into a lot of trouble if we don't report this," another interjected, and several monks nodded.

The monks and Father Lucas felt partially at fault. They wished they had educated Jean better, but it was too late. Ultimately, they could not ignore the incident and protect the brotherhood for the rest of them. However, they decided not to report the incident to the bishop immediately but to wait until Alcuin returned. They wanted to see what he had to say, though they suspected they knew.

When Father Lucas burst into his study with the bad news, Jean was gone. Father Lucas was afraid that Jean might have decided to flee. Could he have gone back to his parents? What would they do then? He looked for Jean everywhere - the dining hall, the church, the library, the yard. Eventually, he found him in his room, sitting on his bed dejectedly. Father Lucas sat next to him. He let his head hang as well. He sat there for a while commiserating, knowing how defeated Jean felt.

Finally, Father Lucas started speaking softly. "The brotherhood decided to wait until Alcuin returns from Aachen and let him decide. But I must tell you, I think he will want to report this to the bishop. And, the bishop will probably want to cover himself by requiring some punishment. We are all sorry. It pained everyone, and there was a lot of debate."

Jean recognized the pain on Father Lucas' face. It was the pain his parents' faces showed when he had done something wrong as a child. He remained dispirited and quiet.

"Until this is resolved, you, unfortunately, must remain in your quarters except for meals. We can't have you interact with the pupils. We could all get into a lot of trouble if we didn't take some immediate action. We hope you understand."

Jean understood. He knew the brotherhood was doing what they had to do. More concerning, though, this was not over. That night, in a panic, Jean wrote to Pierre asking him for help. He had no one else to turn to. Not even his family could stand up to the church on this. Jean thought about it but rejected it. He was sure the church would not let a layperson infringe on their turf, even a Carolingian nobleman. The only option Jean saw was to get Pierre to persuade Alcuin in Aachen. If that did not work, Jean was unsure what to do. He was doomed.

7. Pierre

The letter would not reach Pierre for several weeks. Unaware of Jean's danger, Pierre was busily expanding his influence at the Urbs Regale. He decided to loosen his ties to Alcuin and align himself totally with Theoduff.

Once it was official that Theoduff was to become the new head of the Urbs Regale, scholars at court started kowtowing to Theoduff and, consequently, Pierre. Never short on charm or intellect, Pierre played the game well and rose quickly in stature at the court as one of the important academics. It was ironic since Pierre was not interested in academics. Even when the nuns at the orphanage had recommended him to the monks at the Marmoutier Abbey, they had mistaken his eagerness to learn with academic interest. What was underlying it was a desire to advance, not an interest in academic matters.

The only threat now to Pierre's career was a possible end to religious inquiries and debates. The more control Charlemagne gained over the papacy, the less he needed to win religious arguments.

To Pierre's dismay, the recently elected Pope Leo became so indebted to Charlemagne that the need to win religious arguments became less important. The administration of the papacy, the curia, did not trust Pope Leo since he had no connection with Roman nobility. They accused him of immorality, adultery, and perjury and called an assembly to adjudicate the charges.

Charlemagne resolved the matter by agreeing to preside over the assembly. The presence of the Butcher of the Saxons posed such a threat that none of Pope Leo's accusers testified. Only Pope Leo testified on his own behalf, and Charlemagne used that testimony to absolve him of the charges. In gratitude, the very next day, Pope Leo crowned Charlemagne Holy Roman Emperor and even knelt before him after the coronation. The title that had belonged to the Byzantine Emperor Augustus over three hundred years earlier was now his.

Charlemagne's control over the papacy was cemented, and the papacy further distanced itself from the Byzantine Empire.

It was tremendous news all over the Carolingian Empire. It seemed the only person not celebrating was Pierre.

"Charlemagne will not need our work. The feud over religious matters will end," he fretted to Theoduff. Theoduff was not sure he agreed. He believed that the feud over power might subside, but would never truly end. It might shift to other matters. Still, for the most part, he kept his thoughts to himself when it came to matters in Aachen.

"Charlemagne may not need our work, but he will still need the Urbs Regale. Someone has to educate his children, and he will want the appearance of an academy. Besides, Charlemagne is starting to trust me in other matters." That was all Theoduff wanted to say.

Pierre knew not to ask what the "other matters" were. He knew Theoduff well enough to know there was a lot he did not want to share.

Pierre put his worries aside when Jean's letter finally arrived. He realized that Jean's predicament was grave, but he could not do what Jean requested. He was no longer in a position to persuade Alcuin to do anything. He had shown his allegiance to Theoduff; all bridges to Alcuin had been burned. Even if this had not been so, Pierre doubted anyone in Aachen would risk their career to help a monk in a distant monastery over a heretical text written by a Byzantine.

The only hope Pierre thought Jean had was to appeal to his father to intervene with the bishop before the matter got out of hand. Pierre was more optimistic in this regard than Jean. He had seen plenty of pragmatism in Aachen and knew how bishops yielded if it was in their interest.

Aware that his letter might fall into the hands of an inquisitor, Pierre chose his words carefully.

Jean,

Your situation is distressing. I know you disapprove of Philoponus's views on theology as much as we do here.
The best method to resolve this matter before it takes on unjustified dimensions is to have your father discuss it with the bishop. I am confident the bishop will listen to the man who raised you in the Christian faith.

Pierre

Jean read the letter several times. The way it was written emphasized how dangerous his situation was and showed how thoughtful Pierre had been. He had to take his advice.

Jean went to appeal to his father, both as a son and as a subject. The abbey could not preclude him from doing so. Every subject had the right to appeal to the nobleman in charge on judicial matters. While Jean's issue was religious, he faced punishment that his father could at least arguably intervene in.

It was Jean's mother who again had the final word.

"Family is the most important," she argued with Jean's father privately, but when that did not work, she argued as follows:

"The empire has been married to the church for a long time. As in any marriage, both parties have to respect each other. The church is too extreme here and has to listen to you. Insist on that and then tell the bishop he won't get in trouble in Rome. He can always argue that you, one of Charlemagne's noblemen, pressured him."

Jean's father smiled when he heard this. "Thank God that the church does not have spouses. If they had, they might be in charge in Aachen," he joked.

Jean's father then went to see the bishop in Tours. He argued just as his wife had suggested. The bishop was happy to ingratiate himself with Jean's father, especially if he could fall back on the argument that he was pressured. He only requested that the church keep the book, and Jean would agree to acquire no further ones.

Jean was upset but understood. He tried as hard as he could to put the matter to rest. He apologized to the monks for the trouble he caused them. He wrote a letter to Pierre thanking him for his good advice and telling him that the matter had been resolved. He then spoke to Father Lucas, assuring him he would not do anything of the sort again.

"We hope you truly understand." Father Lucas said. "We have a brotherhood here that you are and will always be a part of. Sometimes, we need to protect it, even if we could harm one of us unjustly, but ultimately, we are here for each other."

Jean then resumed his work with Father Lucas and his teaching tasks. He even immersed himself more in the monastery's religious duties, hoping a routine away from science would benefit him. Unfortunately, this only worked for a short time. No matter how hard he tried, his mind would often wander the way it had during sermons when he was younger. He could not control it. It always ended in his being miserable about where he was. He wanted to learn so much and could not do it at the abbey.

8. Abbasid

Pierre's fortunes turned for the better when new work came his way. While Charlemagne was relatively less concerned with the Byzantine Empire and religious arguments, he was still fighting the Umayyad Caliphate in Spain. The caliphate's main enemy was the Abbasid Caliphate in Baghdad. Charlemagne hoped to develop an alliance with the Abbasids to fight the Umayyads.

Theoduff had grown fond of Pierre and appreciated the young man's political savvy and desire to play the game. He understood Pierre's anxiety about work and sought to alleviate it by giving him an important task. "Alliances are initiated by embassies bearing messages and gifts," Theoduff told Pierre. "We are sending an embassy to the Abbasids, and I suggested to Charlemagne that you draft the letter to accompany it. Do it well, and you will have a new purpose."

"Thank you, sir. I will not disappoint you."

Pierre crafted the letter with enthusiasm over the next couple of days. A small group was organized to take it and gifts to Baghdad. It would take several months for them to make the round trip if they made it at all. Disease and hostile foreign powers made the journey dangerous.

They had also not anticipated the prevalence of common thieves. When the group found rest areas, suspicion arose about what the embassy carried. They managed to fend off some thieves, but a group overpowered them at one stop. The thieves threatened to kill their horses unless they paid them. They gave away some of the gifts they carried to gain passage and continued, not knowing what Charlemagne would do if they didn't.

Eventually, the embassy succeeded in reaching Baghdad. The remaining gifts and Pierre's letter were well received, but there was no immediate response. They returned to Aachen, unsure what they would tell Charlemagne. All they had were stories about the tremendous wealth of the Abbasid caliphate. They spoke of big, clean cities with many palaces, not just for the caliph. No one believed them until a return embassy arrived from the Abbasids a few months later.

Al-Rashid, the Abbasid caliph, had outdone himself to impress Charlemagne. Aside from a letter and the usual gifts, he'd sent an elephant named Abul Abbaz. It took the participants of the embassy much ingenuity to get the elephant over land and sea. Aside from moving the beast, they had to provide it with massive amounts of food and water.

At one point, they came up to a river and hired a barge to cross it, but the barge tipped over under Abul Abbaz's weight. Several of the attendants almost drowned. To everyone's surprise, Abul Abbaz trod water and waited until everyone could hang on. Then Abul Abbaz slowly swam everyone ashore. Unfortunately, what Abul Abbaz was carrying washed away; the group found some things, including some precious gifts, but could not recover any food, including the food for Abul Abbaz. Being grateful to Abul Abbaz for having saved their lives, the group spent several days gathering food before deciding to move on. There was much cursing and arguing about this, but particularly, the non-swimmers of the group stayed loyal to the elephant.

Once they finally arrived, Aachen was beside itself to receive such a strange animal from a far-off nation. Charlemagne enjoyed the frivolity and recognition it signified from distant powers. Several parties were organized for participants of the Abbasid embassy, and everyone at court, including Pierre, was invited. Pierre took the occasion to write to Jean.

Jean,

Things have been quite exciting in Aachen. We received an embassy from Baghdad. They brought an elephant—you cannot imagine the size of this beast!

One of the embassy participants is a man called Akbar. He is our age and works as a scribe at the court of al-Rashid. Scribes are called "kuttāb," and they work in the administration of the caliphate led by the wazīr, the first minister. Unlike the scribes here, the scribes in the Abbasid Empire have no connection to the religious establishment.

Akbar told me that the caliphate had become extremely wealthy from trade and tributes collected throughout Persia. Baghdad, the capital, is built on a river, surrounded by a wall protecting abundant wealth and education, and has many palaces for ministers and wealthy merchants.

He said they have recently established the largest repository of books in the world, as well as the most comprehensive gathering of important scholars. It is known as the House of Wisdom. He insisted that the most important scientists of our time were gathered there, but I'm afraid he did not know about anything they were working on.

He mentioned that they use the absence of a number, called "zero," as part of their mathematics. He said the concept came from India, but I did not understand it. The absence of a number can't be a number, can it?

Pierre

After the embassy left, Theoduff found other projects for Pierre. They continued to work together and often spoke about court politics, particularly the feud about religious matters between Charlemagne and his son Louis. Theoduff had become a confidant of Charlemagne's, even on that matter, but he would find out he was getting too close to the emperor for his own good.

A second embassy eventually arrived from Baghdad, less grandiose than the first. This group included two monks from Jerusalem, reminding everyone that the caliphate controlled the holy city, but this time, there were no lavish parties, and Pierre did not get to meet them. Charlemagne quickly prepared a return embassy, for which Pierre was again asked to craft the message. Unfortunately, al-Rashid died before it arrived, and the alliance between the Carolingians and the Abbasids was not secured.

Charlemagne attempted to defeat the Umayyads in Spain but ultimately withdrew after suffering several crushing defeats. He also entered a peace treaty with the Byzantine Empire, surrendering Venice and the south of Italy.

Charlemagne and the court started focusing on Charlemagne's only son and successor, Louis. Charlemagne's two other legitimate sons, Charles the Younger and Carloman, had passed away.

"I don't get along with Louis," Theoduff confided in Pierre in an unusual moment of openness. "They call him Louis the Pious for a reason; he is just not as pragmatic as his father."

"You are a monk. He must like that," Pierre responded, but knew better. Theoduff had used religion as a means to an end. He was not viewed as a true believer.

It was clear that Theoduff was doomed when Charlemagne made Louis co-emperor. To Pierre's surprise, Theoduff remained at court for another year, until Charlemagne died. However, at that point, Louis exiled Theoduff to an obscure monastery in a distant corner of the empire.

Pierre was alone and had no hope of employment. No one in Aachen would stand up for him. There was no sense of community, only factions seeking power. You were either on the winning team or were lost.

9. The Conversation

Pierre's only immediate option was to return to Marmoutier Abbey. Three years had passed since he had been there last, and he had made no attempt to stay in touch, but he assumed the brotherhood would have to take him back. He was still one of them, which should count for something.

Upon his arrival, he found that the brotherhood was also in a state of upheaval. Alcuin had passed away, and no successor had been named. Choosing a successor was hard. All the senior monks thought of themselves as equals. They had never appreciated the outsider's appointment and wished to avoid repeating the situation, but they did not know how to choose a leader from among themselves.

They had ignored the issue for years, but now that things were changing in Aachen, they were urged to turn to it by the bishop.

Jean was excited to see his old friend despite the circumstances. Upon his arrival, they decided to take a walk outside the abbey. They passed the novices, who were playing Phaininda in front of the abbey. Jean watched them longingly, remembering less complicated and consequential days.

"I am at an end," Pierre confessed. "I have worked all these years to build relationships and succeed. But everything ends with Louis. No one wants to be associated with me. They are all afraid of him."

"Will this not get better with time?" Jean asked.

"It may, but others will be in place by the time it passes."

"You should stay here until things calm down. You are still part of the brotherhood."

Pierre was considering that, but it seemed beneath him. At that time, he saw the monks in the abbey following a routine that was as immovable as the stone walls they were confined to. It did not suit him. Pierre had seen too much. He was not ready to join their unimportant ceremonies, even if it was the safe thing to do. He still had ambitions to live what, in his mind, he called an "important life." He shared none of this with Jean, not wanting to offend him.

"I need to get away. Far away," Pierre said.

"You mean Rome?"

"No, not Rome. Louis's reach is wide and his grip strong." Pierre paused and then continued, "You are also at an impasse, aren't you? Since Philoponus, no more progress?"

Pierre knew that Jean had his doubts about the abbey, even though he had not shared them. In his case, of course, it was not disrespect for the unimportance of the abbey but their unwillingness to improve it through intellectual pursuit.

"Yes, but this is about you," Jean responded.

"Maybe, my friend. But I have an idea that may solve both of our problems."

Baghdad had stuck in Pierre's head since his encounter with Akbar. It seemed like a place more grandiose than Aachen. Akbar's stories about the wealth there, which he could support with lavish gifts, had mesmerized the court at Aachen and always stuck with Pierre. It was the sort of place all of Aachen dreamed about, at least back then. Now, Pierre thought he could go there. He had nothing to lose.

Pierre looked at Jean and shared his outrageous idea.

"I think we should go to Baghdad."

Jean's mouth dropped open. He immediately considered it the type of outlandish idea formed in desperation when someone has nothing to lose and is willing to take outrageous gambles to regain what he just lost.

Before Jean could articulate this, Pierre continued.

"Do you remember I wrote you about Akbar, the scribe I met long ago? He told me the city is abundant with wealth and science. Remember the library of the House of Wisdom I told you about. You even told me that science has only made progress there. It may sound impossible to go there, but embassies have made the trip—why couldn't we?"

Pierre wanted Jean to go. At a young age, Pierre was comforted by the mother he now never mentioned. Comforted that whatever pain arose, he was not alone. Now Pierre was making adult decisions, decisions that might be real mistakes. He wanted company in case things went wrong. Mistakes were best shared.

"My home is here," Jean said, surprising himself a little. He'd wanted to access more of the world, but going to Baghdad was simply outlandish.

"This would not be permanent. We can go for a year or two. You could explore all the scientific discoveries there, and I would be able to earn some money. If I am lucky, I might find a new life for some time."

They walked for a while. Jean could not deny the allure of Baghdad. He knew it to be the science center of the world.

"It is a once-in-a-lifetime chance," Pierre implored. "Adversity creates opportunity. Now is the perfect time."

"How would we fund such a journey?" Jean asked. Surely, it could not be as simple as deciding to go.

Pierre tried to hide his smile. Jean was starting to consider his idea. "First, we would have to get permission from the abbey, and yes, the funding would be a problem. We must travel to Venice and then by ship. That is expensive."

"Yes. How do you propose we acquire such funds?"

"We would have to find sponsors, which would almost certainly mean making promises that will be difficult to keep." Pierre briefly looked at Jean. "I believe the abbey would sponsor part of it, and I was thinking, maybe your family could give the rest? We would promise to earn it back in Baghdad."

Jean laughed. Of course, Pierre had a plan. Pierre always had a plan. "This is crazy," he said, shaking his head, but Pierre could see a little sparkle of the old Jean come alive.

"Crazy adventures are the best kind. Just promise me you'll think about it."

When they returned, the abbey showed its mundaneness. Mass was over, and it was time for dinner. Jean looked at Pierre with a smile, and they bowed their heads as they joined the line that proceeded to the dining hall. No one could imagine the crazy thoughts going through their heads as they sat down.

Jean and Pierre expected at least some monks to join them. Surely, they were interested in Pierre's experiences in Aachen. None did. Pierre felt disrespected, and Jean felt awkward about not being with his usual group for dinner. They were being shunned. Word had gotten around about Pierre's disfavor with Louis.

The next morning, Jean went to see Father Lucas, who, it turned out, had been discussing Pierre's presence with the other senior monks well into the night. The brothers feared falling into the new emperor's disfavor if they harbored Pierre. They were sure it would mean they could not choose a new abbot from among their ranks.

"Can you persuade him to leave?" Father Lucas said. Jean knew it pained him. Father Lucas was not one to cater to politics, but the others insisted he help get Pierre to leave.

"I am not sure I can," Jean said.

Father Lucas looked at Jean with the look he knew too well. Whenever Jean discussed some "blasphemous" scientific idea, Father Lucas would look at him with a look that said, "It is interesting," but "it is out of bounds." Jean appreciated the respect it showed for whatever scientific idea he wanted to explore, but he knew he would have to stop pushing it when he got that look.

Father Lucas wanted something this time and would not accept Jean's answer. He gave him that look and would not let go.

"Unless . . ." Jean finally said. He was, of course, thinking of Baghdad.

The more he thought about it, the more he realized that Baghdad was the perfect place for Pierre and him. It was open to all and open to science. And the only way he would ever get there would be with someone like Pierre, who was good at languages and knew how to get things done. He even had a contact in Akbar. This would be his only opportunity to escape the life he'd conceded to.

"Unless what, Jean?" Father Lucas asked, surprised at Jean's reaction. "Unless what?"

"Oh, nothing. I don't have time. I have to go see my family." Jean said, now smiling, and then turned for the door, not wanting to linger and torture Father Lucas.

"Your family? What about Pierre? We need to discuss this," Father Lucas said indignantly.

"We will. I need to speak to my family first." Jean said as he headed to town.

In the meantime, Pierre was sitting in his chamber, thinking about his proposal. If Jean did not accept it, the idea might die. He needed the abbey's and Jean's family's sponsorship. He wanted the trip so desperately that he had not said anything to Jean about its dangers. Aside from the many threats that faced any traveler, one of the members of the second embassy to Baghdad had died on the return voyage, seemingly of pure exhaustion.

Then there was the political situation in Baghdad, the uncertainty about who would succeed the by now deceased caliph, al-Rashid. Pierre had heard about this in Aachen. Al-Rashid had two sons, al-Ma'mun and al-Amin. Al-Ma'mun was in control of the caliphate's army and had taken it to Merv, the capital of one of the caliphate's provinces. Al-Amin was in control of the caliphate's capital, Baghdad. Neither was the clear leader, and Pierre feared that he and Jean might arrive amid a civil war. Despite these risks, Pierre could think of no reasonable alternative for himself, so he kept his concerns from Jean.

Jean's mother greeted Jean enthusiastically when he went to see her. After the usual hugs, they sat down in private.

"You look like you have something important to discuss," his mother said. "Anything wrong? Not another book?"

"No. But something similar. Pierre has fallen out of favor at the court since Charlemagne died. They also don't want him at the abbey. He has no place to go, but he does have a plan. He wants to go to Baghdad, of all places, to find a new life. And he wants me to go with him."

"Baghdad?"

"Yes. It is not completely crazy. The voyage has been completed by many. The caliphate is quite wealthy. The city is situated by a river that facilitates trade throughout Asia. The merchants there have a bazaar that trades more goods in a day than we trade in years. They have houses made out of marble, decorated with gold and water fountains. But most importantly for me, it is where all the advances in science are happening. They have the most important and biggest library known to man, ever known to man."

Jean's mother did not trust Pierre. She never had. She knew how ambitious he was. She had no use for Theoduff and found Pierre's alliance with him suspicious.

"We know nothing about Pierre—who his family is. Has he ever shared that with you?"

"You know he is an orphan."

"Yes, but orphans usually know where they are from or at least try to find out."

"Mother, this is not the point. I want to go. You promised me an education. My education has ended. They haven't allowed me to learn anything interesting in years."

Jean's mother lowered her voice. "The church focuses on converting people, not enlightening them. I know."

They sat quietly for a while, each thinking about the situation.

Jean finally broke the silence. "Why did Pierre have to come to me? Somehow, it was better when I had accepted that I had no options."

His mother sighed. "Well, now that he is here and you have the idea, you won't be happy unless you go. You want to try. Right?"

"I do," Jean said, bowing his head.

Jean's mother, above all, wanted what was best for her son, and she wanted his happiness. She was not sure a journey of this sort would have a happy ending, but she was sure that Jean would not be happy if he did not try.

"I think you should go to Baghdad," she said to Jean's surprise.

Jean looked up. His face changed from frustration to disbelief to joy. His mother enjoyed that and started laughing.

"Leave it to me. Your father will not like it. You haven't forgotten that you are next in line to your brother, have you? You could be in charge of all this one day."

"Yes, I know, but . . ."

"I know. I understand. Don't worry. I will talk to him. It may take some time; I must choose the right moment."

Jean walked back up the hill to the abbey, realizing they had not talked about the funds he would need. The whole episode had been such a shock—his mother deciding he should go. She only had his interest at heart. That in and of itself made Jean happy.

Pierre was anxious when he saw Jean climbing the hill, but that quickly turned to excitement when he saw Jean smiling. Jean told him he had realized he needed to go to Baghdad. He might regret it for the rest of his life if he did not. Of course, his mother's support had given him the final push, but he did not share that.

Over the next few weeks, Jean divided his time between carrying on his duties at the abbey and dreaming of what Baghdad might be like. He was sure he was exaggerating what it could be like, but he reveled in imagining it nevertheless. The dream became more of a reality when a messenger arrived at the abbey carrying a letter from Jean's mother telling him that she had persuaded his father. But what did that mean? Nothing would be possible without funds.

Jean went to see Pierre.

"My mother sent a messenger telling us we can go, but she has not provided any funds," he said.

"This is good news," Pierre said. "Your mother is a wise woman, and I am sure she has her ways."

Pierre and Jean still had to get approval from the council of senior monks, who would need to provide the official papers to present at various points of their journey.

Fortunately, the council had a distinct interest in getting Pierre away from the abbey as soon as possible. When Jean appeared in front of the council, as tempted as he was, he did not describe the advances of the House of Wisdom or the stagnant nature of mathematics and science in Christendom, though there was nothing he would have enjoyed more. He was politic. He wanted to be able to return.

"My parents are in support. We need only three horses and provisions from the abbey. We may be gone for a year or more." Jean was bluffing. He did not have the funds, and no one knew the requirements for a journey of this sort, but the monks seemed to ignore this.

"We need an understanding that we can both return to the abbey after we have completed our journey," Jean added. That caused the monks some dismay. Of course, they could not refuse Jean a place at the abbey; he knew this. The request was really about Pierre. However, the senior monks were hopeful that by the time Pierre returned, a new abbot would be in place, and having Pierre at the abbey might be acceptable.

Should the bishop question them, the brotherhood imposed only one condition to justify the journey. They required Pierre and Jean to bring back copies of at least three books regarding philosophy or religion that were "useful" to Christian doctrine. Despite his usual stern demeanor, Father Lucas could not help but roll his eyes as he heard this. The other monks noticed, but that disagreement was acceptable amongst the brotherhood.

Pierre was impressed. Jean had done his part masterfully. Pierre was even grateful that Jean had secured his right to return to the abbey, but he did not tell Jean that the only way he could see himself returning would be if they never made it to Baghdad. Of course, they still needed to obtain the required funds, in addition to the horses and provisions the abbey would provide.

10. The Beginning of a Journey

Pierre and Jean spent the next few days organizing the trip. They consulted with Father Lucas, who had some maps to help direct them. The route to Venice was known if one traveled by rivers to the Mediterranean first, but Father Lucas advocated for a more direct, though dangerous route through the Alps. Father Lucas knew some of the monasteries they could stay at along the way.

"Beyond Venice, we have no idea," Father Lucas warned.

He tried but could not find any relevant maps or letters for the last part of the journey.

"Well, at least we have the beginning solved," Pierre yoked.

"I heard that one can board a ship to either Alexandria or Beirut and then continue over land," Pierre continued. "Alexandria is relatively safe. Beirut, unfortunately, is an Arab principality with unclear alliances. The only reason to go that way is that it is much closer to Baghdad. But first, we have to get to Venice."

"I am still unsure about this voyage," Jean told Father Lucas when Pierre left. "Who knows what will await us in Baghdad? Just because they have wealth and science does not mean they will share it. We will be strangers there."

"It will be an adventure unlike any of us will ever have. I traveled when I was young—not to places like this, but I did. Think of everything you will see and the stories you will bring back," Father Lucas said to reassure Jean.

"I suppose I can always turn around."

"Be careful, but take it all in."

Father Lucas did not want to elaborate on the potential dangers. Roads and towns were infested with bandits. Exiled Saxons in particular had made a habit of praying on travelers, even on the roads in the area around the abbey. They would not be able to trust anyone, and for that matter, no one would trust them since they would be strangers wherever they went. Anyone willing to help them might have ulterior motives.

When Jean and Pierre finished organizing, they returned to worrying about the necessary funds. They decided to see Jean's mother and ask if she had considered this.

"Don't worry," Jean's mother said with a knowing grin. "Ask the council about the funds."

It came as a surprise; why had the council not mentioned this?

"But it is nice to meet you, Pierre, and I am glad to have the chance to get to know you." Jean's mother said.

"Quite admirable for you to have come so far as an orphan," she said. She smiled at Pierre in an accepting and complimentary way to allay any fear of disrespect.

"Thank you," was all Pierre said, hoping not to have to elaborate about himself.

"But where are you from? Didn't the sisters at the orphanage tell you anything about that?"

Pierre blushed, and Jean felt bad for him.

Silence followed. Jean's mother smiled at Pierre, expecting an answer, but Pierre said nothing and stared at the ground.

"Apparently not." Jean finally said to break the awkward silence.

Jean's mother gave him a look that he knew too well. It said, "You are ignorant and need to be more thoughtful." Nevertheless, Jean cut the meeting short.

"We will ask the council about the funds, as you suggest," he said and got up. Pierre said his goodbyes and left Jean alone with his mother, knowing what an important goodbye it was for them.

"You be careful. I sense Pierre is a good man, but he is hiding something," Jean's mother said, tears rolling down her face.

Jean was overcome with the emotions of a child about to undertake a defining adventure that he knew was dangerous but that would establish him as his own man. It was the type of adventure that parents hesitate to condone but know they have to accept. He gave his mother a reassuring hug, trying to say that he was an adult.

His mother tried to let go and hope for the best. She feared that Jean lacked the life experiences necessary for the type of journey he was about to undertake.

When Jean and Pierre returned to the abbey, they asked to meet with the council. Pierre was afraid the council did not mention the funds because they wanted to keep them, but Jean did not believe that.

"We were told to ask you about the funds for our journey," Jean said when they were in front of the council. He was a little at a loss for how to exactly say it.

"We have the funds," the head of the council said smugly. "You forgot to ask for them," he said. "We were surprised you forgot and hope you won't forget other things you need for the journey." Then he laughed and threw out a satchel with gold coins on the table before him.

"We wish you the best of luck."

Even Father Lucas, who disdained games, had to laugh at the joke the council had played. Jean and Pierre were slightly embarrassed but laughed as well.

Each council member hugged Jean and shook Pierre's hand; they did not know him that well. It was a fitting goodbye.

Father George, who had always been fond of Pierre, pulled him aside as the council dispersed. For once, he was not smiling.

"You be careful," he said to Pierre with a serious face. It took Pierre by surprise. Father George was concerned about him.

"I will," Pierre promised.

"And make the books you bring back good ones," he joked, even though they both knew that might never happen.

Jean and Pierre started the journey the next day. Pierre advocated leaving "before anyone changes their mind." Initially, the young men traveled through open fields, some forests, and many towns that Jean had heard of from his father. They spent nights at monasteries along the way. Pierre had corresponded with many of them when he had organized synods.

The trip was uneventful until one night, when they were too far away from any monastery, they had to camp. As they packed their horses the morning after, they saw five men on horseback coming up the road. As they got closer, Pierre realized who they were.

"Saxons," he said, gesturing for Jean to stay with the horses. "I will speak to them."

Pierre and Jean had a small fortune with them for the journey. They would never receive the funds again; their journey might end before it even began.

Pierre slowly walked toward the approaching horses, trying to put on a relaxed swagger. The riders, clearly apprehensive, surrounded him as soon as he was close.

Jean could not make out what was happening. Pierre stood in the middle of the horses, looking up at the riders. The horses were so close they could trample him any minute. Jean then lost sight of Pierre in a cloud of dust created by the constant jockeying of the horses. At one point, two riders turned their horses to look at Jean. He was not sure what he would do if they came for him. Now, at least, he could see that the leader was talking to Pierre, who was working some magic. The faces of the riders lost their apprehensiveness. Jean even thought he saw one of the riders smile, not in a mean way, but in a friendly way.

Then, all of a sudden, the gang leader raised his arm and twirled it. The Saxons turned their horses and rode off. They disappeared as quickly as they had come.

Pierre slowly walked back to Jean, relieved, thinking of how he would explain what happened.

"I told them we were monks on a journey to one of the monasteries."

"And that appeased them?" Jean responded, still shaken. He did not believe Pierre, but what did it matter?

"Maybe this is just too dangerous," Jean said. "It has been only a few days, and already this."

"It will be fine," Pierre said sternly. "The decision has been made. We are going. We will be fine. Nothing happened, did it?"

Jean did not understand how it had all been resolved so easily and how unshaken Pierre seemed, but he figured he should be thankful. He tried to put the incident aside.

In the following days, Pierre made sure they spent nights in monasteries, even if it meant turning in before sunset. The letter from the abbey explaining the trip continued to be useful, as was Pierre's ability to charm abbots. He led with promises of stories about Charlemagne and thoughts of what they might encounter in Baghdad. He knew monastic life was driven by routine, and interesting visitors were always welcome.

11. The Alps

Father Lucas had warned Pierre and Jean about the Alps—rows and rows of mountains with deep snow. "Make sure you follow the route," he warned them.

He could not have prepared them for what they encountered. The mountain ranges were enormous; just when they managed to sneak through some via mountain passes, another would appear. All the while, the snow became deeper on the roads.

Then, there was the problem of finding monasteries. Monasteries were usually built close to towns; they needed a community to support them and who farmed the lands they usually owned. There were none in the mountains. Pierre and Jean thought they got lucky when they found a monastery well up a hill in the middle of nowhere.

The monastery was built from wood, not stone. It looked like a large two-story farmhouse with no windows on the first floor and a heavily reinforced front door. There was no bell tower, which seemed sensible since there was unlikely to be a congregation. Still, the place was strange. The only indication that it was a monastery was a large cross that was painted next to the front door.

"I don't feel good about this place," Jean said to Pierre as they approached.

"We have no choice," Pierre said, "Would you rather sleep outside?"

Sleeping outside was an option they would likely have to take at some point in the Alps, but it was uncomfortable and potentially dangerous. At altitude, the weather changed quickly, and nights were cold.

As they approached the monastery, a monk opened the heavy front door before they even knocked. He introduced himself as the head monk.

"We are looking for quarters for the night," Pierre said, and tried to show him the letter from the abbey.

The head monk did not look at it.

"I am in charge here," he said. "I can give you a room, but you are not to converse with the other monks unless I am present."

Then, the head monk ushered them to a room without saying anything except that they could join for dinner once they were settled.

When Pierre and Jean found the dining room, it was unusually small and cold. About twenty monks sat on long benches on both sides of a narrow table. Pierre and Jean found places amongst them. No one was talking.

"We are from Marmoutier Abbey, but I have spent much time in Aachen," Pierre finally said in his usual jocular manner.

"We don't care about Aachen," the head monk said sternly. It was clear he wanted to squash any conversation.

The other monks did not look up. They slurped their soup. It was the only noise in the room. There were no smiles and, indeed, not the banter there would have been at Marmoutier Abbey.

Pierre looked at Jean. This was awkward.

They just ate their meals for the remainder of the dinner, playing with the food occasionally to avoid devouring it too fast.

It was clear to Pierre that the head monk at this monastery was firmly in charge. He did not even seem to have an assistant. There was no clear number two. Pierre's mind wandered. He could not help but think that the absence of a number two usually provided an opportunity for someone. This was the type of place where someone with the right mind could gain absolute power.

"You will be leaving in the morning," the head monk said matter-of-factly when everyone finished eating.

"We will," Pierre responded, even though he was not sure the head monk meant it as a question.

When the head monk escorted Pierre and Jean back to their quarters, Pierre became slightly afraid of him. There was something in his look that concerned him. He was not sure what it was.

"We will be leaving early," Pierre said, shaking the head monk's hand well outside the room.

"I don't feel good about this place," Jean repeated to Pierre when they were alone. "The head monk is like an army general, not like an abbot. Did you see the faces of the other monks? They were afraid of him."

"The head monk is like Charlemagne - firmly in charge," Pierre said. "What is wrong with that?"

Jean resolved not to sleep during the night. He heard some inexplicable noises, and each time he did, he tried to devise a plan for how they could get away if they needed to. He, of course, only knew one way out to the monastery, the way they had come in.

With the first sign of sunlight, Jean woke Pierre.

"Let's get going," he said.

"No need to enjoy the place any further," Pierre joked. "Don't want a quiet breakfast?"

"This place is weird," Jean responded.

They passed the head monk in the hallway as they were leaving. He forced a grin. "If you ever want to join us," he said. Pierre and Jean said nothing. It felt absurd, particularly to Jean.

Pierre and Jean were happy to be out of the monastery, but the next few days were miserable. As they gained altitude, the cold became unbearable. Jean was riding with his hands buried in his armpits, slumping with his head down, trying to collapse inward as though it might help. He looked like he was a hostage on the horse, not holding onto the reins and concentrating on staying in the center of his saddle so as not to fall off.

Pierre did not believe such a posture helped. Instead, he concentrated on fighting the cold with his mind. He told himself that it would soon be over, but could not help moving around in his saddle as he shivered.

Disaster struck when the horse carrying the provisions, dragging itself behind Jean's horse, collapsed. Jean felt the rope the horse was tied to rip out of his hands. It almost knocked Jean off his horse.

"I should never have agreed to this," Jean said as they stood beside the collapsed horse.

"But you did agree," Pierre said forcefully. "We must load the other two horses with our provisions and walk," he continued. "That is all."

"That will slow us down considerably. Do we have enough food?"

"We are probably halfway."

"Then it should be getting warmer, but it isn't," Jean objected.

They unpacked and stayed the night on the mountain, lying under the stars with everything they had covering them for warmth. It was bitterly cold, and they were not moving.

Jean was shivering uncontrollably, and his thoughts turned to what they were doing. It was as though his body was shaking his conviction out of him.

"Why do I have this incessant drive to be part of the scientific community? Where has it gotten me? I alienated the monks at the monastery, caused much expense to my parents, and now might freeze to death on this godforsaken mountain."

Pierre had similar thoughts. "Here I am, finally in charge of my destiny," he thought. "In command of my journey, but it is no good. It is just too hard."

"I think we should turn around," Pierre said to Jean when they got up the next morning. "We should be more than halfway, but it is still getting colder. I think I got us lost."

"That would be a mistake," Jean said, surprising Pierre. "We are on the right path and more than halfway. Easier to move forward than to go back."

"How do you know that?" Pierre asked indignantly.

"I have been tracking the stars and confirmed it last night," Jean responded slyly.

"And you kept that a secret until I asked?" Pierre responded.

"Yes, how does it feel not to be told everything?" Jean retorted. He had heard about the potential civil war in Baghdad and resented Pierre not telling him. Pierre said nothing.

"It has continued to get colder because of a shift in weather, not because we are less than halfway," Jean finally said.

Further encouragement came when the days grew warmer despite the shift in weather. Jean noticed it first. One evening, he muttered that there was no returning now and that they might have overcome the worst. It was intended to make Pierre feel better. He figured they needed to encourage each other. Pierre appreciated it. He replied that he was sure they would make it. When they finally came upon some farmland, they knew they had.

Once they found the farmhouse, Pierre asked the farmer to put them up for a couple of days and provide them with provisions in exchange for one of the horses. The area was so remote that the farmer would not accept coins. They were walking their horses anyway, and one was enough to carry the remaining provisions they needed.

"Not a bad way to live," Pierre told Jean about the farmer's existence.

"He is all alone," Jean objected.

"Don't you sometimes wish you could?" Pierre asked.

"Not really," Jean responded. He did not believe that Pierre felt that way. "You are the one with the need for success in Aachen," he continued.

"And what has it gotten me?" Pierre responded.

A moment of silence set in. "Strange," Jean thought. "Always wanting to be in charge. Is he coming apart?" It was not like Pierre to act this way.

"How are we going to figure out the journey beyond Venice?" Jean asked Pierre to move on.

"I will make inquiries in Venice," Pierre responded. He became more assertive.

"Trade boats go from there. To be honest, I am not sure." Pierre said.

12. Venice

Venice was an impressive collection of small communities distributed on marshy islands. Pierre and Jean hired a ship to take them to the Lido, which Father Lucas had told them was the largest island blocking the lagoon. They were sure to find a suitable monastery there.

On their way, Pierre and Jean sailed by an island called Oliviol. They marveled at an impressive castle on it.

"They are afraid of the Lombards here," Pierre said. "That much I learned in Aachen."

Ships were coming and going around them. The traffic was so heavy that Pierre and Jean's boat had to turn and twist to avoid collisions. They sailed by another large island and saw an impressive cathedral being built. "San Pietro di Castello," the ship captain called out proudly.

It was clear that the Venetian islands were wealthy. It was the most cosmopolitan place Pierre and Jean had been to. Pierre could not help but notice that Charlemagne's preoccupation with empire building over trade had not allowed him to make Aachen the city it could have been.

When Pierre and Jean arrived on Lido, they went to the local churches and asked who might put them up and help them organize a trip to Baghdad. After many inquiries, they were told that a priest, Father Tom, had been to Baghdad and would return there soon. They found him in a small church on a minor road.

Father Tom was a short man with shoulders turned inwards and a head slightly tilted forward. It gave him a defensive, careful appearance. It was also the way he spoke - slowly and as though nothing he shared he had not thought about before. It stood in contrast to his quick and hurried actions. He was busily cleaning up things in the church. He had just officiated a Mass.

"I left the caliphate when al-Rashid died. You don't want to be there amid a civil war." Father Tom said when Pierre asked him about Baghdad.

"I was afraid of that," said Pierre, trying not to look at Jean. "Where does that stand?"

Father Tom stepped to the tabernacle where the hosts for Mass were kept and added some to the silver chalice as he spoke. "Well, it is finally finished. His sons battled it out for some time. Al-Ma'mun won. He laid siege to Baghdad, and his brother was killed, but it wasn't even finished then. What you have to understand about the Arab world is that there are two factions. The Abbasids are descendants of Muhammad's uncle al-Abbas. The Umayyads are descendants of Muhammad's cousin Ali. Both claim the right to lead Islam. So when al-Ma'mun defeated his brother, the Baghdad establishment still rejected him because his named successor was of the wrong faction. Then, the successor conveniently died on al-Ma'mun's trip to Baghdad to resolve the matter. Al-Ma'mun was accepted as Caliph, and I am returning."

"But why? Why do you go there?" Jean asked.

"Well, I belong to a church there. They don't care what religion you are as long as it has a book—strange, that. I mainly work for a wealthy merchant. I copy and translate books for him."

"For him to sell?" Pierre asked.

Father Tom collected things from the altar. "No, though you might think that. Merchants create their own libraries." Father Tom looked at Pierre and smiled. "When al-Rashid was in charge, he started an academic movement and founded the House of Wisdom. Merchants wanted to impress him, so they built their own libraries and participated in research. All of that ended during the civil war, but now that al-Ma'mun is in charge and the war is over, they are building libraries again. Al-Ma'mun claims to have had a revelation in a dream: Aristotle, of all people, told him to undertake a rational inquiry. He is even more determined than his father."

"So you work for this merchant to impress the Caliph?" Pierre asked slightly dismissively. It reminded Jean of the sarcasm Pierre usually saved for the brotherhood. "Do you get paid well for that?"

"Yes." Father Tom said in a tone that implied Pierre did not understand. He did not elaborate. Pierre regretted his dismissive tone. He would have liked him to share more about the riches of the caliphate. Now, that would have to wait for another time.

Pierre and Jean were allowed to stay in the small, sagging monastery next to the church. They settled in a tiny room with barely enough space for two beds. A light breeze filtered through the small window at the end of the room. They were surprised to catch the scent of the sea air. They put their things down and left the monastery to explore the island.

"The most dangerous part of our journey is still ahead. I suppose we have the right to take some time off," Jean said to Pierre.

"A nice change from the deep freeze," Pierre responded.

They had been traveling with purpose for weeks, so it seemed awkward to wander around. But the Lido was a beautiful island—a sand bar, really—with wide beaches. The salt one could smell in the air was subtle, just enough to emphasize that the place was special and near the sea, but not so much as to make you believe you were on a ship, with all the trials and tribulations that usually involved. The island was also full of easy-going, ornate architecture that was enjoyable instead of impressive. There was no attempt to build respect or admiration, as with the things built on the other islands.

The next day, Pierre snuck out of the room early to see Father Tom alone. He found him studying some texts in the small dining hall. He was less hurried than the previous day but continued reading as he spoke.

"We appreciate your help," Pierre said.

"Help, yes. However, I would welcome the company if you'd like to travel with me. It is always safer that way."

"How exactly do you plan to travel - through Alexandria or Beirut?"

"Beirut. It is closer and safe. I am taking a ship loaded with fine wool, glass, and tapestries for Baghdad. I am simply following the merchants making their way—first on the ship, then in the caravan. The merchants are Arab; they will see us safely through Beirut. I know the captain of the ship. He is a British Catholic. I negotiated a price with him and with the merchants. Would you like me to do the same for you?"

"That is a very generous offer, Father." Pierre was somewhat taken aback; he had not expected things to move so fast. "I'd like to ask you some questions first, if possible."

Father Tom smiled gently and nodded.

"Is it safe? Baghdad, I mean. Leadership change is a treacherous thing. Is it possible your employer might be caught up in something?"

"Hard to know. Al-Ma'mun has a vision for his country. Anyone with a vision has enemies. But I believe it is safe, or I would not go." Father Tom paused and then continued thoughtfully. "Al-Ma'mun's rational inquiry into things sounds good, but it is also a power play."

"I am not surprised. I am quite familiar with such tactics," Pierre said, relaxing a little.

"He claims that the Muslim holy book, the Koran, is not the actual spoken voice of God but words created by the prophet Mohammed. This allows his movement to interpret the Koran, which orthodox Muslims take exception to."

"Who does that hurt?"

"The imam."

Pierre was nodding when Jean unexpectedly joined them.

"Do religious interpretations always have to disadvantage someone?" Jean said to join the conversation.

Pierre looked at Jean, tilting his head down and smiling slightly to signal that he thought the question naive. Then he looked at Father Tom, who looked away, not wanting to take a position on this.

"Yes, and Father Tom was saying that al-Ma'mun is undertaking a rational inquiry into how to interpret the Koran."

"Rational?" Jean asked. "Is that possible?"

"Yes. They think so. They love Aristotle. He and the other classical philosophers are well regarded, and al-Ma'mun—"

"Aristotle was not just a philosopher," Jean interrupted. "He was one of the foremost scientists. Did you know he argued that an object's speed is inversely proportional to the resistance of the medium through which it moves? He concluded that a void as a medium is, therefore, impossible. An object would otherwise have infinite speed. I find the concept of a void one of the most important ideas of our time."

"Here he goes again," Pierre said. "His admiration of what do you call it, the zero." He wanted to stop Jean from embarrassing himself.

"In Baghdad, they use a number system that employs the concept of a void. The absence of a number." Jean continued.

The old Jean was back. During the trip, particularly through the Alps, he had become quite introverted and depressed. Even before then, ever since the Philoponus book incident, he had not dared to be this enthusiastic with anyone.

"Don't forget to breathe, my friend," Pierre said with a smile. "The rest here has served you well."

Father Tom chuckled. "You will fit in well in Baghdad."

When they saw Father Tom next, he had negotiated a price for Pierre and Jean to join his voyage to Baghdad, though Pierre was still skeptical. He asked to meet the captain and the merchant in charge of the trip. When he found them to be trustworthy, he paid for the journey. The ship was to leave two days later. Pierre and Jean spent the time enjoying the Lido.

"This has turned out to be surprisingly easy—almost too easy," Pierre said to Jean the day before they left.

Pierre was glad that Jean was with him, and Father Tom had agreed to lead them. They were about to commence the part of the journey that was a complete unknown. Vast lands and seas lay before them with risky circumstances, countless dangers, and unknowns. Pierre did not want to be alone. "Being alone means fewer dependencies and more liberties," he thought. "But that does not compensate for wanting someone with you, especially in uncertain times."

13. Introductions

Pierre and Jean got their first real introduction to Islam on the ship. The merchants and crew gathered on deck for prayers five times a day. They knelt in neat rows and threw their arms forward as they bowed and recited prayers. Catholic Mass was a collection of readings, singing, praying, and communion; this seemed more direct to Pierre, who was watching intently. He was used to gatherings reminiscent of the Last Supper and the early, secretive meetings in the catacombs of Rome. This was a different way of addressing God, more public, more routine-seeming.

"Fascinating. Such devotion and submission to God," Pierre commented when Father Tom approached him.

Father Tom spoke quietly as they watched. "Prayer is one of the five tenets of Islam, known as Salat." Father Tom finished recounting the five tenets, counting them on his fingers. "Shahada is the reciting of the Muslim profession of faith; Zakat is paying a tax for the poor; Sawm is fasting during Ramadan; and Hajj is a pilgrimage to Mecca."

Then Father Tom looked at Pierre. "They are to pray toward the Kaaba in Mecca. It is the shrine where Abraham and his son Ishmael built their first house of worship. On the ship, they can't be sure what direction that is, so they pray toward the south, which is the direction that Mohammed prayed. Mecca is south of Medina, where the Prophet lived."

"We simply don't have such devotion," Pierre said as he continued to watch.

Father Tom's response surprised him. "We have the rosary prayers. Prayers to our Lady Mary, the Mother of God, who represents the mystery of our salvation. God's transformation into our form through Mary. Mary brought God to us so that he could lead us. The contemplation of this in the rosary prayers is a devotion. One that enables us to see the commitment of God to us."

Pierre was a little offended. He was still a monk, after all; he did not need the purpose of the rosary explained to him, though he was impressed with how much of a Christian Father Tom still was after spending so much time in Baghdad.

Pierre excused himself and walked away. The mention of Mary made him think about his own mother, whose great sacrifice he had never spoken about and whose existence he had kept a secret.

As expected, Jean spent most of his time figuring out the ship. The sails, the trade winds, and the navigation were all new to him. He spent time with the captain, trying to make sense of it all. He even stayed up nights to help the captain navigate by the stars.

When they finally arrived in Beirut, Pierre became quiet and apprehensive as it sank in where he had led them. They were in a truly strange place. The city was unlike Aachen; there was pervasive poverty and dirt, but the hustle and bustle of the people was entirely different. It was a port city focused on the Muslim faith and trade. Instead of the Carolingian Chapel being the focal point, minarets were interspersed throughout the city. Instead of bells chiming, men appeared on towers delivering prayers.

They walked by markets with strange spices and fruit on display; only the chickens were familiar. Vendors smiled at them with encouraging gestures, but that was commerce. They knew no one, and it was clear who they were—foreigners who might not belong. From now on, they were unfamiliar.

Pierre was glad that they did not stay in Beirut for long. The camels were loaded with the goods they had brought, and the caravan got on its way. His concerns, however, did not abate; they shifted to their vulnerability in the open. There could be robbers. They were carrying valuable goods. There was no pretending that they were just poor monks on a journey.

Fortunately, they rested in large hostels during the nights, almost like little castles, where even the camels were safely enclosed. Pierre realized that they were primarily vulnerable during the day when they traveled.

Sure enough, one day, they saw some armed riders head toward them—thoughts of the Saxon encounter raced through Pierre and Jean's heads. It turned out to be the opposite, a patrol policing the road.

"Everything has been done in the Arab world to make trade easy and safe," Pierre said. Trade was a focal point in the Arab world, while conquest was a focal point in the Carolingian world.

After the encounter, Pierre started to relax a little and tried to enjoy the open spaces of the desert—vast lands with little vegetation and huge mountains in the distance. It was spectacular; even the heat and the occasional dust storms were novel, the type of adventure to enjoy.

"What can we expect in Baghdad? Can they build a city in the middle of this sand?" Pierre asked Father Tom. Father Tom, by now, had gotten used to Pierre's sarcasm.

"The city is truly amazing. I say that, being from Venice. It is a metropolis surpassing Venice and even Rome in diversity and vibrance. Over one million people live there from all walks of life. Africans, Indians, Asians, and Europeans all pass through or settle there. Canals connect the Tigris River with the port city of Basra, which makes Baghdad a major trading hub. The city has grown so much that it now occupies both sides of the river. A pontoon bridge connects the two parts. It is the most spectacular place I have ever been. I can't stay away."

Pierre and Jean could not imagine a city with over one million people. How could any one place accommodate that number?

Father Tom described the city further.

"The original part of the city, a round fortification with brick walls and four gates, stands on the west bank of the Tigris. It is known as the Round City due to its fortifications, but its official name comes from a vast market district located in the south. The four gates are named after four important areas: Basra, Kufa, Damascus, and Khorasan."

Father Tom explained that the round fortification contained the Caliph's original palace, topped by a huge green roof with a weathervane in the form of a horseman's figure. "The most amazing thing, in my opinion, is that the Caliph does not live there anymore. He has allowed the library of the House of Wisdom and administrative buildings to take over. Imagine that, not insisting on living in the center of things and allowing a library to take over!"

It was clear Father Tom was enamored with the city. Jean liked the idea of a library being in the center of things.

"The fortification does, however, hold a mosque," Father Tom continued pensively. He did not want to elaborate on the upheaval that religious factions caused, even in Baghdad.

"The mosque is large," he continued instead. "But not the largest. That distinction goes to the Umayyad Alid mosque in Damascus. There is relative peace now, but the rivalry between the Umayyads and the Abbasids is never-ending."

"We are aware of that," Pierre said and chuckled. He was referring to his time in Aachen when Charlemagne tried to use this to his advantage.

When they finally arrived in the city, they entered it near the caliph's current palace. It was a large and impressive complex featuring a park that housed wild animals. Next to it were streets lined with new houses made of sun-dried bricks.

"Invasions, including the recent siege, fires, and floods, have destroyed the city so many times that the buildings are mostly new," Father Tom said.

"Aqueducts bring water to all parts of the city?" Jean asked. He was impressed by how immaculate the city was.

The cleanliness, the bright sunlight, and the new brick on the buildings made it gleam. Not just an oasis, a new oasis.

"I see what you mean about other religions being accepted," Pierre commented as they passed a Christian church near the city's center. "I did not think it would be all in the open, proudly displayed like this."

They rode on and noticed a rabbi greeting them. Jean greeted back and then smiled at Pierre. They had never seen a rabbi before.

Father Tom noticed.

"It has been like this for a long time. At the Talmudic academies of Sura and Pumbedita, Jews have maintained centers of learning since Babylonian times. The "ahl al-dhimma" title is given to all religions with central texts like the Bible, and their followers are protected."

It took some time before they arrived in the market district, known as al-Karkh, where the caravan was unloaded.

The center of town was densely built; there was little wind. Jean and Pierre thought the heat in the desert was novel, but here it was stifling. They felt the heat radiating from the walls, the shiny sidewalks, and the sandy roads, really from any surface. This and the bustle of the marketplace they were approaching made Pierre and Jean uncomfortable. People were walking every which way, squeezing by them. They felt a little entrapped and entirely out of place.

"A little overwhelming," Jean said to Father Tom as they fought their way through some narrow alleys. Even Pierre was uncomfortable. Eventually, they got to the center of town and thought they could relax. However, Father Tom told them that he had to leave to meet with his employer, al-Wazi. He was already late. Pierre and Jean would have to find a hostel and fend for themselves.

Al-Wazi's house was just north of al-Karkh, in a part of the city overlooking the Tigris River. The house had two stories and was built around a courtyard with a fountain and a small garden in the middle. Al-Wazi's trade with India had made him wealthy, and his house showed it.

The gate to the courtyard was open. A servant saw Father Tom as he entered. The servant remembered him and greeted him enthusiastically. He escorted him to a reception hall decorated with Chinese vases and silver ornaments. After conferring with the head servant, he escorted Father Tom to a guest room on the first floor and told him to stay the night and have dinner with al-Wazi.

Dinner, held after sundown prayers, was an elaborate affair. Musicians played in the corner of the great room. About twenty guests gathered and were seated in a circle. Food was served in communal dishes placed in the center. The main dish consisted of rice and lamb; other dishes featured a variety of spices and fresh fruit. With the first whiff of cinnamon, Father Tom remembered how much he had missed it all.

It was the usual cast of diverse characters. An overly jocular man immediately looked up to judge Father Tom, not to approve or disapprove, but to figure him out. He smiled. There was a trio of serious scholars hiding their joy, fearing it would adversely affect their status. They were not eating much. There were several business types, some serious, some jovial. They reminded Father Tom of the market sellers in Beirut, superficial but agreeable.

Al-Wazi sat at the far end of the room. Father Tom was seated between him and a Sanskrit translator who translated Al-Wazi's Indian books.

"It is good to see you," al-Wazi said. "You missed a lot during the time you were gone."

"Most of it is good, I am sure, but some is not so good."

"That is now over; al-Ma'mun is in charge. His rational inquiry into everything has taken over. They call it the Mutazilite movement. We have many prominent scholars now, and we are seeking more."

He offered Father Tom some food and then ate some himself.

"Have you heard of al-Kindi? He is probably our most famous. He has written original works on philosophy, physics, mathematics, and other subjects. He just disproved Aristotle's theory on the reflection of light."

"I regret I have not," Father Tom was embarrassed to say. "But I will make sure to find his works."

"How about Jabir ibn Hayyan? I believe he is known as Geber in the West. He has developed new theories of alchemy. I hope to commercialize them." Al-Wazi smiled.

Father Tom had not.

"Then there is Sind ibn Ali, who is reworking ancient texts on astronomy."

Father Tom noticed how confident Al-Wazi was. Things had turned out well for him.

"I could go on. It is all exciting, but we have much to catch up on! Tell me what you were up to while you were gone," Al-Waze asked.

"I went back to Venice to live in the monastery I came from. It was not particularly exciting, but it was safe. I am happy to be back."

"You must have missed our fruits," Al-Wazi said, handing a dish to Father Tom, who smiled.

"Indeed."

They spoke for a while about nothing. It was a conversation more about building a relationship than substance. In his usual self-assured and thoughtful way, Father Tom did not attempt to impress Al-Wazi. He had learned that if he did not try, he usually conveyed enough reassurance.

"We need people like you. We don't have enough. Scholars are advancing new theories every day," Al-Wazi finally said. "I am so glad you are back."

"You know I am only a translator."

"I know, but we must push things forward with interpretations as well."

Father Tom had never interpreted texts before, though he knew that Pierre had, at least to the extent it supported

Charlemagne's views. He suggested that al-Wazi might want to engage Pierre and mentioned Jean.

"I would like to meet them. Pierre, I may hire, but not Jean. I don't commission scientific work."

"Really?" Father Tom said.

"However, he should meet al-Sanad, who comes to my house frequently. Al-Sanad has just been asked to build an observatory to make astronomical observations for the Caliph. The Caliph got a copy of a book entitled Almagest, by the Greek astronomer Ptolemy, in a peace settlement with the Byzantines. He commissioned the observatory to test theories in the book. I am sure al-Sanad would want to meet Jean."

Al-Wazi sat up straight.

"Al-Sanad comes to my house frequently because of my library. Through my business in India, I have obtained copies of old Hindu texts written by an astronomer named Brahmagupta. Brahmagupta calculated the proportions of the sun and the planets to predict eclipses, and al-Sanad is interested in that."

Al-Wazi and Father Tom came to a quick arrangement. Tom would live in the monastery he lived in before and produce one book translation every three weeks he was there. He would be paid twice what he had been paid last time he was in Baghdad. Pierre and Jean were to introduce themselves in a week.

Pierre and Jean did not have such a relaxing evening. They spent the night at a hostel they found. It was noisy, and they were too apprehensive to sleep. They overheard a man and woman fighting in the room next door and then making up in a totally unfamiliar way.

"Not something we would have witnessed in the abbey," Pierre commented to Jean as they lay awake.

"Yet another new experience," Jean commented, smiling. "Wasn't that what this is all about?" he joked.

They met Father Tom in the morning.

"I told al-Wazi about you, and he wants to meet you both in a week. I also went to my church early this morning. They can put all three of us up at the monastery next to the church."

This was the good news Pierre and Jean needed after the night they spent.

The monastery was small, with only six other brothers. Father Tom's suite had a common area with a large table in the center and two tiny bedrooms. He had already spread some books on the table. The room was in the shade of the church. A small garden was visible through a large window, and birds could be heard.

Jean's room was down the hall. It had a bed and a tiny desk that occupied most of the space. The room had a small window and was dark. "I am glad I don't have too many things," Jean commented wryly.

A week after they had settled in, Pierre and Jean were finally invited to al-Wazi's house. They were impressed.

"The house is so clean, new, and airy," Jean said.

"Not worn, old, and moldy, like Marmoutier Abbey," Pierre joked.

"Look at the threshold," Jean pointed out the marble threshold to the house. It was precisely cut and starkly contrasted with the limestone threshold of Marmoutier Abbey, which had been rounded through the ages. The marble was inlaid with green and red stones forming interconnecting flowers.

"Everything is new here," Jean said.

"Everything is built for what is to come," Pierre agreed.

The inside of the house was unlike anything they had ever seen. Every detail was decorated, not with pictures of religious figures, but with intricate geometric designs in tiles on the walls, carpets, furniture, and even on the vases that stood on tables.

"The geometry is mesmerizing. The designs captivate the mind. They are pleasing in a way one can't explain." Jean commented. Pierre was more interested in the people coming to the meeting. He asked Father Tom to introduce him to al-Wazi.

"Al-Wazi, unfortunately, is not here," Father Tom told them when he returned from speaking to the head servant.

"But his oldest son, his daughter, Amira, and al-Sanad are."

He put on a serious, knowing face. The one Pierre remembered from when they first spoke about organizing the trip at his church in Venice.

"You are expected to introduce yourself. Don't just focus on what you have done. Here, they want to know about your family as well. They want to know where you came from." Father Tom instructed them.

Pierre spoke first with some broken Arabic he was starting to pick up and with help from Father Tom. "The Carolingian and the Byzantine empires have been involved in religious debate for many years. During that time, I was employed at the court of Charlemagne in Aachen. I am familiar with interpreting philosophical texts and know Latin and Greek. I hope to be able to contribute to the intellectual movement here. The people who funded our journey expect us to bring back books. We will need access to books and time to copy them. I understand that this would be reflected in our wages."

The scholars at the meeting did not understand why Pierre did not speak about himself. They were also distracted by his blond hair and blue eyes. Baghdad was a cosmopolitan place with a mixture of cultures and people from all walks of life, but Pierre stuck out.

Father Tom was not happy. "Don't make the same mistake as Pierre," he told Jean. "You must speak about your family background; they care more about that." He looked at Pierre, a little upset since he had ignored his instructions.

"I am the son of a nobleman of the Carolingian Empire," Jean started. He felt a little awkward. It was unusual for him to speak of his background, but he trusted Father Tom.

"I grew up in a regional capital my father was in charge of, but it was nothing like Baghdad." Jean continued, but then he wanted to pivot into an introduction much like his friend. It would have been awkward for Pierre if he had not.

"I have studied Aristotle and have heard of the great work of al-Kindi and the mathematician al-Khwarizmi. I look forward to learning the Hindu decimal system used here. I have long been fascinated with the use of a zero in the number system and look forward to using it. Coming to Baghdad has been a dream of mine. No place on earth is as advanced in science and mathematics. It is wonderful to be here."

On the way out of the meeting, Pierre teased him. "They will not hire you just because you are eager to learn. They want us to work."

"You could have spoken more about your background." Jean retorted, raising an eyebrow at Pierre and resolving that he would find out why Pierre never wanted to talk about his family. He remembered his mother finding that unusual.

14. House of Wisdom

A few days later, Jean received a message that he should attend a scientist's meeting at al-Wazi's house. The sessions were organized so that scholars could lecture on their current work. Visitors were allowed, and other scholars would come if they were interested in learning about the subject being discussed.

The meeting was in a large room in the back of the house. It was not the room where al-Wazi held his dinners but another equally big room with ornate carpets and decorations. Jean had thought that austerity encouraged intellectual pursuits, but now he changed his mind. Maybe being in ornateness was a way of underscoring that their pursuit was worth adulation. He liked the setting.

Scholars sat in a horseshoe with a focal point towards one wall in the front of the room, where the lecturer was to sit. Jean was stunned to discover that the great mathematician al-Khwarizmi was attending. In his introductory remarks, Jean had spoken highly of al-Khwarizmi but did not expect to meet him so soon. That may be why they had invited him, despite being an obscure newcomer. When they met, al-Khwarizmi described the astronomy book he was working on, Zij al-Sindhind. Jean told him about the Bede book that Alcuin had brought to Marmoutier Abbey. The two got along well.

Jean also met the physician Hunan ibn Isqhaq.

"I hear you have studied Aristotle," Hunan ibn Isqhaq said.

"A little, mostly his theories on moving objects."

"You know, al-Kindi has improved on some of them. I am not that ambitious," he smiled.

Jean took an immediate liking to him.

"I am working on the geometry of the eye," he continued. "I have found some texts of Gallen, Hippocrates, and, of course, Aristotle to be helpful."

Hunan ibn Isqhaq surveyed the room in an approving, appreciative manner. Nods were exchanged. Then he looked at Jean again.

"Did you hear al-Khwarizmi will lecture on a new mathematical procedure? It might be useful for my work."

"The collaboration here is fascinating," Jean responded.

Amira, al-Wazi's daughter, was the only woman present. She had been at Pierre's and Jean's interview. Jean recognized her but did not dare to introduce himself.

Al-Khwarizmi started the meeting with a mathematical problem. "You and I both have a basket of eggs. If I give you one of my eggs, we would have the same number. If, on the other hand, you give me one of your eggs, I would have twice as many as you. How many eggs does each of us have?"

Everyone in the audience quickly solved the problem through trial and error: 7 and 5.

Al-Khwarizmi agreed but then explained that there was a systematic way to solve this problem that did not involve trial and error. He used a board to write down the formulas "$a - 1 = b + 1$" and "$a + 1 = 2(b - 1)$" and then manipulated the two equations such that he could solve for a being 7.

"This abstraction and method allow one to solve the problem without trial and error. The advantage of a systematic approach is that it is faster than trial and error and allows for more complicated formulations where trial and error would be impossible."

He handed out pieces of paper on which he had written examples of his algebraic approach to problems. The scholars in the room studied them; some consulted with al-Khwarizmi. The room filled with enthusiasm. It ended with all agreeing that the approach was helpful to them.

When the lecture was over, Jean wandered around the room to see if he could meet other scholars. To his surprise, Amira introduced herself.

"I think al-Sanad will contact you," she said. "He was impressed by your enthusiasm."

Amira was well-informed.

"Isn't he building an observatory?" Jean asked as he was trying to compose himself. He tried not to stare into Amira's soft, subtle brown and black eyes, whose nuances he could not capture.

"Yes," Amira responded, turning her head slightly. "The observatory is being built at Daryr Muran Monastery at Mount Oasyun, near Damascus. He wants your help."

"Really? That is great, I mean. Astronomy has always fascinated me." Jean said, a little flustered. "We would have gotten lost in the Alps if not for astronomy, but I am getting carried away."

Amira enjoyed Jean losing his composure.

"The Abbasids have strong roots in it. The Zoroastrian religion, which predated Islam, focused on the stars. It was one of the few ancient religions with only one God. But it is not recognized. It does not have a book."

Amira said this so matter-of-factly that it left Jean with the impression that she was looking at her society from the outside.

"How curious that she would mention an unrecognized religion as part of their heritage to a stranger," Jean thought. "And how curious how the book requirement seems to have marginalized precisely that religion."

But before he could ask Amira about that, she left.

"Who was she? Part of the establishment, but not really?" Jean wondered.

He forced himself to think about the "systematic approach" they learned in the meeting. "If you can devise a system, things become easier," he thought. He reconstructed the algebra they learned in his head. After a while, however, he could not help but think about Amira.

The next morning, Father Tom, Pierre, and Jean sat at the table in their common area, and Jean spoke about his meeting. He told them about the algebraic approach and about potentially working with al-Sanad. He also told them about his encounter with Amira.

"She may be testing you with the Zoroastrian comment," Pierre said. "Be careful. Also, we are supposed to be copying books, remember, not doing work on an observatory."

Jean could tell that Pierre was frustrated. While Jean felt confident that he would find work, Pierre had no prospects. Al-Wazi had said nothing after their meeting. Pierre did not know what he would be doing or how they would produce the needed books. He had little to do besides fret over the volatile political situation in Baghdad.

"Things here are even more unstable than we expected," he continued. "The caliph and the imam continue to be at odds. The Mutazilite movement continues to marginalize the imam, and he is fighting it."

Jean nodded but said nothing. He wanted to talk more about how exciting his meeting at al-Wazi's house was, the openness and access, and the intellectual interchange. He also wanted to talk about Amira, but knew that conversation would fall flat given Pierre's mood.

Soon thereafter, as Amira had forecasted, Jean got a message from al-Sanad to join him at the observatory near Damascus. The observatory was encountering problems. Their observations of the sun and the moon were inconsistent with prior recorded facts.

"Not sure what I can add," Jean told Pierre.

"And it will be hot in the desert," Pierre responded. "It was fun the first time, but I am glad I don't have to go there." Pierre was still upset about not having any work.

"Yes, hot. Don't they know that we are better at cold facts than hot intuitions?" Jean joked.

On top of the heat, the sand also made the trip uncomfortable. Jean struggled as he made his way to Damascus. The desert stood in stark contrast to the pleasures of life in Baghdad.

"How can anything be measured accurately in these conditions?" Jean thought, and that thought made him a hero in the end. When he arrived, he developed a hunch that the conditions in the desert might impact the measurement instruments.

"We place instruments inside where I come from," Jean told al-Sanad. "Are you sure they are accurate?"

It turned out he was right. The heat was slightly bending the metal. Jean had the early success he needed to be accepted by the other scientists.

From Damascus, the group traveled to the plains of Sinjar, about 70 miles west of Mosul. There, they undertook another experiment commissioned by al-Ma'mun: determining the Earth's circumference. Jean thought the experiment curious since the Earth was still considered flat in the Christian world.

"I am enjoying the desert," Jean told his companions instead of quibbling. It was the joy of being respected that had overcome him. The desert was as miserable as ever.

When the group arrived at the plains, they took an initial reading of the sun's angle from the ground, then one team headed north, and one team headed south while carefully recording the distance traveled. Once they traveled enough distance to change the sun's angle from the ground by one degree, they noted the distance traveled. They then used geometry from the Greek mathematician Eratosthenes to determine the Earth's circumference: about 20,160 miles.

In the meantime, Pierre's fortunes took a turn. At first, al-Wazi had resisted hiring him; he did not trust him. However, when it became clear that Father Tom was not making enough progress with interpretations on his own, al-Wazi asked him to team up with Pierre. Al-Wazi agreed to pay Pierre and organized for him to copy books from the library of the House of Wisdom in his free time.

Father Tom and Pierre developed a routine. They spent the mornings translating and interpreting books. Father Tom tended to church matters in the afternoons, and Pierre worked on copying books for Marmoutier Abbey. He made good progress, quickly completing two books.

It was progress, yes, but Pierre was not happy. He was alone, and while earning good money, he could not see any prospects for advancement. He was a lowly scribe in a foreign country. It was not the life he was accustomed to.

He decided to try to find Akbar, the scribe he'd met in Aachen. He assumed Akbar might have risen in stature by now and might be able to find him a more important position.

As he walked the streets of Baghdad, Pierre was reminded what a foreigner he was. The constant stares at his blue eyes and blond hair made him feel like he was not human, more like he was a curiosity. He hated it and made no eye contact.

Pierre looked for Akbar in front of the wazīr's, the first minister's, offices in the town center. He waited outside, hoping that Akbar still worked there. Sure enough, after a while, he saw Akbar walking out of the building.

Pierre recognized him immediately. He walked with his usual ease and constant smile. Pierre had always admired that, but to his surprise, he was now envious. Akbar still had the position that Pierre had lost. Pierre almost turned around, unsure if he could face Akbar and admit how far he had fallen.

"Pierre!" Akbar said when he saw Pierre. It was too late.

It was a meeting neither could have imagined, and Akbar wondered, at least for a moment, if he was imagining it in the heat.

"Is it really you?" Akbar said.

Pierre had to smile at that and then proceeded to explain how he and Jean had ended up in Baghdad.

"Aachen was the most exciting time of my life," Akbar said.

"And mine," Pierre said with a hint of frustration.

"I could never go back there now. I hear the new emperor—what is his name?—would not want Arab visitors."

"His name is Louis, but he is known as Louis the Pious. You are right: he is not known for tolerance. If it were not for Louis, I would still be in Aachen."

"Is it true that al-Ma'mun arrested the imam?" Pierre then asked, always wanting to be informed.

"Yes, it is true," Akbar said flatly.

"How serious is that? Will there be a civil war?"

"Unclear, but I don't think so. The risks are too great for both sides."

Then they went back to reminiscing about Aachen - a topic more enjoyable to both.

After a while, Pierre confessed his frustrations to his old friend. "I am having a hard time here. I have a job as a scribe for a merchant. Not what I am used to. I also know no one here."

"I understand. You want to make a career here. But while we may be open to trade, science, and religions, you would be hard-pressed to rise here to the position you once enjoyed."

Pierre slumped. "You don't think there is a way for me to work for the wazīr with my language skills?"

"Maybe, but even here, people trust their own. You could not advance far in politics."

"I suppose not," Pierre said, defeated.

Akbar was right. Pierre had risen to the top of the Carolingian Empire as an orphan. But to assume that he could do it again in Baghdad as a foreigner was overly ambitious.

Over the following weeks, Pierre often thought about Aachen. It had all come so suddenly. He was summoned to Aachen. Theoduff had taken him under his wings, and he had risen to the top with him. Aachen was not a particularly attractive town, Charlemagne was not particularly impressive, and there was constant infighting, but it was the pinnacle of power.

Reminiscing entertained Pierre for a while, but eventually, the joy subsided.

Pierre resumed his lowly routine. He started the day translating texts. Painstakingly finding the right words, translating sentences without thinking about the deeper meaning of the paragraph. He translated what he was assigned. It did not interest him.

He would take a break for lunch, sometimes with Father Tom, sometimes alone.

Then he would resume his work. In the afternoons, he copied books. He copied them as he was taught, without considering any meaning, even the meaning of the words. He just copied individual letters in a delicate but continuous flow. Letter after letter. No need to know the word. It was endless. Letters kept coming.

It all consumed time, but Pierre had an infinite supply of that. What was worse, he did it all in his room. Day after day.

"I don't know how the farmer in the Alps does it," he thought. He felt like him - all alone. It did not suit him.

He thought about seeking Akbar out again, but it reminded him too much of the time of his life he could never relive, and Akbar told him he had little hope of gaining meaningful employment there.

One night, Pierre had a dream about returning to the abbey: A storm brewing outside, wetness in the air - the smell of wetness. It was autumn, and the leaves were turning. Fresh, wet air was blowing leaves of a multitude of colors. The monks were conferring, debating, smiling, teasing each other, and laughing. Pierre could not be sure of what. Was it about him? He was sitting alone in the dining hall, but he heard them. They were in the church. Laughing in the church. Was this right? They could not contain themselves. Their faces filled with joy. Then, three monks appeared in front of him. Still laughing. They handed him a blanket. What for? It was warm. There was warmth, warmth despite the storm.

Pierre woke up smiling. He liked the dream. He wanted it to continue. He tried to fall asleep again to continue and force it back, but it did not work.

Over the next few weeks, Pierre tried to fall asleep during the day. He was not physically tired but hoped the dream would come back. It never did.

The only thing Pierre thought of to break his routine was to join Father Tom in Mass.

"I am surprised to see you at Mass," Father Tom told Pierre afterward. He was thinking of how Pierre had shunned the religious duties before.

"It reminds me of the brotherhood," Pierre said. That surprised Father Tom even more.

15. Jean's Success

When Jean returned, al-Sanad reported the findings directly to al-Ma'mun, but Jean was allowed to report on them at the gathering of scientists at al-Wazi's house. It was a significant achievement, and Jean felt he was gaining respect as one of the scientists. He was happy that Amira got to see his presentation. He was now part of the House of Wisdom, she admired.

"You just arrived in Baghdad a few months ago, and already you have been away from the city for more time than you have been here," Amira teased him.

"I would not know what to look for in the city, how to enjoy it," Jean responded, reveling in the continued lighter tone of the conversations with Amira.

"And yet you were able to find things in the desert."

They both laughed.

After the meeting, Jean found himself thinking about Amira again. She was well educated and part of the establishment, yet sarcastic—a free spirit.

He returned to his quarters in the monastery, where he met with Father Tom and Pierre.

"I like what you've done to the room," Jean said when he entered. The room had no decoration; it looked as barren as it had always been. Father Tom and Pierre saw it as temporary. They were not staying in Baghdad. Pierre did not appreciate Jean's sarcasm.

"I am working away. I am almost done with a third book. I am earning money, which is already enough for a return journey. If we wanted to leave tomorrow, we could. What are you doing?"

"I did not know that you even wanted to return to Marmoutier Abbey, at least not so soon," Jean retorted.

"We may not have a choice. The imam was arrested. Have you thought about what that may mean?" Pierre said with an agitated voice.

"You want me to work. Fine, I will ask al-Wazi if I can join you." It was a crazy idea, given his recent successes, but it was all Jean could think of. He was upset.

"Good. You can see what it's like; join our little routine," Pierre said, looking at Father Tom, who'd been listening to the conversation.

"Why don't you join Pierre and me for Mass?" Father Tom suggested, in an upbeat tone, to change the conversation.

Jean gave Pierre a surprised look. "No, thank you. I have other things to do."

Jean wanted to daydream about Amira. He went to his room and lay on his bed. He never had or was allowed to have feelings for a woman, but there was no one to enforce that here. Father Tom might be the only one to say anything, but he did not have to listen to him. But if he were to court Amria, he might have to convert.

Jean's mind was racing. "Did it matter if he had to convert? They accept Moses and believe in one God. They don't even dispute the existence of Jesus. When Mohammed ascended into the seventh heaven from the mount in Jerusalem, he was reported to have seen Moses, Abraham, and Jesus."

Jean stopped himself, surprised at how wild his thoughts had gotten, when he heard a crowd outside on the street. The crowd shouted slogans about the holiness of the imam. He went into the hallway to take a look. Father Tom and Pierre were there listening intently to the commotion, concern written on their faces.

"These demonstrations have become quite passionate," Father Tom said.

Jean went by them to go outside.

"It is not safe," Pierre warned.

Jean went despite that. The crowd was an angry mob of students with disrespectful faces. There was nothing holy about their expressions. Some students looked at Jean as they passed, but did not stop. They pushed forward in a river of emotions, headed for a confrontation. They wanted their grievances heard in the center of

Baghdad, where they were sure to be met by police or, worse, by the military. The conflict between the imam and al-Ma'mun was heating up.

The following scientific meeting, held at al-Wazi's house, featured a lecture by one of al-Khwarizmi's scientists on the ongoing work on an atlas of over 2,000 places. Jean's help in measuring the Earth's circumference was integral to this project. Jean attended the meeting because he was interested in the topic and wanted to ask al-Wazi for a job. And, of course, he hoped to see Amira.

When he arrived, he wasted no time approaching al-Wazi. "I have been selfish. I can't justify not earning money and letting Pierre do all the work. I need a job. Can you help me?"

Al-Wazi started laughing. "You want a job?" He walked away, shaking his head. Jean was not sure what that meant. Had he offended him?

Jean approached Amira, slightly disoriented and unsure how many more scientific meetings he would have time for if he got a job or be invited to if he offended Al-Wazi.

"You accused me of not seeing Baghdad," he started, referring to their prior conversation. "It may not offer anything better than what is present here," he continued, flattering Amira, who took note. "But, I will let you convince me," he said to prompt her.

Amira put on a slightly devious smile and widened her brown eyes. She was up to the challenge.

"Let's take a look," she said. "You wait outside."

Jean was stunned by how quickly Amira decided to take him up on his challenge. A few moments later, Amira, chaperoned by one of her brothers, appeared, and they went off on a sightseeing tour of the city. Amira took her task seriously. She told Jean about the history of Baghdad. Baghdad became the capital of the Abbasids after Mashallah, a Jewish astrologer, had interpreted celestial signs for al-Mansur, the Caliph's grandfather. The astrologer currently close to the Caliph was Musa ibn Shakir, whose three sons Jean had met at the observatory.

They walked through the various quarters of the city. Different professions, nationalities, and religions dominated different areas. The market quarter was the most vibrant. Jean and Amira were constantly approached to purchase various items. At the old fort in the city's center, they saw well-dressed scribes who worked in the administration. Jean mentioned that Pierre had recently seen Akbar, who had become prominent enough in the administration that Amira knew him by name.

Finally, they went to the library of the House of Wisdom.

"My father was told that it houses the biggest collection of books in the world," Amira proudly proclaimed.

As they entered, Jean marveled.

"No one on Earth could ever know as much as is written in these books, fascinating."

He told Amira about his incident with the Philoponus book.

"Really? They could not accept the text for what it was?" Amira asked.

"Right, it made no sense," Jean said. "No one saw it that way. Can you believe that?"

"Let's see if we can find it. Come on," Amira said, excited about the search.

Jean waited for a moment and smiled while he blew on his black curly hair. Since being at the abbey, he grew it out. It made him look casual, and he wanted to be that way with Amira. Before they went to the librarian to find the book, he looked at Amira intently, appreciating being with her. She gave him a warm, discerning smile in return.

"No, I am sorry, Amira, it has been lent out," the librarian who knew Amira said with a smile that showed Jean that he was not the only one who admired her.

When the day was over, Jean went back to his quarters. He did not want to speak to Father Tom or Pierre and went to his room.

He just wanted to lie on his bed and think about his afternoon with
Amira.

16. Pierre and Jean's Differences

When a messenger arrived at the monastery with a pouch of gold coins, Jean was surprised. Who could have sent it? It came with a letter from al-Sanad.

Jean,

I am sorry that I did not explain how things work. When al-Ma'mun commissions a project, we aim to please him. When we are fortunate to be successful, he rewards us.

Not knowing this must have been distressful for you. I am sorry. Here is your share of the great Caliph's appreciation for our work.

Let us talk about our next project soon.

al-Sanad

Jean immediately went to see Pierre. This was his independence.

"Here you go," Jean said proudly and handed over the coins he had earned. In the back of his mind, he heard his mother's warnings about Pierre and her concerns about his secrecy. Despite this, Jean felt he should trust Pierre.

"I got paid well for the project. We should pool our resources."

"I don't believe it," Pierre said, clearly pleased but not without jealousy.

"And now I want to tell you about Amira." Jean went on to describe the afternoon they had spent together. Usually, he could not stop talking about science. This was new.

Pierre was not amused. "The fight between al-Ma'mun and the imam is escalating. We will have to leave soon. The last thing you need is to get entangled with a woman."

"What if we stay?"

"Stay? For the civil war?" Pierre looked at the ceiling of the room. "He has lost his mind." Then he looked at Jean. "If you want to court Amira, you will not only have to leave the priesthood; you will also have to leave the faith. You would be required to convert to Islam."

While Jean was sheltered in the womanless grounds of Marmoutier Abbey, Pierre had seen in Aachen what happened to priests who got embroiled in affairs. Either the woman was ruined or the priest left the priesthood, or both.

"I am willing to convert," Jean said boldly. "Mohammed laid down rules about acceptance, while Jesus laid down rules about forgiveness. I am not sure which is more important." It was a petty turn of words, and Pierre took it as such.

"Right now, probably acceptance," Pierre said flatly, making light of the comment.

Father Tom chimed in to add some seriousness. "The Koran has forgiveness, gentleness, virtue, justice, civility, and more. But that is not the issue. You are missing the point. You should consider who you are before you run off after your heart."

Jean did not relent. "Baghdad is a melting pot of Hellenistic, Sumerian, Persian, and Indian learning. There is nothing like it in the world. Every day, we meet Muslims, Christians, Jews, and even Zoroastrians and Sabeans. We can be part of this. I want to be part of this. Marmoutier Abbey is a community of defenders of the existing order; they might as well be dead."

Pierre took the comment as an emotional outburst born from frustration and did not respond. Instead, he looked hard at Jean and then, in a rational, emotionless voice, said: "Mohammed fought the Quraysh to take control of Mecca. He established the Dar al-Islam, the abode of Islam. We are from the Dar al-Harb. You must believe in the Dar al-Islam if you want to court Amira; you know that. You are getting involved in something you can't finish."

He looked at Father Tom, who nodded reluctantly. Jean said nothing.

Pierre finally let out an exasperated sigh. "At any rate, I am not staying."

Jean did not heed Pierre's warnings. Over the following months, he started courting Amira regularly. They would roam the streets of Baghdad. Whenever they encountered a demonstration, they looked the other way and smiled. It all seemed silly to them. They were in another world.

The only thing they spoke about was each other and their past. Amira's father had encouraged her to pursue academics; he had paid for private lessons and encouraged her to be part of the scientific meetings at his home, and she had developed a mind of her own and her own perspective. It made it easier for her to accept Jean as a non-Arab and for Jean to feel at home when talking to her.

"Is that why you are so sarcastic?" Jean asked Amira at one point. "You have been encouraged to have your own mind?"

"Are you?" Amira responded.

"Not like you," Jean responded.

"But you are funny. You laugh about most things." Amira responded.

It did not take long for it to become clear to both of them that they belonged together.

Just as Pierre had predicted, al-Wazir insisted that Jean convert to Islam if he wished to marry his daughter. He did this not out of pride or conviction in his faith but because he wanted Amira's husband to fit in everywhere.

Father Tom continued to insist that conversion would be a mistake. Jean had been brought up as a Catholic and belonged to that faith. As much as he liked to think otherwise, Jean would realize that the Catholic faith was in him. He would recognize that what Jesus Christ had shown him was now part of him. The stories of Jesus forgiving Mary Magdalene, of Jesus asking the first person who was not a sinner to cast a stone, or of Jesus touching Lazarus were part of his soul.

"The two religions are not that different," Jean insisted. "Muslims gather on Fridays, Catholics on Sunday; Muslims fast during Ramadan, Catholics during Lent; Muslims undertake pilgrimages to Mecca, Catholics to various shrines; Muslims pay a zakat, Catholics make donations; Muslims pray five times a day; I pray twice a day."

"You pray twice a day? I did not know that," Pierre said when he heard this. But he left it at that. Pierre repeated that if Jean wanted to marry Amira, he had to convert, and he could never return to Marmoutier Abbey. He would remain in Baghdad for the rest of his life.

The decision came to a head when al-Ma'mun declared a mihna: an inquisition. Al-Ma'mun ordered an interrogation of anti-Mutazilite clergy. Ibn-Hanbal, a renowned traditionalist, was arrested. Tensions were running high in Baghdad.

Pierre announced that it was time to leave. He had copied more than ten books by then, more than needed. The books would be treasured at the abbey. He and Jean had earned a lot of money. There was enough to pay for the journey back, repay Jean's family, and enough for Pierre and Jean to live on if the abbey would not take them back.

Jean did not want to leave.

"That is what was agreed," Pierre said.

"I am sorry, things change," Jean said.

"That is convenient," Pierre growled. "Amira just blinds you."

"We always made fun of the brotherhood, and now you want to go back," Jean responded.

Then, he tried a more conciliatory tone.

"Why don't you want to stay?" Jean asked his friend.

Pierre wondered if he was glorifying the past, but then he quickly rejected that.

"I don't feel at home here," Pierre confessed, a little downtrodden. "I am just not part of this. I need to be part of something now. It is time." He wanted to say he needed friends, but he suspected Jean would not believe that. It was not how he had portrayed himself, even to Jean.

Jean was surprised and felt a little guilty. He had been so focused on his doings that he oversaw how Pierre's life had become almost like Jean's life had been at Marmoutier Abbey - uninspiring.

"With your earnings and the books, you will be a hero at the abbey. I'm sure there will be a life there for you." Jean said to encourage Pierre to do what he felt he needed to do.

Father Tom surprised Pierre and Jean by agreeing.

"It may be time for the two of you to part ways. We all want to belong somewhere. As blasphemous as it may sound, religion is part of belonging. You belong at the abbey," he said to Pierre. "Jean belongs here. You belong in the Catholic Church; he will belong to Islam. If our religion were more accepting of science, maybe we would not have lost him."

Pierre nodded reluctantly. The two embraced.

"Not sure I foresaw this," Pierre said, and Jean smiled.

The next day, Jean asked for final permission to marry Amira. Al-Wazi told him he would first talk to his daughter.

"I suspected this might happen. Letting you be educated risked you not sticking to the conventional ways," Al-Wazi said to Amira when they met privately. "Though I did not expect you to choose a Christian from the Carolingian Empire." He said it with a sweet smile that showed Amira he would not object to the marriage.

"He is more of a scientist than a Christian," Amira said, trying to console him.

"Well, that is good, and he told me he would convert," Al-Wazi said.

"He did?" Amira asked.

"Yes, it will make things easier. Jean will need to fit in."

"I suppose you are right," Amira said. She gave Al-Wazi one of her disarming smiles.

"How can I refuse such a smile?" Al-Wazi said.

When Pierre and Jean met next, Pierre gave Jean two-thirds of the money he had accumulated.

"It is only fair since I will be taking the books back. You take most of the money, and I will take the books. The abbey will want them."

Pierre smiled. "I made sure they are the right kind of books."

Jean was surprised. "This is too much." He said, referring to the money. "I could buy a house with this." He felt a little guilty about doubting Pierre's honesty when he gave him the gold he received from al-Sanad.

"So you are ok with me staying," Jean said.

"Do I have a choice?" Pierre responded. "You learned to be independent young, Jean, avoiding the need to belong there - a scientist, not a nobleman."

"I suppose that is why I came in the first place," Jean said. "And you?"

"I belong there as much as I have been trying to fight it. I want brotherhood." Pierre responded.

17. Goodbyes

Pierre was late for the wedding festivities at al-Wazi's house. The guests were divided into men and women. The wedding couple was nowhere to be seen. Jean and Amira had retreated into separate rooms to sign the wedding contract.

Al-Wazi had decorated the house with so many flowers that their sweet smell made it feel like spring. A band was playing Arabic tunes that Pierre still did not recognize. Servers delivered exotic fruit juices for the guests.

Almost all the academics Jean knew were present, along with business people, mainly from the Arab world and India. Father Tom was speaking to al-Khwarizmi, and Pierre decided to join them.

"I heard the caliph summoned you to search for God in numbers," Father Tom said to al-Khwarizmi.

"Yes, it is true. His Highness is fascinated with mathematics and feels the divine must be present."

"I don't know much about mathematics. What do you think, Pierre?" Father Tom asked.

"It is a great compliment to science that such a question would be asked, and it is a credit to you, al-Khwarizmi. The Caliph is the greatest pursuer of knowledge known to man."

"Well said. I am trying to persuade myself that His Highness will not be upset if I fail."

"I suspect that more inquiry could then be needed," Pierre said with a smile.

Al-Khwarizmi chuckled. "Father Tom tells me you will be leaving us to return to Christendom. Are you certain that is what you want? War and political infighting have taken over there."

"That may be. But I will return to the monastery near Tours, where Jean and I grew up. It is where I belong."

Pierre did not mention that Father Tom was likely to leave soon as well. Father Tom was also concerned about the political situation. But Father Tom's plans were not Pierre's to share.

Jean emerged and began making rounds amongst the guests with a broad smile. He wore a red traditional Arab coat and radiated joy.

The men broke out into a line dance behind Jean. Holding hands, they slowly advanced, shaking their shoulders and stepping in unison. They kept a communal rhythm matching the music, smiling and enjoying. The music picked up, and they threw their shoulders and bounced in deep steps, gyrating up and down together. Jean was part of it. He had studied it. The other men enjoyed him being part of it, dancing as they were.

"You could make changes and find a way to belong as your friend has," Al-Khwarizmi told Pierre while they watched Jean.

"No, I have had too many changes in my life. I need to hold on to something," Pierre said, looking at the floor.

Al-Khwarizmi and Father Tom conversed with some of the other guests, and Pierre went to the fountain in the middle of the garden, hoping to speak to Jean eventually. When they finally met, Pierre congratulated Jean and said he admired his decision. It was a bold move.

Pierre knew that al-Wazi might be in danger depending on the alliances he chose. Jean, a foreigner, might become suspect as tensions in the region rose. Jean and Amira had not considered this in their decision.

Pierre knew the time had come to tell Jean about his family background. He could not leave Baghdad without doing that. But the wedding was not the place. It was Jean and Amira's day. They agreed to meet at Jean and Amira's new house in a few days.

On their wedding day, Jean and Amira slept in separate rooms in al-Wazi's house. The next day, Amira was escorted to the house at the edge of town, where she would live with Jean, who had been waiting there for her since early morning. There were so many newcomers to Baghdad that it had been challenging to find a place, but they were pleased to be settling near the river with a view of the old fortification with its impressive library.

Pierre marveled at the view as he made his way to the house a few days later. He stood in front of the house and stopped. He noticed the library of the House of Wisdom in the background.

”I see," he said to himself. "What a perfect location, and Amira agreed to it!”

Then he went to the front door.

"It is good to see you," Jean said as he opened the door. He proudly ushered Pierre into the sitting room. Pierre had brought a package that he put on a small side table.

"I am impressed! What a great house, and I like the view."

"Thank you. We are happy here.”

Pierre took the opportunity to get acquainted with Amira. They spoke about the history of Baghdad and her family. Pierre quickly understood why Amira was the right woman for Jean. She was intelligent and inquisitive and did not care much about the politics in Baghdad. When Amira left the room so Jean could spend time alone with Pierre, Pierre spoke first.

"There is something I have never told you. I am embarrassed because of how long we have known each other and all we have been through. I am sorry I have waited so long to tell you the truth. Jean, I am a Saxon."

Pierre looked straight at Jean, whose face had fallen slack with shock.

"My parents, Tielo and Mathilda, had five children. I was the youngest. My father was the leader of a Saxon settlement northeast of the Rhine. When Charlemagne's army overran the settlement, my mother showed true strength. She convinced my father to concede to the Carolingians and to be baptized as a Christian. It saved him from immediate death and the family from ruin."

Jean kept quiet.

"My mother then persuaded my father to relocate near Tours. She hoped this would ease his embarrassment of having been baptized. The Carolingians were happy to accommodate this. They were trying to integrate Saxons into their empire by having them scattered throughout it. Unfortunately, my father was a proud man who was resistant to change. He started to organize other Saxon men in the Tours area to rob Carolingian travelers."

Jean's eyes widened, and Pierre grinned.

"My father became a robber like we encountered on our trip. That is what saved us. The band we encountered knew of my father."

Pierre chuckled, then became more serious again. "My mother was sure that my father would eventually be caught, and she would not be able to provide for us. She decided the only way to save me was to bring me to an orphanage. It was the perfect way to integrate me into Carolingian society, as long as I never admitted that my mother was alive or anything about my heritage."

Jean could not believe what he was hearing. "What courage. You were cut off from supporting or even being with her for the rest of her life."

"She ended up being right. My father was caught and killed. I thrived at the orphanage and attended the school at the abbey." Pierre paused and then continued. "I occasionally got messages to her. I saw her last in a forest when Sigewulf brought me to Aachen. I fell behind on purpose so I could stop and speak to her. She was very ill then, and she is not with us anymore."

Jean laid a hand on top of his friend's. "I don't know what to say. What a sacrifice your mother made for you! But, of course, it could not have been easy for you, either."

Pierre shrugged. "At any rate, I played my part and never spoke about my heritage. I spent my life integrating into the Carolingian Empire and rose very close to the top. It all became a part of me, just like my mother had planned."

Pierre took a deep breath. "Can you see now why I belong there, not here? I can't change again, not again, and I want to belong somewhere."

Jean nodded. "Of course, my friend. Of course."

Pierre rose and picked up the package he had placed on the side table when he came in. He handed it to Jean.

"I think this will be familiar to you," he said with a smile.

Jean looked curious as he unwrapped the package to find a book. He opened it to the first page and laughed aloud. It was a copy of the Philoponus book Jean had gotten into trouble over.

"I found it in the library of the House of Wisdom and copied it on the side."

Jean's eyes filled with water.

"It must have been why Amira and I could not find it. Thank you!"

"Now you can finally read Philoponus openly," Pierre said.

"I, too, have something for you," Jean said, got up, and walked to a table in the corner of the room. "You are a true friend," he said, picking up two letters. "Interesting how we both end up without parents because of our mothers' best intentions for us," Jean said as he walked back to where Pierre was sitting.

Pierre gave a wistful laugh.

"Thank you for all you have done for me," Jean said. "Without you, I would not be here. I have a letter to my parents explaining why I cannot return. Please give it to them as soon as you return."

Pierre took the letter with both hands. "I know it was not an easy decision. I will deliver it as soon as I arrive."

"I will miss you," Jean said. "It won't be the same without you."

At that moment, Pierre saw in Jean a maturity and calmness he did not know he had. He paused and looked at his friend with admiration.

"Think of me as the number 0 in your set, the absent number still there," Pierre said jokingly.

"You will never be absent from me," Jean said. He pulled himself together.

"I have also prepared another letter for you. It recognizes who you are and how I have come to know you. It explains how fairly you have treated me regarding our work and earnings. I am asking my parents to treat you as they would me. To help you as though you were their son."

Pierre was moved and somewhat stunned to hold a letter that allowed him the backing in the Carolingian society he had always wanted. He was unsure he wanted it now, but he appreciated it.

18. Pierre's Return

A few days later, Pierre left for Marmoutier Abbey. The return trip was uneventful, though the journey was lonely. Pierre missed his friend. He met up with some other monks traveling to Venice.

The Alps again were a formidable obstacle, but at least Pierre knew the route. He stayed at the farm Jean and Pierre had stayed at, again admiring the lone farmer for what he was able to do. Pierre could not be that solitary. He learned that in Baghdad.

When he got to the abbey where Jean and he had stayed at the edge of the Alps, he stopped. "I used to admire how firmly the head monk is in charge," Pierre thought. "And how one could easily become the number two."

However, Pierre figured out the look that the senior monk had given him, which scared him when he was there with Jean. It was the cold look of someone trying to evaluate you, not to get to know you as a person, but to find a weakness. This brotherhood was one based on fear.

Even though it was late, Pierre was resolute when he walked past the abbey. He did not want to be part of something like that. How far he had come. He chuckled about looking forward to the bickering at Marmoutier Abbey. "At least they care for each other, even if they fight over petty things," he thought.

Marmoutier Abbey looked the same when he arrived on his horse on a rainy day. Novices were playing Phaininda in front of the abbey. They stopped only briefly to look at him and then resumed the game. Pierre stayed and watched them for a while. The players worked together, advancing the ball and taking the pushbacks together. It did not matter; being in the moment with your team was fun. "A new generation of monks enjoying each other's company," he thought. "Enjoying a reprieve." Then he smiled. "I have had my reprieve, and what a reprieve it was. Now it is time for me to be home."

No one at the abbey expected him, so he just walked in. As he entered, he admired the worn-down limestone threshold, thinking of how it contrasted with the edgy marble thresholds in Baghdad. Centuries of monks had worn it down, knowing they were welcome within. He took a deep breath to appreciate the moldy smell, which now held some extra sweetness. Then, he noticed the warmth and smell of cooking from the dining hall. He headed there.

It was there that he found Father George quietly studying a book.

"Still into those books," Pierre said, so Father George would notice him.

Father George looked up.

"Pierre," he said with a smile that was big even for him. "You are back!"

Father George asked about every detail of Pierre's journey, not because he was particularly interested in Baghdad, but because he wanted to know what Pierre's life had been like.

Pierre finally asked about the abbey. They had gained independence from the court in Aachen and renewed the brotherhood among the monks.

"They elected me as the head monk to appease the bishop. I am not really in charge; no one is," Father George joked. "You know how it is here."

Pierre knew. It was what drew him back to the abbey.

Father George was glad that Pierre was back, but he also admired Jean for building a new life where he could pursue his dreams. He gathered the senior monks who came to the dining hall one by one to greet Pierre. They spoke into the night.

The next day, they gave Pierre a robe. He put it on gladly and, with it, looked like them. Pierre helped officiate the morning Mass, reading the prescribed scriptures even though he was tempted not to.

Pierre delivered Jean's first letter to Jean's parents as soon as he could. Jean's mother was sad but not surprised to hear about Jean's decision.

"He always sought his own way; I suppose he had to," she said. "I am glad he is happy, though I am sorry not to get to know Amira."

"He has become a respected scientist," Pierre said. "We will all miss him."

Pierre never used the second letter, which could have restarted his career; it was no longer important to him. He did not have to prove himself anymore. He became a welcome part of the brotherhood. He taught languages. At dinner, his unusual experiences in Aachen and Baghdad, along with his sarcasm, entertained everyone.

Pierre occasionally thought about his unusual past. He concluded that it no longer mattered. He fit in. He was amongst friends. "I am the zero that completes the set," he often joked.

Afterword

Marmoutier Abbey was overrun and destroyed by the Normans in 853 AD. The Carolingian Empire ended around 888 AD, yielding to internal civil wars and continued invasions. Academic achievement did not prosper in Europe until the Renaissance in Italy in the fourteenth century.

A civil war never broke out in Baghdad. Al-Ma'mun was killed in a military excursion soon after his mihna. The House of Wisdom flourished in Baghdad until 1258 AD. Mongols invaded the city and destroyed the library. It was reported that the Tigris turned black from the ink of all the books thrown into it.

Al-Khwarizmi became known as the father of algebra. Europeans would dignify mathematical postulates for the next seven hundred years with the phrase dixit algoritmi: "So says al-Khwarizmi."

Part II

Machiko

Japan, End of the Edo Dynasty, circa 1800 AD

1. Nara

Machiko sat in the large living room of her parents' farmhouse, listening to her parents argue about a donation for the Buddhist temple in Nara. Her father, Bunji, did not care for the monks because of their concern for power and influence. Her mother, Asuka, however, was practical and had made donations in the past to stay on the temple's good side. It was not a matter of charity.

Machiko contorted her delicate face. It was an attractive face, but its natural state was too serious for her age. She had no siblings. It was also hard for her to make friends since her family was by far the wealthiest in the area.

Machiko continued to frown as though it could impact her parents in the other room. She wanted the fighting to stop. It was unusual for her parents to fight, and she wanted that harmony back. She liked the idea of donating to the temple and wished she could make the donation herself, but at fourteen years old, she had nothing to give. She would be wealthy one day and inherit her parents' wealth, but that lay in the future.

"You can make the donation," Bunji finally said, "but don't let Machiko know." Bunji thought Machiko needed to learn how to be commercial, not generous. He never asked Asuka what the donation was for.

When breakfast was ready, Machiko went to join her parents. They smiled, pretending they had not fought. As they ate, porters gathered outside, ready to carry the three of them on the day-long journey to Nara.

Machiko and her parents would each ride in a kago, a blanket tied at both ends to a long bamboo pole carried on the shoulders of two porters, while the traveler sat in the blanket.

After they completed the awkward balancing act of getting into their kagos, they passed through Akeno, the farming village. Akeno consisted of one main street and a few dozen houses, mostly occupied by merchants. It was surrounded by rolling hills covered with rice fields, next to which most farmers lived. Machiko's parents' farm started at the end of town. It continued as far as one could see, yet they added to it constantly.

Machiko hated this part. She did not want to be seen. She crouched down and pulled her arms over her body so that the blanket of her kago would pull up until she could not be seen. Everyone in the village knew that her family was wealthy and influential. These trips made it more visible. One could see they had business in Nara.

As they passed through the center of Akeno, the porters suddenly pulled to the side of the road. A samurai and his entourage were passing through on horses; respect demanded that everyone make way for them. Despite the delay, watching a samurai procession was always interesting. They wore expensive kimonos and impressive swords.

Machiko pulled her blanket down slightly. This samurai was a particular treat. He wore his full body armor, decorations jutting out from the torso, with huge shoulder pads and a helmet that went past his shoulders. All this gave him a foreign, almost nonhuman look. He didn't make eye contact with anyone and rode his well-groomed white horse quickly through the center of town. Four lesser soldiers on brown and black horses followed him.

"That armor is an expensive badge of honor," Bunji whispered to Asuka.

Asuka gave him a stern look, but he did not stop.

"A badge for things they did a long time ago."

In prior years, samurai had shown complete obedience to their masters and were likely to die young in battle. The discipline and bushido code they followed were respected to that day. However, the Tokugawa shogun united Japan, and there had not been any fighting for a long time. Samurai were no longer needed, but their position was still respected, and they retained considerable influence.

Once the procession passed, the porters continued through Akeno. Machiko hoped that the commotion would distract villagers from noticing her family. She was relieved when they got through to open, recently harvested fields.

Bunji greeted a farmer. "You will even find chores in an empty field," he said, complimenting the farmer on his work ethic. "I am traveling to Nara to avoid the idleness at the farm." It was an exaggeration. Bunji oversaw an army of hired hands, collections from tenant farmers, and the acquisition of new equipment. His work continued even after the fields were harvested.

It was autumn, and Machiko liked the crisp air with its earthy smell. The countryside looked manicured - groomed, empty fields and colorful, exhausted trees. The summer heat was over; a long winter break was coming. It all created a sense of calmness.

Machiko's family always took a break at a spot two-thirds of the way to Nara, where the road forked next to a little stream. The spot was in a valley surrounded by open hills topped with pine trees, no houses. Machiko liked that it was in the middle of nowhere, pure nature.

The porters rested on boulders next to the stream and complained about their aches while Machiko's parents tried to hide theirs. Kagos were as uncomfortable to be in as they were to carry, but it was how one traveled.

Machiko's parents walked down the road to stretch their legs.

"It is beautiful here," Bunji said to Asuka, who nodded.

"We are fortunate, and we can afford to make some small donations to the less fortunate. I wish there were a better way than making them through the temple."

The reason Bunji did not want to donate to the monks at the temple was similar to why the shogun moved his headquarters away from Nara, which used to be Japan's political and religious center. The shogun thought the monks at the temple were selfish and had become too powerful. Asuka had not told Bunji that the donation was actually for Machiko's benefit - not a true donation and not earmarked for the less fortunate, as Bunji assumed.

Machiko wandered off along the stream, oblivious to her parents' continued discussion. She was deep in contemplation, appreciating every part of her surroundings. Mist hovered over the shimmering water of the stream. Machiko found several spots where the current twisted over flat rocks, creating little whirlpools. Eventually, she got close to a small pond. Frogs lined the edge, and Machiko always tried to approach without disturbing them. It never worked; they all jumped in before she got close.

"Sorry, frogs, no need for you to jump," she said as though the frogs could understand her. When the ripples on the water from the frogs cleared, Machiko sat on a rock and took in the restored calmness. It was her favorite place. Machiko had told her mother about it, but she never came along, not wanting to prolong the trip for the porters.

Machiko did not feel it was right to touch the pond. She watched, wanting not to interfere but to appreciate what was there. Making the frogs jump in was bad enough. She watched until she heard the porters getting restless. Then, she hurried back, knowing she had prolonged the trip. Seeing her special place was worth it. It was one of the few things she demanded.

"Did you see any frogs, little one?" one of the porters asked her.

Frogs were considered good luck on journeys. Times were uncertain, and they wanted to hear that they had good fortune.

"Many frogs," Machiko reported happily.

Nara became visible as soon as they passed the next set of hills. At the edge of town, they encountered terrible slums. Factories had gone up where fields used to be. Strange, large buildings rose behind courtyards with high fences. Seeing the machines inside was impossible, but you could hear and smell them. They demanded to be the center of things even if they could not be seen. One could hear their heavy pounding and the insistent supervisors yelling, nothing else.

On the road, workers were coming and going. They walked lifelessly without interacting with anyone. Farmers usually walked in groups, talking to one another. Factory workers were different. They were not present. They walked in a mindless state, their heads down, in unison, in single files, as though they were mimicking the machines they served - conforming to repetitive motion.

Next to the factories, makeshift buildings housing workers leaned against one another. Machiko saw children playing in the dirt. They looked miserable. Machiko frowned, wondering why anyone would live there. There was no harmony, no peace, and certainly no joy.

Machiko overheard the porters confirm this. "What a sorry place," one porter said. "Strange, really," another agreed. They picked up their pace. Once they crossed a bridge over a filthy stream containing factory waste, the neighborhood reverted to what they were used to: nice, clean houses. Then they reached the center of Nara, the sophisticated and stylish part that was also strange to the porters. Beautiful, large houses were built side by side, interrupted by elaborate shrines and temples. Rows of trees lined the streets. Well-dressed people could be seen among the crowds.

Machiko watched a woman drag her delicate pastel green kimono through the dirt, oblivious to the harm she was causing it. "It must have taken workers hundreds of hours to produce it," Machiko thought, "but not caring set her apart. Was that intentional?"

They headed to the home of Toshiro, an old friend of Bunji. The men had met many years ago when Toshiro owned a small farm-supply business. Bunji had been one of his initial customers, and most of the machinery on the farm had come from Toshiro. The farm's success was a direct result of this alliance.

Toshiro grew the farm supply business into the biggest in Nara. He started a construction company that built factories, and recently started a trading house that sold many of the goods made in those factories.

Toshiro continued accumulating wealth and moved to a newly constructed house. Bunji and Asuka had not seen it but heard that it was one of the largest in the city. It sat on a street lined with cherry trees near the town center. As they approached, Machiko's parents felt inadequate in their kagos. They could not see the house yet, but even the neighborhood was intimidating. They told the porters to let them out around the corner from the gate to the house and sent them back to Akeno.

"I can't believe how much wealth he has amassed," Bunji commented to Asuka as they walked to the front of the house. The house dominated the already wealthy street, even though it sat back from the street more than the others, behind a large courtyard.

"The new way is rewarding people," Asuka said. Machiko took note. Her mother was referring to trade, which, while traditionally disrespected, created a lot of wealth for people like Toshiro.

One of Toshiro's servants came running out of the house after they rang a small bell next to the gate to the courtyard. He seemed distressed that he had not noticed them earlier and bowed several times. He took the sack with their belongings and led them across the courtyard into the house.

Even though new, the house was built in the traditional Japanese style, with curved roofs and a labyrinth of sliding doors. However, it had two stories. It was richly appointed with traditional Japanese wall paintings and smelled of recently replaced floor mats. Machiko took in the smell with a deep breath. Her parents knew not to.

They were led to a reception room to the right of the entryway. A senior servant appeared and told them that Toshiro would, unfortunately, not be able to meet them until dinner. Then, they were led back into the hallway and up the long stairs to their room on the second floor. It all seemed formal but appropriate.

Their room was large. The mats for them to sleep on had not been rolled out yet, so it was empty. The sack with their belongings had been placed under the window at the end of the room. The room overlooked the courtyard, and a subtle breeze blew through it. As soon as they were alone, Asuka started changing into better clothes.

Machiko could not help but marvel at Toshiro's wealth. She loved how beautiful the house and the courtyard were and wanted to see more. She imagined what it would be like to live in a place made purely for comfortable living, with servants tending to her needs. She saw herself walking down the stairs in a fancy kimono as servants scurried out of the way. She felt the subtle breeze and imagined the smell of fancy food served to her.

It was a pleasant daydream. But Machiko stopped herself. She was raised better than to aspire to comfortable living. Machiko felt a little guilty about how self-absorbed she had become.

"Don't waste time. Get ready. We are going to the temple," Asuka ordered, noticing how absentminded Machiko was. Asuka had already managed to change and left the room to make the necessary arrangements.

It always amazed Machiko how quickly her mother could change from looking like a down-to-earth farm owner to a sophisticated, well-dressed woman. Even her hair, with a few twists, took on an elegant look. Machiko hurried. She was frustrated that she would probably not look sophisticated and that they had to go to the temple so soon.

When Asuka told the senior servant she needed to go to the temple, he insisted they take one of Toshiro's norinomos. Norinomos were carried by porters, similar to a kago, but had a wooden box to sit in instead of a blanket. Asuka smiled and gladly accepted. It was more suitable for a stylish arrival at the temple.

The temple knew that Asuka was coming that day. Ordinarily, the head of the temple, Tomeo, would receive her, given the likely size of her donation, but he was busy with politics. Seiji, one of the temple's rising stars, greeted them when they arrived. He was in his early twenties, smart and ambitious, with fast darting eyes and a constant smile. Seiji's primary focus was to become Tomeo's assistant, a role that carried prestige and might lead to further promotions. He liked interacting with people, and they enjoyed interacting with him. His excitement about what was happening in Nara and Japan always rubbed off. He would share a lot, which inevitably meant that others would share a lot with him. He was exceedingly well-informed.

"She has grown into a young lady," Seiji commented as he approached them.

Machiko bowed her head.

"I hear the harvest was good," Seiji continued, stopping for the customary bow in the middle of the temple gate as they passed through.

Statues of Agyo, the protector god, flanked the inside of the gate. Agyo was always shown with strong arms, one waving away evil spirits and the other holding a big spear. Machiko was mesmerized by the crazed look in Agyo's big eyes.

"They are perfect for scaring away bad spirits, aren't they?" Seiji said, noticing the effect the statues had on Machiko.

Machiko smiled shyly.

Next, they passed by a belfry, a square building open on all sides, with a bell hanging in the middle. Machiko was too shy to ask what it was for. Why would the temple need such a large bell? Was it to gather spirits or to warn of approaching enemies?

They made their way to the censer, waving incense smoke toward themselves to cleanse before entering the temple's main hall. It was Machiko's favorite part of visiting a Buddhist temple. She loved the smell of the incense, and waving it toward herself was fun. She had made a habit of doing it twice. Asuka noticed but did not mind. She would grow out of such games soon enough.

They entered the temple's main hall, which contained a massive statue.

"This is Amida," Seiji said, "the Buddha who presides over a heavenly paradise. Worshippers may be able to join him upon rebirth."

Machiko could not tell the difference between the statue of Amida and the many statues of Siddhartha, the original Buddha. Again, she said nothing.

When it was time to pray, she prayed that Amida had ushered not her ancestors but those who had recently died in Akeno into his paradise. It was a kind thing to do and showed how much she loved her village and cared for others.

Then they went outside again. A large wall and immaculate gardens surrounded the back of the temple complex. Stone paths overgrown with moss led through them, shaded by massive huckleberry trees covered with lichen. It was a surprisingly serene place in the middle of Nara. Machiko thought it was beautiful and did not mind when her mother asked for a moment alone with Seiji. "This place calms one down," she thought; it was not unlike the pond she enjoyed so much.

"You are right," Asuka said while alone with Seiji. "The harvest was quite good. As you know, when it is good, we save for times when it is bad. I hear you are starting to get donations from merchants."

It would be a huge embarrassment for Seiji if Asuka did not make a donation. Asuka wanted to create that concern in him. It was the only way to get something in return.

"Yes," Seiji said, taken aback. "But Tomeo does not like us dealing with merchants. He believes in the old hierarchy. Bushido samurai at the top, farmers and tradespeople in the middle, and merchants at the bottom. He does not interact with merchants. I have gotten to know many of them, though, and I like them. They are making a lot of money. Unfortunately, they are not sharing it yet. I think they are the way of the future."

"The way of the future requires educated people," Asuka commented, and then came to the reason for her visit. "We need educated men and women to run things. I need Machiko to have a sound education. The only way to do that is for her to attend the girls' school here at the temple."

Seiji was shocked.

"That would be unusual. The school is for orphans and apprentice nuns."

Asuka put on a kind face. "Even though the harvest can't always be good, I will make twice our usual donation and plan to continue at that level from now on."

Seiji smiled. He would be a hero at the temple for obtaining such a donation. The fact that it was from a farmer would also please Tomeo. Lastly, if he were able to get Machiko into the school, it would show his influence. It was a challenge he wanted to take on. "All this might help me become Tomeo's assistant," he thought.

"Leave it to me," he said to Asuka. "It will be hard, but I will see what I can do. Why don't you come back tomorrow?"

Asuka was confident Seiji would figure out a way. She left the temple smiling, thinking about what she had to figure out next. She still needed to persuade Bunji to let Machiko go to the school.

2. Dinner

Toshiro often entertained guests at geisha establishments, but it did not suit him. He had little appreciation for music. He felt the parlor games the geishas used to entertain guests were silly. It was a spectacle - an art form, but a spectacle. After a while, he always developed the same feeling. The contrived music, the randomness of prescribed winners in parlor games, and the obligatory flattering smiles by the geisha were just wrong. He much preferred a meal at home with good conversation. He knew Bunji felt the same, so they usually settled on that.

Having dinner at Toshiro's house also allowed Toshiro's wife, Lika, and Asuka to participate. Both women were admired by their husbands for their intellect.

"They told me that you can come too, but you must be quiet," Asuka told Machiko. Machiko was always encouraged to ask questions at home, but she understood this was different.

The event occurred in a large room behind the staircase at the bottom level of the house. The room could easily seat thirty guests—unusually large for a traditional Japanese house, though not for the new houses of the successful merchant class. Bunji and Asuka considered the room strangely impersonal and out of place.

One wall was decorated with a mural of thick pine trees, a symbol of strength and permanence. The other walls were undecorated, so they would not take away from the impact of the pine tree mural. "One focal point without the option to decide that another is more interesting," Toshiro had requested. He wanted to portray power. It was good for business.

Bunji, Asuka, and Machiko were admiring the room when Toshiro arrived with Lika.

"How was the harvest?" Toshiro asked when he entered. He skipped the bowing. They were old friends.

"With modernization and good weather, we produced a record crop with fewer hands," Bunji answered gladly. He tilted his head slightly and produced a smile that almost looked mischievous.

"We just don't need that many farmhands anymore," Asuka added. "The new generation is moving to the cities at any rate."

Toshiro appreciated her forthrightness, but Bunji searched for something else to say, not wanting the conversation to drift to Asuka.

"We continue to buy farms at attractive prices. The small farmers can't compete with our costs. Record crops help us. Prices move down, and farmers realize they can't compete."

As he spoke, Bunji sneaked a quick look at Machiko. He was not sure she was ready to learn the harsh reality: their family benefited from the misfortunes of others. It was customary to celebrate good crops in Akeno.

The concept that good crops might cause misery did concern Machiko. Why did prices move down? Would it not make it easier if goods were cheaper? How is it that more leaves some with less? Machiko frowned her forehead. It was an expression her mother knew well. Machiko was either upset or did not understand.

"Modernization is important. Some areas of Japan are starving; we need more food, and modernization helps that," Asuka said. It was for Machiko's sake, not for Toshiro's, but Toshiro did not know that. Not sure how to react, he changed the subject.

"I am focused on my trading business. The goods produced by the factories at the edge of town need to be distributed throughout Japan. The factories make such large quantities that distribution has become important." It was the topic Toshiro liked to talk about most, at least recently.

They were interrupted by two women bringing in food. Toshiro's chef had gone out of her way to make a meal with the freshest autumn ingredients: mackerel pike, newly harvested rice, and mushrooms with ginkgo nuts. It was exquisite.

Toshiro had, of course, profited from helping Machiko's parents modernize the farm. That was how business worked. However, now he had another idea of how they could benefit each other.

"As you know, record crops mean record taxes. The government in Edo will want their share. We merchants still don't pay taxes; we are considered too low in the social hierarchy to tax." Toshiro chuckled. Lika slightly shook her head. They were making a lot of money right under the government's nose without being taxed. Talking about it might put an end to it.

"You should invest in a merchant business," Toshiro told Bunji. "Here is my idea. Osaka's port is not far from here. Goods are shipped up and down the East Coast from there. I am telling you, goods produced in the factories need national distribution. Take plows; they are best produced in large quantities in factories. Factories can pass on their lower costs, but must produce large quantities. I am opening a trading house in Osaka to buy and sell in bulk. You should invest with me."

They were interrupted again. Persimmons that resembled the fall colors in Nara were served. Everyone admired them.

"At some point, I want to open a trading house in Nagasaki for trade with China," Toshiro continued.

Machiko's parents did not know how to respond to the investment proposal. They knew how to manage the risks of a farm: keep enough reserves for two failed crops. They knew little about trading houses but had done well trusting Toshiro.

"Let us think about it, but we would be honored to invest with you," Bunji finally said, despite his reservations.

Then sake was served. Toshiro and Bunji became louder as they felt the alcohol. They were also intoxicated with thoughts of economic opportunities. Toshiro ventured into a topic he could only discuss with good friends.

"The samurai are bankrupting the country," he said matter-of-factly.

"The daimyo appointed by the shogun for the Nara region has done a good job persuading the shogun to continue to repay them for their past loyalty and service," Bunji added. "The government granted them lands that they are not taking care of. They are amassing debts to support their extravagant lifestyle—debts funded with taxes on us farmers."

Asuka did not like how open Bunji was about this. She could have used the opportunity to bolster the importance of staying on the temple's good side. The temple had played a role in persuading the daimyo and, ultimately, the shogun to continue supporting the samurai. But Bunji had agreed to the donation, and the conversation was quickly becoming a rant.

"One in ten citizens in Japan are samurai class—this is not sustainable," Toshiro said. "With their bushido honor code, they would make good businesspeople to deal with, but they won't lower themselves to join us merchants." Toshiro waved his arm dismissively.

"It is a problem that needs solving at some time, maybe not yet," Lika said. Then, she looked at Asuka, but she did not smile. That would have been too much. They both knew it was time to end the samurai discussion and that Lika's comment might do it.

Toshiro started talking about foreigners. The shogun issued strict instructions that no foreigners were allowed in Japan. Some Europeans had traded with Japan for some time, but that was now forbidden. The only sanctioned trade was with China. Ordinarily, one did not speak about this topic either. Why would one? However, the alcohol was having its effect.

"Eventually, we have to open up. We may not be competitive right now, but we never will be if we don't open ourselves to new opportunities." Toshiro was sure about this. It was just a matter of time. Bunji was not so sure. Toshiro, as usual, was two steps ahead.

This was Asuka's opportunity to make a point she wanted Bunji to hear.

"To be competitive, we will need to improve our educational system. We will have to be smarter than them." She meant the foreigners.

"We may see the transition from farms to factories now, but in the long run, the transition will be to the educated."

Bunji took note but did not respond. He suspected there was a reason Asuka was saying this. There always was.

Toshiro perked up. "That is certainly true. We need engineers and smart managers. How much time do you spend figuring out the equipment we sell you and managing the farm?"

Bunji did not like thinking of work and was getting tired. He decided to get lost in the sake and think about this later. Toshiro went along with him.

Lika and Asuka continued to speak about their children's education, but in a way that did not interfere with their husbands. Machiko took note.

Was her mother right? They already saw a transition to offices on their farm. Machiko worried about where she was going to get her education. She did not know that if things went her mother's way, she would find out soon.

3. Machiko's Education

The next morning, Machiko and her mother returned to the temple. Seiji was all smiles. He had persuaded the nuns to accept Machiko as a student.

First, he spoke to Tomeo about the donation, hoping that Tomeo would try to influence the head of the orphanage. However, Tomeo did not like such obvious connections between donations and favors. Therefore, Seiji went to see the head of the orphanage. He told her that Machiko would be perfect for the orphanage.

"She is choosing to be an orphan for the benefit of an education," he said. "What better way to show the other orphans how fortunate they are? In all their misfortune, they should realize that being at the orphanage is a small blessing. They are receiving something others are giving up a home for."

Matsushima, the head nun, grinned when she heard this. She suspected that Seiji was not concerned with the orphans. Still, his point was valid, and she agreed to meet Machiko to see if she was so eager to learn.

"I think it will work. Matsushima, the head nun, has requested to see us." Seiji told Asuka when they met at the temple gate.

"There is only one thing: Matsushima will accept Machiko only if she expresses a genuine desire to learn and be at the school. Do you think Machiko can do this?"

"I think so," Asuka said.

Asuka liked that the head nun was selective and not purely focused on the financial support they had promised. Little did she know that the financial support was going solely to the temple, not the school.

They walked across the temple gardens. The school was on the other side of the temple walls. As they walked, Asuka explained to Machiko what the visit was about.

"Your education at home will come to an end. Already now, you are reaching the limits of your tutor's capabilities. The nuns at the school here can build on all you have learned."

Machiko was shocked. Now, she knew why her mother had spoken about education at the dinner.

"I don't want to leave home," she said, even though she had fretted over her education the night before. Machiko then gave Asuka as upset of a look as she thought she could get away with.

"I like Nara; the temple is beautiful. But I like home. I don't know this place. When would I see you?" Machiko continued with a shaken voice.

"We would not be far away, and there is no time to discuss this," Asuka responded. She felt that the less said, the less of an opening she would give Machiko.

"You will tell the head nun that you want an education. We can discuss this later," Asuka insisted, even though she was not going to accept Machiko's opinion.

They entered the school through a gate in the main temple wall. The school was small and, unlike the temple, purely functional —one plain building for teaching and sleeping, a small building next to it for the five nuns who ran the school.

Matsushima was standing in front of the main building. She was a middle-aged nun with a sober, authoritative presence. Machiko had imagined she would be like Seiji: young, outgoing, and engaging. Instead, Matsushima seemed like a harsh leader focused on running things and keeping good old-fashioned order.

"You must tell her that you want to learn," Asuka whispered again to Machiko, "You must!"

"I hear that you are great supporters of the temple," Matsushima said, greeting Asuka. Seiji winced a little, realizing Matsushima had figured out more than he thought.

Asuka bowed deeply, respecting Matsushima.

"Thank you for seeing us."

Matsushima bowed and then wasted no time, turning to Machiko. "I hear you want to come to school here?" She said it with a slight and disarming smile.

"Learning is important, and I want to read more books," Machiko said. She was doing her part.

"She has command over most of the important Chinese characters," Asuka interjected, happy about what Machiko had said, but then Machiko continued:

"The Buddha wants everyone to seek enlightenment," Machiko added.

Asuka did not know how that would go over. Was Machiko doing this to sabotage her acceptance? Asuka stared at Matsushima, waiting for a response.

Matsushima raised an eyebrow. "Wanting to be educated is good, but quoting the Buddha about enlightenment may have to wait."

Asuka smiled. "Smart woman," she thought.

Matsushima pulled Seiji and Asuka aside with a face that had surprisingly softened after Machiko's remark. "Is it possible you would want her to become a nun?"

The question surprised Asuka.

"We have made no plans for that, but time will tell what her calling will be."

It was not completely truthful. The last thing Asuka or Bunji wanted Machiko to become was a nun. They wanted her to take over their farm.

"I have spoken with Tomeo about this, and he thinks education is the way of the future. It cannot be limited to nuns," Seiji said.

"This is not my concern," Matsushima said harshly, then paused to think.

"Machiko is smart and will benefit from an education, but it will be hard for her to fit in." Matsushima took a deep breath.

"We must ensure that she does not receive special treatment," Matsushima said resolutely. "If she comes here, I can't allow you to see her during the school year. It would be too disruptive to the orphans."

Asuka was taken aback.

"I can look after her and report back to you," Seiji promised. Now that he had begun this endeavor, he wanted to see it through.

"Very well. But I still need to get Machiko's father to agree to this. Let me discuss it with him." Asuka responded, wanting to buy some time.

Asuka did not speak to Machiko on their way back to Toshiro's house. She felt it was a wasted discussion since Bunji might not allow Machiko to attend the school.

Meanwhile, Machiko's mind was racing. What would it be like to live in the orphanage? How hard would the nuns push her? Would she see her friends? She would not be able to roam the way she did around the village and the countryside. Nara, with its factories, had places that seemed scary. What would she do in Nara?

"You can't say anything to your father," Asuka finally told Machiko. "I need to find the right time to raise it with him."

Machiko gave her mother one of those looks that she had only recently learned. It was not the upset, frowned-up look. It was the look of a child growing up and questioning her parents' sanity - the look of disapproval wrapped in a smirk. Then she hoped that her father might say "no" and all this would disappear.

Asuka said nothing. It was hard to accuse Machiko of a look. She was also starting to question whether she was doing the right thing. Not seeing Machiko would be an issue.

When they returned to Toshiro's house, Toshiro was in the courtyard speaking to Bunji. They had spent the morning discussing the investment in the trading house.

Machiko was happy to see that the porters with three kagos were waiting to take them back to Akeno. After the meeting, she was not sure if she would be going back.

"If you invest in the trading business, you will be able to do away with the kagos," Toshiro said, not knowing that Machiko's parents would probably never splurge on norimonos.

Then Toshiro turned to Asuka with a knowing smile. "I hope everything went well at the temple." He winked.

"It was good to see you," Asuka said. She suspected Toshiro knew what she was up to but had not told Bunji. Toshiro was always well-informed and was close to the temple. He had to be. The temple was close to the authorities, and sometimes Toshiro needed them to get things done.

Bunji, Asuka, and Machiko got into their kagos and headed down the street. What came next surprised them. It started to rain, and the streets emptied quickly as though they were on fire. Farmers were not afraid of a bit of rain, but people in the city appeared to be. Within a few moments, they all disappeared. Only the workers headed to the factories remained. The factories demanded that they be on time for their shifts no matter what the weather was like.

When they got to the part of town with the factories, they saw the workers line up in the rain without complaint. That was also strange. Farmers did not mind rain but would not stand still in it.

Machiko stared at a man with torn clothes stained with factory grease. The rain was washing grease down his muscular arms. His face was emotionless, not eager for anything. On the other hand, his body leaned forward with a powerful, straight back, ready for work. Machiko had never seen this before. Farmers' bodies and faces usually matched.

Machiko was frightened. "So strange," she thought. She was glad when her parents told the porters to hurry through.

Once outside the slums, they soon reached the place with the stream and the pond. They kept going. The porters wanted to get home. Machiko looked back and watched the rain leave its mark on the trees and the stream. The place was beautiful, even in the rain. She looked forward to seeing it the next time they went to Nara, even though that might be the time for her to start her schooling.

The next morning, while Machiko waited for her tutor, Tomo, in the living room, she could overhear her parents again. They were concerned with the progress the farm had made in their absence. Then they reminisced about how impressive Nara was and what a good time they had at Toshiro's extravagant house.

"He certainly has been successful," Bunji said.

"Maybe we should invest with him; he has advised us well so far," Asuka said.

"He is asking for a lot of money. We would be stretched. Two bad harvests, and we could end up like the others," Bunji said.

They stopped discussing it when Tomo arrived. After greeting them, Tomo went to the living room to see Machiko for her lessons.

Tomo came from a samurai family. Her father was injured in a battle with a foreign vessel that had attempted to land near Nara. He had not been well-connected, and Tomo's family had become impoverished when he refused to take a position beneath his status. He passed away unhappy and feeling abandoned. Tomo did her best to support her mother and younger brother by teaching. It was an honorable position and perpetuated the status that her father could not let go of.

Bunji, Asuka, and Machiko felt sorry for Tomo. They often talked about it over dinner. Bunji advocated giving her some extra money. That charity, he could see himself making. But Tomo could not accept it. She was too proud.

Machiko smiled at Tomo when she entered the living room. She always wanted to please her. It was all she could do for her. She reported on her trip. "It was so exciting. We saw Toshiro's extravagant house and visited the temple. What a great place. Beautiful and serene, right in the middle of Nara. We also visited a school next to the temple." As soon as she said it, she realized she should not speak about the school. Asuka had told her not to talk about it, and Tomo was sure to be distressed to learn that her position might end. Machiko, concerned, started to ramble.

"The temple there has lots of books. I told Matsushima, the nun in charge, that it would be great to read them. They have lots of Buddhist books. It may be interesting."

Tomo sensed what this was about and stopped Machiko. "Reading Buddhist books, really? Let me tell you an old Buddhist story about that." She smiled. She wanted to save Machiko from her miserable state. The story was all she could think of at the moment.

"The story goes that there was a master and a holy book. The master insisted that everything be written in the book and that his followers live by it. They would consult the book for advice whenever they encountered a new situation. One day, they were walking with their master, and he fell into a river. He could not swim and asked his followers to rescue him. When they insisted on first consulting the book, he drowned."

Tomo felt bad. She made the same mistake as Machiko, speaking before thinking. She did not want to discourage Machiko's education in Nara. That was not the samurai way. It was not what her father would have done. She quickly figured out a way to correct it.

"Now it is time that you learn my favorite poem—much more important than the silly Buddhist story. It is by Matsuo Basho, who died almost a hundred years ago.

It goes as follows:

Old pond
Frog jumps in
Sound of water

Can you write it?"

Machiko tried.

古池
"Old pond"
蛙
"Frog"
飛び込む
"Jumps in"
水の音
"Sound of water"

"Good, except you need to add a ya, like this や, after frog to indicate a pause."

Machika was getting close to knowing the two thousand kanji she was expected to know. Her mother was right about that at the temple. For the rest, Machiko and most educated Japanese spelled out the words instead of using one of the forty thousand kanji that represented them.

Tomo was not particular about Machiko's penmanship. She just wanted Machiko to be able to read and write. She never emphasized the beauty of calligraphy, which suited Machiko's parents. Tomo was as matter-of-fact about that as they were. The purpose of writing was to communicate, not to entertain.

Machiko did a reasonable job writing the poem; it was not pretty, but correct.

"Now, can you interpret it? What do you think it is about?"

"I don't know. Is it about nature? Is it about good luck?"

"Almost. It is about change. There is beauty and good fortune in introducing change to an ancient pond. Like your education in Nara. Just don't get carried away with books."

"Beauty in introducing change—I like that," Machiko said. "Beauty in introducing change."

Tomo later spoke to Asuka. She told her that she would support Machiko being educated in Nara. She wanted to make sure that she knew that, in her opinion, this was the right thing to do. Her ability to educate Machiko further was nearing its end. Machiko deserved an education in a place with the required materials and more advanced teachers.

Asuka was not happy that Machiko had told Tomo. She was having second thoughts. She was not sure Machiko would do well alone in Nara and needed to decide if she would try to convince Bunji.

Tomo went to the Shinto shrine in town. It was unusual for her. She was brought up with the traditions of Shintoism, but kept them to a minimum. She avoided introspection or appealing to the spirits in nature. Shintoism believed that nature had spirits; trees, rocks, etc.—they all had spirits. You could appeal to those spirits for harmony or to help. All this seemed too abstract to Asuka. But this time, she had a particularly important decision, and going to the shrine would give her time to think.

When she was there, she followed the traditional rituals. Washing her hands and mouth at the fountain, as was required before entering, calmed her down. Before approaching the boulder with the most powerful local deity, she made a customary donation. She took her time. She approached the rock slowly, then clapped her hands twice, the second time holding her hands together in front of her. She started praying and contemplating. Her face was solemn and empty, and her body position gave nothing away. There was no need to express, just a need to think. Eventually, only one thought kept crossing her mind—education can do no harm, education can do no harm. She decided that must be the right thing to do.

She raised the subject with Bunji as soon as she got home.

"I am not sure she needs to learn anything we can't teach her," Bunji said.

"We are unsure if we should invest in Toshiro's trading business because we don't understand it. We have to do it based on trust. Machiko needs to be able to do better. She needs to be educated so she can keep up with future developments. There is a world out there that we don't understand, and Machiko needs to learn about it."

Bunji said nothing. He respected Asuka enough to know that he should think about it. Bunji was also quite upset about potentially losing Machiko. He had learned a long time ago that it was better for him not to argue when he was that upset.

A few days later, after he had thought about it, he agreed to let Machiko go. It was the future, as Asuka said.

"But only for one year," he insisted, and Asuka did not mind that. She was still unsure about the whole idea.

Asuka wasted little time. She informed Tomo, who stepped up her lessons to prepare Machiko. They still had the winter; lessons for her at the school were to start in the spring. She knew if Machiko were to succeed, she would need to study a lot during that time. She balanced this with looking for a new position. There were no teaching positions available in Akeno, so she had to go to Osaka.

"It is hard to find a job," she reported to Asuka a couple of weeks before Machiko was to leave for Nara.

"Let us know how you fare once you get settled," Asuka said.

It was a sad situation. Even if Tomo found a job in Osaka, she would still have to figure out how to move her mother and brother there. By the time Machiko left, Tomo had not found a job, and it was unclear what would happen to her.

4. School

Machiko was greeted at the temple by Akio, a monk of Seiji's age. He was tall and skinny like Seiji, but his eyes were deep and steady. They did not dart like Seiji's. They were also hidden behind glasses. Akio was contemplative and less enthusiastic than Seiji.

"Seiji is too busy to meet you. Let's head to the school. Matsushima is waiting," he said in an unwelcoming, hurried tone. He started heading through the courtyard, almost leaving Machiko behind. Machiko hurried to keep up. Akio was upset. He was competing with Seiji to become Tomeo's assistant. He minded greeting the child of a donor that Seiji took credit for, while Seiji was probably off courting another donor.

Akio was an orphan, born to a single mother who had passed away. He had never met or been told who his father was. All his life, he heard others speak of their parents and where they came from. Good or bad, it gave them a reference point that he was missing. "I feel so naked, empty, unconnected," he would often think to himself in despair. Then, he would try the Buddhist teachings of shedding needs, but it was hard.

He was thinking of this as they were walking. "Knowing my parents is an emotion, a need I should be able to overcome. But, no matter how hard I have tried, I can't. I feel empty. Of course, I shouldn't; I have the temple and might become Tomeo's assistant. But, the Buddha would probably not approve of my pride if I became Tomeo's assistant."

Akio finally gave himself a break. "At least, I have not done anything untoward to get the position, which cannot be said of Seiji." Then, he stopped his self-flagellation altogether, realizing he had ignored Machiko.

"I will help you get settled," he told Machiko with a consoling smile. "Don't worry, you will like the school, though I am not sure what the girls will make of you. None of them has your background, but they are good kids," he said, and Machiko smiled.

They got to the little gate in the wall that connected the school to the temple. Because of her travels, Machiko had arrived just before the middle of the day. Lessons were already well underway. Matsushima came out of the classroom to greet Machiko and quickly introduced her to the class. The class was in the middle of mathematics lessons, a subject in which Machiko was weak. Tomo had focused too much on reading and writing.

The class comprised seven eager classmates. They ignored Machiko as she sat down, and she did not make eye contact with any of them. Machiko was happy when the lesson resumed.

Unfortunately, Machiko did not understand the concepts being taught. It also finally sank in that she would be in a foreign place for several months. She would not see her parents.

When the lesson ended, the students exited the classroom and entered the courtyard outside the school. Mimika, one of Machiko's classmates, introduced herself.

"I came here to become a nun, along with two other girls," Mimika explained. "What about you?"

"I am not sure if I will be a nun," Machiko answered. She did not want to share her background.

"I'm sure you'll like it here," Mimika continued, producing a smile. "We all do." It was true in part. They were all glad to have each other and to escape the misery they usually came from. But they all missed having or being with their parents. Machiko knew most had no options but did not want to admit it because it would cheapen the school.

"I did not understand anything they taught in the math lesson," Machiko confessed.

Mimika immediately agreed to help her after they completed their afternoon chores.

"Will lunch be served in the classroom?" Machiko asked Mimika. Mimika nodded, and they went inside. Mimika thought that

Machiko must be a strong person not to complain about being sent to the school.

Lunch was a simple affair with rice and some vegetables. No one was allowed to speak.

After lunch, it was time for afternoon lessons. Matsushima told an old Buddhist story about a man and four wives.

"In parts of Japan some time ago, women could have several husbands, but this story is set in India, where men were allowed several wives and where the Buddha lived. So, a man knew he was dying and wanted his wives to come with him to the afterlife. When he asked his first wife, she said, 'You always loved me, and now you are dying. It is time for us to separate.' The second wife said, 'You only loved me for selfish reasons. I refuse to go.' His third wife said, 'I pity you and am sad. I will accompany you to your grave, but my duty stops there.' Finally, his fourth wife said, 'You have neglected me all your life, but I will go with you. We can't be separated.'"

None of the students understood what the story was about. Matsushima explained that the first wife represented our bodies. When we die, we must be separated from them. When no one knew who the second wife was, she explained that it was the man's wealth. He loved it for himself all his life, but he could not take it with him. One of the students guessed that the third wife must be the man's friends. They would come to his grave but could not join him. Machiko suspected that the fourth wife had to be something spiritual; otherwise, why would Matsushima tell the story? But she could not figure it out. Matsushima told them that the fourth wife represented the man's soul. It would stay with him even if he had neglected it.

A lively discussion followed. The students enjoyed the story and generally appreciated interpreting it and discovering its meaning.

When the lesson was over, the students did their chores. There was a wide variety - anything that needed doing at the school. Mashiko was asked to sweep the courtyard. She ran into Mimika, who was taking out some trash. When they finished their chores, Mimika helped Mashiko with the math lessons. As she did, Machiko noticed the genuine joy in Mimika's eyes. Mimika liked helping. It was not pride or the expectation of receiving something in return. Losing herself to selflessness came naturally to her.

They stopped the lesson when it was time for dinner. Dinner, again, was a solemn occasion where no one was allowed to talk. The students stole occasional glances from each other but otherwise did not interact. No one, not even Matsushima, knew why that was the custom. Matsushima assumed it might be to honor food. She perpetuated it mainly because it taught the students discipline.

After dinner, they had free time. Machiko wanted some time alone and wandered around the courtyard. Behind the courtyard, she discovered a Shinto shrine.

It was not unusual for Buddhist temples to have Shinto shrines next to them; most Japanese worshipped both religions.

Tomo had taught her about Siddhartha, the original Buddha, who had given up being a prince to live among poor monks. "Most Japanese like Buddhism for introspection and for teachings of selflessness that lead to a better afterlife. That is why most Japanese get buried Buddhists. Shintoism has spirits to appeal to. At Shinto shrines, you can ask for things. That is why most Japanese get baptized and married there."

That had always stuck with Machiko, and it was what she thought about when she saw the shrine behind the temple. She was interrupted when Akio entered the courtyard through the little gate in the temple wall. He came to check up on her.

"How was your first day?" Akio asked.

"We learned about the man with the four wives," Machiko said glumly.

As they were talking, they could hear chimes from the Shinto shrine.

"I like the sound of those chimes," Akio said, trying to cheer Machiko up.

"We did not care much for the shrine in Akeno," Machiko responded.

"Really? I thought farmers cared a lot about appealing to nature's spirits. For a good crop and all."

"A good crop is not always good for everyone," Machiko responded, but did not elaborate. She frowned. Before Akio could ask what she meant by that, Machiko asked him a question.

"I saw a belfry at the entrance of the temple. Do you know what it is for? When is it rung? Is it to summon spirits or to warn of danger?" Machiko asked.

Akio smiled, realizing Machiko wanted to change the subject. "No, nothing like that. It is rung once a year, but then 108 times. Once for every one of the 108 temptations of man. Can you believe there are 108 temptations? I look forward to experiencing them all!"

Machiko laughed, and Akio was happy he had managed to cheer her.

Soon, it became dark, and they had to turn in. Akio said good night, and Machiko went back into the classroom. They slept on mats rolled up in one corner of the room during the day. Machiko took a spot next to Mimika.

"Since you are new, you might be asked to recite the four Buddhist noble truths at the beginning of class tomorrow. One student always recites them, and then we jointly recite the eightfold path," Mimika told her.

Machiko barely knew the four noble truths and spent the next few minutes reconstructing them in her mind. Once she did, she fell asleep.

The next morning, Matsushima did indeed pick her to recite them.

She stood up and spoke quietly. "Life equals suffering. Suffering is caused by desire. To rid oneself of suffering, one must rid oneself of desire. Desire can be eradicated through the practice of the eightfold path."

Machiko had done well. She was grateful to Mimika for the warning. After Machiko finished, all the students stood up and, together with the nuns, recited the eightfold path.

1. Right outlook: to know the four noble truths.

2. Right resolve: to overcome illusions caused by belief in an individual self.

3. Right speech: to refrain from untruth and frivolity.

4. Right conduct: to avoid harming living beings and to relieve suffering.

5. Right livelihood: to have an occupation in keeping with Buddhist precepts.

6. Right effort: to show determination to reach salvation.

7. Right mindfulness: to realize the dangers of discontents that arise from various physical and mental states.

8. Right concentration: to be free of distractions and illusions and to be alert and receptive.

It was a little awkward, but it made the nuns feel good, and the students knew it. They proudly recited the path and pretended to understand what they were saying. In fact, they did not. They understood that Buddhism was about ridding oneself of desire so one could become selfless and enlightened. The eightfold path was more challenging both in its meaning and in terms of the multitude of obligations it entailed. Matsushima suspected this and decided to spend a lesson on each at some point.

During the break before lunch, Machiko learned more about the backgrounds of the students in class from Mimika. One of the students was there because her father had stopped supporting the family after he took a job in Edo. Another had lost her mother in childbirth; her father moved them around Japan after he sold his farm, and they ended up quite poor. For both of those students, the only option was the sisterhood. One girl's father had died in a factory accident, and her mother could only afford to support her brother. All the stories were sad. Machiko was the only child with a happy childhood and wealthy parents. That was why Matsushima had not allowed Machiko's parents to visit her: the other girls either had no parents or had parents who could not afford to see them.

Machiko and Mimika did not talk about each other's backgrounds. Machiko thought Mimika might not want to elaborate on her past if it was as sad as the others. Machiko did not elaborate on hers because she did not want to share how fortunate she was and admit that she was unhappy despite that. Machiko was having a hard time being alone.

One day, to cheer herself up, she went to the censer on the temple grounds. She wanted to play with the incense the way she always had, scooping it twice, but it had lost its appeal. She could not find the joy in it anymore.

She tried to find Seiji. Her mother had told her he had promised to look after her, yet she had not seen him since she'd arrived.

"Seiji is always busy. He even skips prayers to meet with samurai," Akio told Machiko when she ran into him instead. Akio picked up a stick, made a fierce face, and waved it through the air like a sword. "Seiji loves the samurai. He would like to be a fighter if he could."

Machiko reluctantly produced a smile. "He also likes the merchants," Machiko said. "I heard him tell my mother that."

Akio looked away. This hurt. He did not like Seiji's growing influence. It could mean that Seiji and not he would become Tomeo's assistant. Then, as always, he tried to stop himself from coveting the position. It was an un-Buddhist temptation.

"Have you learned the three temptations the Buddha overcame before he became enlightened?" he asked Machiko.

"I think so. Mara, the god of the underworld, tempted him with his daughters, an army, and a mirror."

"Yes, but do you understand why those things were temptations?"

"I think I understand the first, but I am not so sure about the second and the third."

"Mara's army of soldiers marching on Siddhartha represents overcoming fear. The Buddha trusts that the self, your soul, cannot be harmed. Think of it like this: If you are sure of who and what you are, then physical harm won't impact you."

Machiko nodded.

"In the third temptation, Siddhartha is given a mirror and promised power. It represents the temptation of believing in oneself too much and insisting that the world should conform to oneself."

Machiko was not sure if she understood the third temptation. But before she could ask a question, Akio went on.

"There is a chance that Tomeo will see Seiji as having succumbed to the third temptation."

There it was again. Akio could not let go of it. He felt guilty for having twisted the story to be about Seiji when it was also about him. Machiko was surprised to hear him speak so negatively of anyone and wrap it in a Buddhist teaching.

"Is it possible to not focus on oneself?" Machiko asked. She did not want Akio to feel embarrassed. She liked him. It was a way to let him out of his predicament. They were becoming friends.

"I don't know," Akio said. "It is hard."

Akio and Machiko spent a lot of time together. They seemed inseparable. At one point, Akio even shared what bothered him most about his life."I envy you for having parents and a home to go to," Akio told Machiko, confessing his emptiness. It was an honest observation and not meant to evoke pity.

"I am sorry. But you do have the temple and the other monks. That is like a big family." Machiko responded.

"It is not the same," Akio said sadly. It was then that Machiko finally understood the sadness she often saw in Akio's eyes.

What Machiko could not see and what Akio did not tell anyone was a fact that made the pain almost unbearable for him. He knew that his father was probably still alive. Sometimes, Akio played a game in his mind, imagining what it would be like if one of the men making offerings at the temple was his father. He would pick one at random and imagine the conversation they might have. It was a sad game rooted in deep pain.

5. The Summer

When the first semester ended, Machiko's parents sent porters to fetch her for the summer. On her way back to Akeno, she asked them to stop at her favorite spot. The pond's green waters blended into its surroundings. It was calm. As usual, all the frogs jumped in before she got there. She could make out a few lurking under the water, waiting for her to pass.

Machiko became contemplative. She thought about all she had learned during the school year. She felt sorrow for the girls in her class with their sad backgrounds. She decided to pray for them the only way she knew, the Shinto way. She appealed to the spirits in nature for them. Then she thought about Akio. She felt sorry for him, but did not feel it was right to pray for him to become Tomeo's assistant. Instead, she prayed to ease his pain about his father.

As she was leaving, she thought about others - the factory workers. Many of them were the parents of children like the girls at the school. She turned around, went back, and prayed for them. "Ease their pain, ease their pain," she said repeatedly. In her mind, she saw their miserable existence, their empty faces, and their beaten-down bodies. "Ease their pain."

She ran back to the porters as quickly as she could. As she looked up, running towards them, she saw the porters' smiling faces. She could not help but think that even though they had a hard job, their faces, like the farmers' faces, were happier than those of the factory workers. She felt good about praying for the factory workers, but had reservations. What had she really done except utter some words? She wondered if that was something to be proud of.

Machiko did not hide herself when she passed through Akeno. She wanted to see what had changed, even at the risk of being seen in her kago. She saw some farm boys she knew on the street. One of them was Nakayama, with whom she was friends. He had a tough life, taking over his parents' farm from an early age and working it with minimal help. Despite that, Nakayama had a cheerful, easygoing way about him that Machiko admired. Machiko enjoyed seeing how relaxed he was with his friends - his shoulders down and moving slightly on his feet as though dancing as he talked and laughed. His friends were interacting with him, just enjoying talking about whatever they were discussing. Then, before Nakayama could see her, Machiko slid down in her kago. She did not want him to notice that she had stared at him.

She reemerged and looked out when she was on the long road approaching her parents' farm. It was a beautiful summer day. The air was warm but not hot - easy to breathe, and it contained the smell of the rice fields. It was a smell that was especially intense when it was warm. The afternoon sun gave everything a deep color. Akeno was greeting her with all its might.

Machiko's parents were waiting for her in front of the house. They were wearing clean clothes, not work clothes. Bunji's hair was short. He always had it cut before special occasions. He must have thought of her homecoming as such. Machiko was overcome with emotion. She laughed and cried at the same time. Her parents embraced her and would not let her go.

"What is this?" Machiko finally asked to stop the hugging. She pointed towards the house. A new wing had been added. She wondered if it was a dining room like the one at Toshiro's house. It was not. That was not her parents' way.

"It is where we administer the farm. Your father and I now spend all day on administrative matters and need space to do it in. Things are going well, though we are probably a little overextended," Asuka responded.

"Thus the clean clothes," Machiko thought.

Machiko told her parents what she was learning at school and the people she'd met. She told them about the circumstances of the other children and inquired about Tomo. Unfortunately, they had not heard from Tomo.

As they caught up, they noticed how much Machiko had matured. Machiko showed seriousness and determination in her speech. It was not conceit, quite the opposite; she often qualified what she said for things she did not know or understand. It was more that she had seen hardship and knew that things mattered and could not always be taken lightly.

"Let us show you around the farm," Bunji suggested.

. "Besides the house, we have added a building with a silkworm farm; the building you see that is half finished is where the silk is to be spun."

Machiko took a closer look. Big round bamboo wheels where silkworms created their larva stood in the middle of the new building.

"We harvest the silk from that. All you have to feed them are mulberry leaves. And this type of worm creates larvae twice a year," Bunji proudly explained.

It seemed a little awkward to Machiko to rob the silkworms of their lavae, not to let them see through what they had started, but much of farming was that way, wasn't it?

"This seems like a great investment," she said. "I saw a lot of wealthy people in Nara wear silk."

"Yes, we have invested heavily in the farm," Asuka said proudly. "We probably should have slowed down after investing in Toshiro's trading business, but there are many good opportunities."

Machiko worried a little about hearing her parents continue to complain about being overextended, but she trusted that they did the right thing.

"I want to learn about everything you are doing," she said. That pleased her parents. A routine was established. She would rise early, do chores around the house, and then work most of the day in the office, entering bills in a ledger. While she did that, she could overhear her parents running things. She learned a lot.

In the evenings, the three of them would have dinner together. Machiko would ask many questions, now mostly about the farm. Then, they would sit outside the house, overlooking the surrounding fields. All was harmonious until it became clear that

Machiko was learning things beyond reading, writing, and math in Nara.

One evening, as they sat outside the house, Machiko told a story she had learned at school.

"The story tells of a rich person who invited priests to his house and gave them lavish gifts to gain merit. Yet, the Buddha did not give merit for this. He said that there are four types of offerings: one in which the gift is large but the merit is low, one in which the gift is small and the merit is small, one in which the gift is small but the merit is large, and one in which the gift is large and the merit is large. The first is a gift by a deluded person who takes life to sacrifice to the gods and celebrates doing so. The second is a gift from a person who keeps much to himself and offers little. The third is a gift from someone who can afford little but gives with an open heart and love. The fourth is a wealthy person who, with an unselfish spirit, makes donations and starts institutions for the needs of others."

Bunji was upset. He wanted to avoid Machiko becoming too giving even before going to Nara. She needed to learn the harsh realities of life. It was hard to accumulate wealth and equally hard to protect it. If this story was any indication, she was learning the opposite.

Machiko noticed the upset expression on her father's face. In a way, it reinforced her thoughts. At her age, she was trying to establish her own ideas. Utter rejection reinforced them more.

Before Bunji could say anything, Asuka defused the situation. "That is a nice story. The institution we support is the temple."

Bunji did not like that answer. The temple was not providing for the needs of others. However, he was unsure what to say.

Asuka then tried to change the subject. "We are so glad you are here. You must learn how to run the farm. One day it will be yours."

But this did not improve things.

"I am not sure I am up to that," Machiko answered.

"Nonsense. Of course you are, and you will," Bunji erupted. "You will run it just like your mother and I do. If there is anything you need to know, it is that a farm needs to be run by its owner. We have seen too many samurai fail at being absentee farmers. You will be the farm's owner and need to run it. We know you will be good at it."

"That is not what I mean. I like what Matsushima does. I was thinking—"

"This is why I did not want her to go to Nara!" Bunji shouted.

Asuka looked hard at her husband, then turned back to her daughter. "What is it about what she does that you like?"

"The girls at the orphanage need help. Many of them are not orphans. They just come from families that can't support them."

"There is lots of time for you to decide what to do," Asuka said.

Machiko said nothing but frowned. Asuka noticed.

"She is meeting Nakayama tomorrow after work," Asuka said, smiling at Bunji. Asuka wanted to encourage Machiko and Nakayama to continue their friendship. Bunji was oblivious.

"We should be investing more in the farm," Bunji said. Now, he was the one trying to change the topic. He also wanted Machiko to hear that running the farm was not without worries. "We have used up our resources. I am not sure how that trading business investment is going."

"It will be fine," Asuka said.

When Nakayama and Machiko met up, Machiko was nervous. She was intimidated, maybe a little captivated, by his good looks. She had always noticed them, but they caused more of a distraction now and made Machiko slightly uncomfortable. She did what she usually did when she was uncomfortable: she started rambling. She spoke about the temple and the Buddhist teachings she was learning. After a while, Nakayama stopped her.

"All that contemplation and meditation. Do you really think it is worthwhile?"

He did not want to offend her, but if one had to be spiritual, he preferred appealing to spirits to take action, as he did at the Shinto shrine. He could appeal to them for good crops, friends, or good fortune. He did not understand the Buddhist preoccupation with introspection and selflessness.

"What is your favorite Shinto story, then?" Machiko asked, secretly hoping it would stump Nakayama, but it did not.

"Okuninushi," Zakari responded without hesitation.

Okuninushi was a god who, with his brothers, went on a journey to court Princess Yakami. When the brothers encountered a badly bitten rabbit, they told it to bathe in the salty sea and blow itself dry in the wind. Okuninushi had fallen behind because he was carrying his brothers' bags. When he encountered the rabbit, it was in terrible agony because of the salt and wind. Okuninushi told it to wash himself in fresh water and roll in the scattered leaves of the cattail plant. The rabbit healed and predicted that Okuninushi would marry Princess Yakami. When this came to pass, Okuninushi's brothers tried to kill him, but every time they tried, his mother petitioned the creator gods to resuscitate him. Eventually, Okuninushi created Japan and was victorious over all his brothers.

"So you are for the underdog?" Machiko asked.

"Maybe, but I think most people are when they hear stories like this."

"There are a lot of underdogs in Nara."

"I have heard. It isn't surprising. All these changes that are building big cities leave many people behind. Cities are tough."

Nakayama told Machiko he had heard that Tomo was having difficulty in Osaka. She lived there with her brother and mother, but she'd had to take a factory job and was struggling with it.

"It is true. Life is easier in Akeno," Machiko said, lowering her head.

6. A Society in Transition

On Machiko's return trip to Nara at the end of summer, they stopped at Machiko's favorite spot, but not for long. The porters noticed that Machiko had matured, and they no longer treated her like a child. They would not get the joy from seeing her return from the pond like they used to. They wanted to move on.

Machiko rushed to the pond, so much so that the frogs were still jumping in when she arrived. It created a flurry of waves on the pond, and the splashes occurred almost simultaneously, amplifying their noise. "That is unusual," Machiko thought. Then she realized that she would lack the serenity to enjoy the place. She turned around, mimicked the serious faces of the porters, and they went on their way.

At the outskirts of Nara, they noticed that more factories had gone up, and most of the existing ones had been expanded. Before, the factory buildings were spaced apart; now, they were crowded together. It left little room for the makeshift shacks in which many factory workers lived. Masses of lifeless faces on the road were making their way to or from the factories. What did it matter? None of them looked up to see who was in the kago.

The streets of Nara seemed tense. There were more people, yet it was quieter. The temple had more activity than usual. Crowds were coming and going. Usually, there were more monks than lay people at the temple, but now it was the reverse. The crowd around the censer frantically waved incense smoke toward themselves, and a crowd prayed insistently in front of the central statue. The monks were walking a little faster than usual.

Akio was nowhere to be found, so Machiko walked through the temple to the school. When she arrived, Matsushima was happy to see her. The nun had grown quite fond of her. She admired how reserved Machiko was and how she had stayed humble despite her privileges. She had missed her during the summer. They spoke about Machiko's time in Akeno, the many evenings with her parents, and

Nakayama and his Shinto ways. Matsushima was happy to hear about Machiko's time away from the temple and let her talk for a while.

Then Matsushima turned to less fortunate news. There had been riots in Osaka. The farmers there were struggling and could not afford to pay the taxes they owed. Since the crops were not promising, many were giving up—selling their farms and heading for the cities, where they would encounter low-paying jobs and limited housing.

"We took in three more children. We should have taken more, but we simply couldn't. They are only five years old. We have never taken in any children that young who were not orphans. Their parents simply could not support them."

"They gave up their children at that age?"

"I don't know what is happening, but things are getting worse."

"The children must miss their parents terribly. Five-year-olds without their mothers."

"Yes, but there was no alternative. They needed help," Matsushima said matter-of-factly and then changed the subject.

"The only good news is that they made Akio Tomeo's assistant. Justice prevailed." Matsushima never liked Seiji, but this was the only time she hinted at it.

"That is great news. I can't believe it. I must go see him." Machiko said. She excused herself. Matsushima understood. She knew how close Akio and Machiko were.

"Unbelievable, but well deserved. Congratulations!" Machiko said, smiling at Akio when she finally found him.

"Thank you. It is such an honor. They told me they had noticed how committed I have been. It seems like a strange reason, almost as if they didn't want to tell me the truth. What does that even mean?"

"Did you celebrate?"

"No, not really. No one to celebrate with," Akio said, looking down.

"Does this mean one day you will run the temple?" Machiko said enthusiastically.

"No. That is not a good aspiration."

"Was Seiji upset that he did not get the position? Of course, he was."

"I have gotten the sense that Tomeo feels threatened by him."

"Threatened? How?"

Akio would not answer that. Instead, he asked Machiko about her summer.

"I have to tell you later," Machiko said. "Matsushima wants me to help the new children. I need to go meet them."

Machiko left in a hurry, looking forward to meeting the new students. She found them in the school courtyard, but the other children already cared for them.

"You must be hungry," one of the students asked one of the new kids. "I have some food that I kept for you."

Another student was playing hide and seek with another one of the new kids. The student was too old for the game, but the new kid was not.

Machiko watched jealously from a distance over the following weeks. She noticed the joy the other students got from taking care of them. In all their misery, charity created a special bond. It created what a family has: trust, respect, and selflessness. It created it for the giver and receiver. Machiko wanted to be part of that, but couldn't. She got there too late.

Instead, Machiko was to learn more about the temple. Matsushima received a letter from Bunji asking if she could deemphasize the religious part of the curriculum for Machiko and instead teach her practical skills. The evening when Machiko had told her Buddhist story had stuck with him. Since all the children were taught simultaneously, Matsushima could not entirely accommodate this request, but she figured out a way for Machiko to learn some additional "useful" skills. She knew that Machiko's parents would be pleased if she asked Machiko to keep the books for the school. With that, Machiko not only learned accounting but gained insight into the temple's administration. The accounts were presented at a monthly meeting presided over by Seiji. Much discussion would ensue amongst the senior monks about donations and where the money was spent. It provided an insight into the underbelly of the temple.

At the first meeting that Machiko attended, Seiji, always one for gossip, told Machiko that the emperor had continued to insist that the samurai class be taken care of.

"He invited them in all of their regalia to the palace. Can you see them bowing in their outdated uniforms?" Seiji chuckled. "The emperor says it is the nation's moral obligation, even if it means higher taxes for farmers at a time of poor crops."

Machiko did not want to get into such a disrespectful conversation and felt it was wrong. Seiji had courted the samurai the way he had courted the merchants, and now he was disrespecting them.

"I recently saw your mother," Seiji continued. "I hear they are having a harder time expanding the farm, given their recent investment in a trading business?"

Machiko hated how well-informed Seiji was. She could not resist a little jab. "I heard that Akio became Tomeo's assistant."

"Some of us know things about Tomeo. He won't always be in charge," Seiji said, looking away. It was the sort of comment Machiko knew he would deny, but could not help uttering. When he looked at Machiko again, his face contorted with such meanness that it scared Machiko.

"Let's look at the books," Seiji said.

After the meeting, Machiko wandered around the grounds. She wanted to decompress. She saw Akio speaking to an impoverished farmer. Akio noticed Machkio from the corner of his eye but did not acknowledge her. The meeting with the farmer was too serious. The farmer was trying to figure out how to bear his guilt over his situation.

"I don't want any handouts; I just don't know what to do. I have not planned correctly, and now I can't feed my family. They don't say so, but I don't know how they can respect me," the farmer said, not caring if he was overheard.

Akio did his best to console the farmer calmly and reassuringly. Machiko could not make out what he was saying. When the farmer left, Machiko approached Akio.

"You must feel good about helping like that. Don't you?"

"I suppose," Akio responded and shrugged his shoulders.

"I wanted to help the new orphans at the school, but I was too late. Instead, I am stuck with the books and Seiji," Machiko said.

"Sorry to hear that, but I am not sure I am helping any of the farmers. We talk about how to focus their spirits on positive things. How to balance their lives. How pains and desires must not develop into suffering. You know, the Buddhist teachings. They may leave a little better, but they always come back."

"You are helping them, even if only for a little while. You are doing what you are supposed to—tending to their souls," Machiko said. She frowned, her face not sure if she believed that.

"OK, let's try that out," Akio said.

"Take the story of the gaki, the person with a big stomach but a small throat. He can't nourish himself. I often think about it. The story is to help people temper their desires. I am meeting people with the opposite problem. They have a small stomach that they can't fill. How can I tell stories about a gaki tempering its desire when people are in real need? What good does that do?"

"The Buddha's concern is helping people find their own salvation. You are at a temple. You are doing what you can. You are tending to souls, not stomachs," Machiko said to console her friend.

"Really? Listen to yourself. You can't really believe that." Akio responded, trying not to offend her. "At some point, we need to figure out a way to really help people."

"Yes," said Machiko. Her face finally lost its frown. "I would like that. We should."

Akio and Machiko only met occasionally over the next few months, as Machiko tended to her studies and the school's finances, and Akio tended to the poor. However, the onslaught of people needing help continued, and as their plights became more and more dire, Machiko and Akio became increasingly disenchanted with Buddhist teachings.

Matsushima encouraged Machiko to keep searching in the scriptures and said her desire for answers indicated her spiritual calling. Machiko was not sure. When Masushima granted Mashiko's parents' request for their daughter to come home for the matsuri harvest festival, she was happy to get away. She needed a reprieve from it all.

The guji, the main Shinto priest of Akeno, a representative of the farmers and a representative of the village, chaired the festival. Bunji avoided going to the Shinto shrine except when something important was happening in his life. He was not religious. Despite this, he had been elected the farmers' representative for the festival. It was a great honor, and that is why Matsushima granted Machiko the request to attend.

The Shinto shrine at the edge of town contained a boulder with the most powerful spirit in Akeno. It was where Asuka had gone to pray for guidance about Machiko's education and sometimes, in the years before, to pray for a good crop.

During the festival, the venerated boulder was paraded in a mikoshi, a portable shrine. The mikoshi was a palanquin constructed and decorated like a miniature house, only in this case, it was a house you would see in Nara, not in Akeno. It was elaborate, featuring exquisite wood carvings and a bright red finish. The boulder was placed inside and paraded as a form of giving special thanks to the spirit for the harvest.

On the festival's first day, children from the village were allowed to carry the mikoshi without the boulder around the village. It was an honor, and the children did it respectfully.

Then, usually in the afternoon, the guji chanted a few prayers that no one understood. He purified the shrine with a branch from a sacred pine tree and prepared it to hold the important boulder. It was not placed in the mikoshi yet - not before the evening celebrations.

For the evening celebrations, a big fire was lit in a field outside the village. The adults started drinking and singing. Everyone enjoyed themselves.

Machiko loved the festival and wandered through the crowd, enjoying everyone's happiness. She ran into Nakayama, who was his usual happy self, but only a little more so since he was drunk.

"I love the festival! I love Akeno!" he said when he saw Machiko.

"Wonderful to see you. Yes, a great festival," Machiko responded.

"Are you here for long?"

"Just for the festival because of my father."

"I will be one of the porters of the shrine."

"Congratulations," Machiko said. "Great honor."

She smiled. A happy, warm feeling that she was not used to came over her. Was it the feeling of being with someone she had known since childhood? Or was it Nakayama's easygoing, self-assured nature she had come to like?

"You should probably be drinking with the other porters then," Machiko said. It was a selfless comment. She would have liked to spend time with him.

Nakayama's face lit up. The prospect of more drinks and Machiko's kindness encouraged him.

"Maybe I should." He turned around and started walking away.

"It was good to see you," he said, turning around after a few steps. He smiled. Then he disappeared with his usual smile in the smoke from the fire obscuring everything.

The next morning, Bunji put on his best kimono, which he never wore. He headed to the shrine early, wearing a mask over his mouth to avoid breathing on the kami—the spirit—while in the shrine.

"Purity is key. Breath carries human imperfections and a physicality that disturbs the kami's purity," the priest had reminded Bunji days before. Bunji did not like all this concern with purity, but what did it matter? It was an honor to be chosen.

When he arrived, ten porters, including Nakayama, were already there. They wore white loincloths and headbands. They barely greeted Bunji, wanting to hide their hangovers from the night before. Bunji was embarrassed about his get-up. No one made eye contact. Even Nakayama was uncharacteristically shy.

The ceremony started with the guji clapping his hands and issuing a prayer. A drummer situated just outside the shrine beat his drum. The sound resonated over Akeno. The guji stepped out of the shrine and bowed his head left, right, and left again. There was a pause. Then, the porters lifted the mikoshi, now containing the boulder with the kami. The priest had put it there early in the morning. Bunji, together with the representatives from the village and the guji, then started walking and leading the procession down the steps in front of the temple and through the village. Bunji had a hard time acting deferentially to the guji and respecting the kami, but he tried.

The villagers stood in front of their houses watching the procession; many were hungover from the celebration the night before. Kids followed the procession, making noise, but otherwise, it was a somber affair, especially compared to the earlier revelry.

Machiko and her mother had come to the village to watch. Bunji did not greet them when he walked past them. He wanted to keep a serious demeanor.

When Machiko finally got home with her mother, she found a letter from Tomo:

Dear Machiko,

I was honored to hear about your progress in Nara. You are a virtuous and patient person. My friend Bako, who still lives in Akeno, told me how proud you are making your parents. I never had any doubt about that.

I now live in Osaka. At first, I worked in a factory, but I recently found work as a bookkeeper at one of the businesses in town. My father would probably not be happy that I am employed in the merchant class, but circumstances change.

I hope to visit Akeno eventually, but it is impossible right now.

Please write me soon. I want to hear about all you are learning.

Respectfully,

Tomo

"Things have not turned out well for Tomo," Machiko told her mother.

"Yes, and her brother died from an illness that they could not afford to treat," Asuka responded.

She wrote Tomo a letter back, hoping to see her, but she realized that the chances of that any time soon were low.

When Machiko returned to school, she continued to become more disenchanted. Akio was spending more time tending to Tomeo's needs. He also feuded with Seiji, who had dared to undercut Tomeo since he had not been made his assistant.

"Seiji controls a lot of donors, and many people owe him favors. Tomeo has a hard time standing up to that."

Machiko hated hearing about these intrigues. Being an accountant for such an organization was not what she wanted. She also never got to help the younger children at the orphanage. It was a lonely, empty existence - a routine devoid of purpose. As soon as the school year was over, she returned to Akeno.

She applied what she learned in Nara to the farm. She helped in the administration and soon became indispensable to her parents. There was joy in that, even though it was not particularly rewarding either. At least she avoided the hypocrisy of the temple. Machiko never returned to school.

7. Twenty Years Later

Machiko ended up marrying Nakayama, attracted to his more traditional ways at the time. The things she saw in Nara, both inside and outside the temple, caused her concern. In contrast, Nakayama exuded such confidence and appreciation for the Akeno ways that Machiko knew he would create a stable life for her. Being the conscientious person he was, he made sure that she understood what exactly that meant before they got married. He wanted a traditional Shinto life. Machiko somewhat reluctantly agreed.

They had a son, Kiyoshi, who was exceptionally bright and quickly required schooling outside Akeno. Unlike his mother, he was schooled at a Shinto seminary.

Machiko's parents had passed away. Machiko inherited their farm and business holdings. When the farm was combined with Nakayama's farm, it became the largest farm in the region by far. Machiko and Nakayama moved into Machiko's parents' house. They were extremely wealthy.

Like their parents, Machiko and Nakayama hoped that Kiyoshi would one day take over the farm, but it seemed less and less likely every year. Kiyoshi liked the seminary and was studying to become a Shinto priest. Machiko saw the irony in her now wanting to preclude her son from studying away, the way her father had, but she did not object.

It was a hot summer day when Nakayama came home early from negotiations to buy farm equipment. He was not feeling well and went to lie down. He had felt ill for several days but thought it would get better. That day, he developed a severe stomachache. Machiko helped Nakayama to their bedroom and asked for a physician to be called. She knew it must be serious since he had come home early.

The doctor diagnosed that Nakayama was suffering from a severe intestinal infection. He gave them some medication. Machiko spent the next few days tending to her husband.

"I know life has not been easy for you," Nakayama told his wife. "You have a yearning to get involved. To get out and help. All the stories we heard about the factory workers. I am sorry, I was just not able to deviate from our ways. Now, it is time for Izanami."

"Don't talk like that," Machiko said. "You will get better."

"It is the cycle of life. Nothing to be afraid of." Nakayama said.

Nakayama was referring to the myth of Izanagi and Izanami. Izanagi and Izanami had a daughter named Amaterasu, the sun goddess, whose grandson, Ninigi, and the storm goddess Susanoo gave birth to Jimmu, the first emperor of Japan. When Izanami died, Izanagi found her in the underworld, badly deformed. Izanagi could not bear it and left her for good. Izanami then vowed to kill a thousand people per day for every day Izanagi was not with her. Izanagi responded by creating 1,500 people per day to make up for this.

"Poor Izanami," Nakayama said with a smile. He was trying to comfort Machiko by making light of his situation.

Then, he continued what he wanted to say about his life.

"It just is not what farmers do. It was not our place to go to Nara and help. We agreed that the traditional life was the way, simple farmers with a good family," Nakayama said.

Machiko nodded and held Nakayama's hand.

"We did pray at the shrine," she said, even though neither Nakayama nor she considered that "doing."

A few days later, Nakayama passed away.

Kiyoshi came home from the seminary for his father's funeral. Machiko was glad to see him.

"My son," Machiko said when he arrived. She said it proudly, the way a parent would.

She reached out and embraced Kiyoshi.

"I am so glad to see you. We have a lot to catch up on. But first, we must figure out how to bury your father the Shinto way. No one knows how. Everyone wants to marry with hopeful Shinto traditions but be buried with contemplative Buddhist traditions." She remembered how Tomo had told her that. "I guess we are fortunate that you decided to become a Shinto priest."

It was the always practical side to Machiko that Kiyoshi was used to - always concerned with what had to be done, not taking time out to be sad.

"We wash the body. It needs to be pure. Then we make food offerings. We place the clean, pure body in a pure wood coffin. The cremation should be over a well-organized fire. Not something put together hastily. Then we purify the grave site where he will lie, and we purify the bedroom where he lay when he died. It all has to be done with a lot of respect - minding purity."

He reassuringly looked at Machiko. He was proud to have learned something useful. "I will take care of it."

It seemed a little procedural and too concerned with purity for Machiko, but she said nothing.

While watching the fire, Machiko kept an honorable face. She did not cry. When it was over, she thanked the few friends who came, the priest, and Kiyoshi. It was Machiko's way of asking for time alone. She walked out to the open fields behind the gravesite until she would not be seen, and then she sat on a rock.

"What a life, Nakayama," she said as though he were there. "Never disturbing things, upsetting no one. You were such a good man."

"He was a good man," she thought. "Is that what one says about someone who keeps to the rules - he was a good man! Good, however, because of the many things he did not do, that he could have done, as opposed to good because of what he did do."

Machiko felt a little guilty about that train of thought. She tried to stop herself from contemplating the good they did not do. This was not the time. To force herself to stop, she got up and returned home, where she found Kiyoshi.

"Tell me about the seminary," she said before Kiyoshi could ask any questions about how she was doing.

"It is a solitary place. People come to hang Ema prayer plaques and for baptisms and marriages. They mostly stay away. There are no regular ceremonies for them to attend. It is peaceful. I often take walks in the woods."

Kiyoshi forced a smile, wanting his mother to see that he was happy.

"Do you like that? Not a lot gets done." Machiko said.

Kiyoshi knew that she did not care for idle time.

"I like it. It suits me." Kiyoshi said, displeased that he had caught himself getting defensive. Machiko did not intend that.

"Who do you think should run things now that your father is gone?" she asked, to move on.

"I think you should, like your mother did."

"But what about after I am gone?" Machiko asked.

"You trust Zakari."

Zakari was the main office administrator - a son of a local farmer whose farm Machiko and Nakayama had bought. He proved to be exceptionally good at figures and organization.

"I do," Machiko agreed. "But you will own the farm? Will you not stay and learn to run it?" Her father had always said that the owner of a farm had to run it. Kiyoshi answered by not responding to his mother's question. It was the wrong time, at any rate.

It was not until late autumn, with the harvest completed, that Machiko had time to think about her life again. She decided to go to Nara. She told Zakari what she needed.

"I don't want porters. I want to walk. It will give me time to think. But I need at least three changes of clothing - one formal for dinner. Please have that packed and delivered to Toshiro's house with a note on when I will arrive."

Zakari noticed that Machiko was not in her usual matter-of-fact way. The tasks were not different from other organizational tasks, but Machiko had a particular enthusiasm and joy on her face when she told Zakari what she needed. Her forehead was relaxed, her face assumed an unburdened eagerness, and she produced a lasting, comfortable smile. It was almost as though she had become the child she had never been. Zakari liked this side of her.

Machiko did not tell anyone that she would stop at her favorite spot. It was the main reason she did not want porters. It would give her time to think at the pond where the road to Nara forked.

The pond was as beautiful as ever. When she arrived, the frogs jumped in. That had not changed. As she sat by the edge for a while, she could see them reemerge from the water. That was new. She never had enough time to see that happen. It was calming. She also noticed birds overhead settling into the trees. "Given enough time, the place becomes more interesting, calm, and inspiring," she thought. Truly undisturbed.

She sat there for a while, taking it all in, until thoughts about things she wanted to do slowly started to preoccupy her. She thought about Nara and the difference she could make if she did more than pray at Shinto shrines. One thought in particular kept crossing her mind: She was given a body to act. Everyone is. Frogs have bodies to jump. We have a mind to think and pray, but a body to act. Resting there by the pond, she realized that resting was not what she was meant to do. She was meant to act. Do things.

"I must be the first frog to jump in and disturb the water!" She said to herself. "The first frog."

Machiko got up, took one last look at the pond, and, driven by renewed energy, stridently walked to Nara.

She hurried through the slums around the factories at the edge of town, not because she was afraid, but because she did not need to see anymore. She knew the plight that had been created. She walked straight to the temple and asked for Akio. She did not want to walk with him in the gardens when he came to the gate. Instead, she walked with him through Nara's busy streets. It seemed more appropriate, given what she had in mind.

"There have been a lot of changes at the temple," Akio reported. "It hurts me to tell you, but Seiji is now the head of the temple. With his connections with the samurai class and the merchants, he became powerful—too powerful. Most of the donations came through him. There were even samurai who advocated for him. That has never happened before. Temple leadership used to be an internal matter."

Machiko remembered how Seiji had told her that he knew something about Tomeo. She was sure that had something to do with it, but did not tell Akio. After all, she did not know what it was.

"How is Tomeo taking this?"

"He abdicated before it would have been embarrassing for him. He still wields influence, as you can imagine, but it is not the same." Akio slumped. "There is more. Matsushima passed away. The school gained a reputation for being the best in Nara. The wealthy merchants now send their daughters here. I guess your mother was a trailblazer. No more orphans."

"So, who takes care of the orphans?"

"I don't know. No one seems to care. I don't know where I would be if the temple had been this way when I was an orphan."

"And you, what are you doing?" she asked.

"I continue to tend to farmers and increasingly factory workers. Farmers come because of the droughts and taxes, and factory workers have all sorts of issues. There are a lot of destitute people."

Machiko took that as her opportunity to discuss what she had come for.

"You see poverty every day. You have been frustrated for a long time about being unable to help. I know you help spiritually, but you yourself have said that is not enough. A long time ago, you said we should find a way to help, really help. That is what I want to do."

"You want to make a donation to the temple and ask Seiji to distribute it to the poor," Akio said halfheartedly.

"No," Machiko said emphatically. She tilted her head to the side and spoke directly to Akio, but in a way that she could not be overheard. "Seiji and the temple have not shared their wealth with the poor for a long time. You cannot trust them. You know this."

Machiko then raised her voice a little.

"I saw the temple gardens when I was at the gate waiting for you. They are as pristine as ever. The temple is freshly painted. All the monks are wearing well-maintained "simple" robes and are fed well. No suffering there."

Akio conceded with a sad nod.

"A worthy place to visit and honor the Buddha," Machiko continued, even though she did not have to. "Except everyone just gets to visit; only the monks get to live there."

Akio looked at her with slight disapproval. He agreed but lived there as well, and Machiko did not have to carry on denigrating the temple. She had made her point.

"Mind you, the same is true for Kiyoshi's shrine," Machiko said. "They are all focused on power."

"Very well, Machiko. But what do you want to do? Do it yourself? Do you know what it will entail? It will be costly. You need food and people, and when the money runs out, it will be over."

Machiko was ahead of Akio. She had grown up watching her parents organize businesses. Any real effort to help the poor would have to involve an organization. It needed resources and a mission that would persist.

"Yes. I thought about that. I want to create an organization of people who help each other. We help the poor, and when they can, we ask them to help others."

"You mean the poor feed the poor."

"No, we help some to get onto their feet, and then they, in turn, help in whatever way they can. If we can get enough to do that, we can make a difference."

"Isn't that a bit optimistic?" Akio asked.

"I don't think so. We start with my money and get some people on their feet. When they are doing better, we ask them to join the movement. It won't be perfect, but it won't be just a handout."

"I guess it could work," Akio said, shrugging his shoulders, unsure. Then, he let out a sigh. "And you want me to be part of this?" He asked.

"Yes!" Machiko said. "I can't start this on my own."

Akio understood that Machiko would not want the temple involved, but he could not be a part of it unless it was. Seiji would not allow such a movement to be run any other way. How would it be viewed if the Buddhist temple were not in charge of such an effort?

"I can only be part of it if it goes through the temple," Akio finally said. "That is who I am. I owe it to them. They took me in as an orphan."

"If I get Seiji to release you from your duties as a monk, would you come to live on the farm?"

"The farm? How can we help the poor from the farm?"

Machiko had an idea, but did not know if it could work. Instead of sharing it, she put up her hands to stop Akio. "You are right, but these are details I can work out. Would you join me?"

Akio could not see himself repaying the charity the temple had shown him by leaving it to help an organization that would be viewed as undermining it. Seiji's blessing would not change his mind. He did not respect his authority. Akio was about to reject the idea, but then thought about the loneliness inside him that had never gone away. He had been searching for something, some purpose to fill that void. Machiko's idea would be a fulfilling undertaking. It would provide the purpose and the direction he had been missing. He could focus on the future as opposed to dreading the past. He agreed to think about it and to speak to Tomeo.

That evening, Machiko had dinner with Toshiro, one of his sons, and his wife. It was a simple affair. They served hinachirashi, a dish consisting of scattered sushi rice, mushrooms, and carrots. The conversation centered around Machiko's farm and other businesses. One of the businesses Machiko's parents had started was a sake brewery. Toshiro had advised that it was a good business extension for a rice farmer. The production of sake was relatively easy after they acquired the necessary equipment, but obtaining the stoneware bottles proved challenging. Machiko wanted to know if it made sense for them to manufacture the bottles. After a while, Toshiro and his son decided that it probably would not, and Toshiro's son said he would look into finding a reliable supplier.

"You know," Toshiro said to Machiko, "the trading house in Osaka is doing well. As I suspected, trade has picked up tremendously. National distribution is the way of the future."

"Really? I had almost forgotten about it," Machiko said.

"It is worth more than any farm could ever be," Toshiro said, looking at his son, hoping he would take note.

Machiko was stunned and then remembered that her parents had not gotten any documentation for their investment. Was Toshiro going to honor it once he looked into it?

The next morning, Machiko returned to the temple. She had made an appointment with Seiji to keep up her mother's annual donation. Her mother had taught her to stay on good terms with the temple. Stopping the donation would surely disturb things.

She met Seiji in his office. It was decorated with exquisite vases and a wall painting of turtles, a sign of lasting strength. The office smelled of new tatami mats. Machiko knew that smell from Toshiro's house, and the office's opulence also reminded her of it.

Seiji was sitting behind a desk piled high with papers.

"We all knew you would head up the temple at some point. Congratulations!" Machiko said.

Seiji looked up from his papers. "It is a lot of work. Thank you for continuing your mother's donation."

"I noticed poverty and suffering on the outskirts of Nara when I traveled here," Machiko said, knowing that raising the subject was enough.

"Poverty is an unfortunate by-product of the industrialization of Japan. The nation will become wealthier, but some will not be able to transition quickly enough."

"Can the temple help?"

"We can, and we are. Your friend Akio is spending a lot of time with the poor, tending to their souls."

"I mean, can you not provide them with food?"

"It is not our place. Even if we wanted to, you are keeping up your donations, but none of the other farmers are. Their tax obligations are too high. The samurai are also not doing well. We are relying on merchants to donate, but it is not enough. They have not gotten used to donating yet."

"Something has to be done," Machiko insisted.

Seiji said nothing and instead waited for Machiko to give him the donation.

"Thank you," he said when she did, and then returned to his papers. The meeting was over.

Machiko felt a little defeated as she walked through the temple grounds, but her steps became faster and more resolute once she left Nara. She came to her favorite spot and did not stop. Instead, she walked down the road where the road forked by a stream. She did not go the way to Akeno. She wanted to find the owners of the land with the pond. She noticed the fields around the land were poorly maintained and thought the owners might be interested in selling.

When she found the farmer's house, the farmer, whose name was Fumito, invited her inside.

"We know who you are," Fumito said when he sat beside his wife after Machiko was seated. Machiko's parents had bought up many farms in the area, and Fumito suspected that this might be why Machiko came.

"We are not interested in selling," Fumito said. He wanted to get a good price. Machiko knew what he was doing. She had been in many of these situations.

Instead of playing games, Machiko made a fair offer for the run-down farm, which, as Machiko expected, was quickly rejected.

"I will double the offer," Machiko said.

Fumito caught himself with a surprised look on his face. He hoped Machiko did not notice.

Machiko did, but did not mind paying too much. It seemed wrong to her to buy her beloved land at a bargain price. It was the first time Machiko had made a significant purchase, not as an investment. Strangely, it felt better to pay more than it was worth. "It is worth more to me than its farming value anyway," she thought. "It is a sacred place."

Machiko was surprised and a little infuriated when Fumito started to hesitate. He wondered why Machiko was willing to pay so much. Was he missing something? Maybe he should hold out for more.

"It is my final price," Machiko said quickly and sternly, getting up to walk out. She had to put a stop to Fumito.

Fumito looked at his wife, who gave him a stern look, urging him not to lose this opportunity.

"What will I do without a farm?" he asked Machiko, still holding out.

"We will hire you," Machiko said. "There will be plenty to do."

Fumito took a little time to pretend he had to consider the offer. Then he gave in.

When Machiko returned home, she told Zakari that he should make arrangements for the purchase. Zakari knew precisely what to do. He was a little surprised at the price and how far away the farm was from Akeno. They might be unable to run it as part of the main farm's operations. They would not attain the benefits of being part of the larger farm. However, it was not his place to question Machiko's decision, so he did as she asked. Machiko also seemed resolute, more resolute than he had ever seen her.

8. The Initial Movement

"You will upset a lot of people, " Tomeo told Akio when he approached him about helping Machiko's movement.

"It is the first time I have been enthusiastic about anything," Akio responded. "It is so obvious, right in front of us. Praying and contemplating are not enough. We need to do something."

"I can't condone you doing this. Plus, do you even know how long this will last? Even if the authorities don't intervene, Machiko may give up on this. She will soon realize she is handing out money, her money."

"I want you to be supportive," Akio said. "I don't want to do this and leave the temple without your permission. You took me in as an orphan, and I owe you for that."

Akio was surprised to see that this stumped Tomeo. Tomeo got up from the chair he was sitting on and paced the room. Then, after some thought, he said:

"You are right; you owe us, but let me see if I can square it away with Seiji."

Akio could not believe it, but took no further time to contemplate the conversation. Instead, he sprang into action. He spoke to a warehouse owner he had become acquainted with at the temple. The owner agreed they could use part of the warehouse as a weekend gathering place when there was little activity. Akio then told everyone he knew who might be able to help that they should come to the warehouse in a couple of weeks. He also told them that they should recruit others to join their effort. The group would feed the poor who could not provide for themselves.

He wrote to Machiko, asking her to be at the warehouse at a designated time. Upon receiving word, Machiko asked one of her employees to buy the necessary equipment: big bowls, plates, spoons, and carts to haul them. She also asked them to set aside some of the rice they were storing. Machiko found starting new ventures difficult, but this seemed simple and enjoyable. There was no pressure to make a profit.

Tomeo, as promised, went to see Seiji. He did it as part of his regular visit. Since Seiji was in charge, they met weekly. It was a little-known fact that Seiji tried to hide. Tomeo had insisted on it when he agreed to step down.

"How are collections?" Tomeo asked.

"Not as good as they should be, even from the merchants," Seiji responded.

"What about Toshiro? Has he not increased his donation?"

"He did. He is doing well. He told me he prioritizes dealing with merchants that adhere to an honor code, like the bushido code. It makes business easier. Can you believe that?"

Tomeo chuckled and then switched to what he wanted to discuss with Seiji.

"Akio came to see me. He wants to join Machiko to help the poor."

"She can't," Seiji said.

"Well, it seems like it will happen," Tomeo said. "But I have a way to stop him."

"What will you do?" Seiji asked. "Tell him he can't."

"I don't think that will work. I will tell him that we discussed it and that he owes us."

"Do you think that will work?" Seiji was surprised.

"Yes, he told me he feels guilty about that," Tomeo said. "I just need to tell him that that concern is real. It would be immoral to leave when we took him in."

"Really. And you would do that?" Seiji said.

Tomeo nodded reluctantly, and Seiji produced a devious smile. They did not look at each other.

"But you must find a way to stop Machiko," Tomeo said, to move on.

"I will talk to Toshiro. He knows her. Not sure he will help us, given his bushido thing." Seiji scoffed.

"If he won't help us, I will take it up with the authorities. Let them do the dirty work," Seiji continued.

"Could that get Akio into trouble?" Tomeo said.

"Don't worry, Akio will be left alone. I will make sure of that."

Seiji knew about Tomeo's special bond with Akio. It was something he held over him when he had to. Tomeo was relieved to hear it.

Akio was stunned when Tomeo forbade him from joining the movement. Tomeo made him feel guilty about leaving the temple. However, Akio told him he had to at least follow through with the meeting he had already organized. It did not mean he was leaving the temple.

When it was time, he went to the warehouse early. He could not be happier about what he was doing, despite the uncertainty of whether he could continue. He greeted everyone as they came in. Most were factory workers from Nara. They entered and lingered, not knowing what to do.

"Take a seat," Akio had to tell them. "The chairs are for you."

They quickly found seats but said nothing, even to those they came with.

When Machiko arrived, they stared at her. While she didn't wear an expensive kimono, it was clear to everyone that she was wealthy and likely in charge.

The silence was awkward. As Machiko reached the front of the room, Akio introduced her as the donor. Machiko thanked everyone for coming and spoke of the difficult times that many were facing. Farmers could not feed their families if they paid taxes, and factory workers could not keep up with city rents. Sick people were not provided for.

"The purpose of this organization is to step in and help. I will provide the food, and we will jointly cook and distribute it. We will all work together."

It was a simple message. The only unclear part was why Machiko needed to participate. One of the factory workers dared to ask.

"Why are you helping cook and distribute the food?"

"The work is just as important as the result. The food benefits the poor, but the act of helping benefits me and you; it benefits our souls."

Akio was one of the few who understood what she meant. There were no more questions. The rest was straightforward. Everyone knew people in need. Everyone felt that helping was the right thing to do and that it was time for someone to step in.

Akio announced that they would meet again in a week. Some of them would need to prepare food, others would need to transport it, and yet another group would need to distribute it and return the equipment. All were asked to line up to receive their tasks, along with the corresponding times and meeting places. As that happened, a commotion started in the back of the room.

Akio, at first, could not tell what it was. Then the crowd parted, and four police officers and a police captain named Teijo made their way to the front of the room.

Teijo was tall and slender but muscular. He lacked the brutishness that many police officers in Nara recently wore to defend themselves against the growing disapproval of authority. He was the son of a samurai, respected by the establishment for the family he came from, and well-respected by others for his earnestness. He had risen to captain at a young age. He was younger than most of the officers with him.

It was clear he was headed for Machiko. Akio stepped in front of her. It was unusual for the police to deal with women, and he felt he was more responsible for the meeting than Machiko; he had organized it. But Teijo pushed him aside and told Machiko that he had come to take her to the police station.

The room became tense. Why would he want Machiko to come with them? What had she done?

Machiko knew. She remained calm and said she was happy to come to the police station and clear up whatever the concern was. She left the building with the four officers and Teijo, trying to smile so the volunteers would not worry.

When she arrived at the police station, it was obvious that Teijo's superiors had carefully planned her arrest. They were all at the police station waiting for her, even the police chief. The police chief had even spoken to the daimyo. At first, the daimyo was reluctant to sanction the arrest, knowing of Machiko's family, but he could not afford an uprising in the region.

"Gatherings of this sort need to be licensed," the station head said while the police chief made sure to nod in a way that would be noticed.

"The gathering was not a demonstration, and it was held on private property. More importantly, it was about distributing food to the poor."

"This type of meeting will create a perception of discontent. People may start criticizing the system. You must understand that."

Machiko knew not to argue that the system was failing many. "All we want to do is help. It will create goodwill."

"We have seen riots in other parts of the country. I hope you understand and cease these activities."

Before Machiko could argue any further, the police chief rose to signal that the meeting was over. "You are free to leave, but cannot return to the meeting."

Bewildered and uncertain about what to do next, Machiko decided to go to Toshiro's house. Was this already the end of her new movement? If they were willing to arrest her, they might be willing to incarcerate her. Then, they might try to take over her farm. They would argue that she could not run it. It would be all part of the destruction the authorities usually visited on opposition.

Machiko could have gone to see Akio, but she figured he might prefer her not to visit him at the temple right away. Something else bothered her. It was unusual to arrest a woman. Why had they not arrested Akio? He had organized the meeting. The police clearly knew a lot about what was happening. They surely knew that Akio was the main organizer. She did not know that Tomeo was protecting Akio.

When she arrived at Toshiro's house, she told him about what had happened. Toshiro was not surprised. Seiji had spoken to him, but he politely refused to intervene. He said he could not stop Machiko, at least not yet, and assured Seiji he would do him a favor another time.

Toshiro tried to calm Machiko down and asked her to stay the night. Over dinner, they began discussing the latest business ventures. Toshiro wanted to give Machiko time to compose herself. But eventually, they got to the day's events.

"Did you attempt to include the establishment in your undertaking?" Toshiro asked even though he knew the answer.

"I could not involve Seiji. How could I? He would only use the money in other ways. I thought about the Shinto shrine where Kiyoshi is. They are busy trying to win favors in Edo. The last thing they want is to get involved in something controversial that might undermine that."

"Well, you clearly thought about it, but you might want to rethink involving Seiji. It may be the only way."

"I hate the idea of involving the very institution that has been ignoring the poor for so long. I am also afraid that, at best, they would distribute whatever I give them. It would end when the funds run out. This needs to be a sustainable organization. We need volunteers, members who want to perpetuate the cause."

Toshiro thought about this and took the honorable route.

"You are right. I can't argue with that," Toshiro said. He knew it would be a battle for Machiko, but it was a battle she had to fight if her movement was to sustain itself. He also knew it would upset Seiji that he did not stop her, but he had to take that risk.

Machiko was excited to share with Toshiro what she had in mind.

"We already have factory workers helping. We are creating a movement, whether it is considered religious or not, in which followers focus on helping others. And by helping, I mean doing, not consoling!"

Toshiro smiled. He could not help but think how pleased Machiko's parents would have been to know that their business and organizational talent had rubbed off on her.

"That makes sense," he said. He found himself thinking about how he could help her, how he used to help Machiko's parents, but that would have to wait.

In the morning, Machiko met with Akio to consider the next steps. It might have been too soon after the incident, but she wanted to meet with him before she left Nara.

"Tomeo summoned me as soon as I returned to the temple. He expressly forbade me not only from leaving the temple but from helping in any way."

"I am sorry," Machiko said.

"Seiji apparently said the temple is about helping people lead a Buddhist life. Siddhartha lived with less than any of the poor. My duty is to tend to their souls. Can you believe that?"

"He only says that because he sees our movement as a threat. We will be viewed as doing what they have refused to do," Machiko responded.

"He reiterated that I owed it to the temple to remain. Since I was an orphan."

"I am sorry," Machiko said.

Machiko calmed herself. "But, what happened to the people who came to the meeting?" She asked.

"They quickly dispersed. They were scared. I am not sure they would ever come back if we were to organize another meeting. The warehouse owner also told me that we could not meet there again. He does not want to get in trouble with the authorities."

"Give me some time," Machiko said.

When Machiko returned to Akeno, she did something she had not done since her husband's death. She went to the Shinto shrine in town. After completing the obligatory rituals, she tried to pray, but no thoughts came. Instead, she noticed the birds chirping and the fresh air. It was a beautiful day; she had not noticed it before. There was so much beauty in nature, and it would always be there. She could always take refuge in that. Slowly, she regained enthusiasm. She knew that what she was doing was right and that it would give her and others joy. Even though her plans had been thwarted, even beginning to bring them to fruition felt better than anything she had done. She just needed to get away from Nara's intrigue.

What if, she thought, we organized outside the city and we only serve food on the outskirts? Their mistake had been in bringing their movement to the center of town. There was no need for that.

The vision Machiko had was to build some dwellings on the land by the stream she had bought. She could live there. They could have their gatherings there and organize trips to distribute food no farther than the edge of town. It would require an investment, but it was what they needed. She also liked the thought of living in her favorite spot.

It did not take long to draw up the plans. After years of adding buildings to her parents' farm, she had all the necessary contacts. She met with architects and asked them to design three buildings. The first would become her home: small, one-story, overlooking the pond. The building should be square and have a veranda surrounding it, with sliding doors that open to the pond. The second would be a two-story barn. Instead of dirt floors, she wanted wooden floors. The challenge would be to build an ample floor space where a lot of people could gather without too many columns obstructing the view to the front of the room. The third would be a one-story building with a large kitchen and several separate rooms, each with its own entry. She envisioned that one of these rooms could be for Akio, should he join her.

Construction commenced in the spring and finished in late summer. Machiko named the place Tomo after her tutor.

Machiko invited Akio. He could not wait to see the place, including Machiko's small new house, which was constructed so perfectly.

"Have you urged the people in Nara to be patient?" Machiko asked him.

"Hard for them," Akio responded.

Akio could not avoid staring at everything in Machiko's new house. He immediately noticed that she had planned it according to Zen Buddhist architecture. The main room with the sliding doors faced south, overlooking the pond. The stream was visible to the west, and you could make out the road to Nara to the east. The tallest hills were to the north. It could not have been laid out any better for a Buddhist to meditate and contemplate the transcendent. It was a little strange since Akio had not known Machiko to be otherwise enchanted with Buddhism.

The smell of the house was wonderful. Machiko had placed the best quality tatami mats in the main room. It was the smell she'd admired as a child when she first visited Toshiro's house, and the smell of Seiji's office. Machiko told Akio that if she got up early, she could enjoy the sunrise and watch the mist over the pond. At dinner, she could watch the sunset. It gave her strength.

Akio was impressed with the barn, the largest building on the property. The architects had extended the tops of the columns so that they could be placed farther apart. They had also left half the room's ceiling out so that if you stood on the second floor, you could look down onto the first floor. It was the perfect auditorium for a large group of people.

Finally, the kitchen building was simple and functional, built to cook large-scale meals. The bedrooms in the building were small but nice.

Looking at all of it, Akio got worried. The buildings were purpose-built for the movement at a significant cost. What if it did not take off? But Machiko was serene. Even the act of constructing the place had given her joy. It was a hopeful act, and it was good.

Akio and Machiko went to have lunch in the main room of her new house.

"So you're sure about this?"

"As sure as I have ever been."

"What will the authorities say? They will not like it."

"We will have to take that chance. We are at least as far away from prying eyes as possible."

"Why the big auditorium? There should not be any speeches. You should not criticize the system."

Machiko looked at Akio but did not respond.

"You still think people will come after what happened?" Machiko asked.

"I think so," Akio responded. "Did you ask Kiyoshi to join?" Akio asked.

"I am afraid the Shinto priests have had the same reaction as your Buddhist superiors. We are on our own. It is all the more reason you are needed."

Akio knew not to inquire any further about Kiyoshi. He could sense that it was hurtful to Machiko. She had hoped that Kiyoshi would see the importance of charity and at least try to persuade his temple to support their venture or join her, but he had not.

When they were younger, Machiko avoided speaking about her parents to prevent hurting Akio. She had sensed the deep pain it caused him not to have any parents, particularly not to know who his father was. Now, it was Akio's turn to show a similar sensitivity. Instead of voicing his disappointment in Kiyoshi, he changed the subject.

"You know, Seiji forbade me from being part of the movement. I would have to leave the temple."

"You would be doing more good."

It was not unusual for priests to leave temples, but it was usually to get married, not to start a cause seemingly at odds with the institution.

"I have to think about what the temple has done for me. They took me in when I had no one."

9. The Second Organization

The next day, Akio awoke to the smell of rice boiling in the kitchen. Fumito, the farmer Machiko had hired, was cooking a large batch of food to distribute that day. Machiko asked him if he preferred to continue farming the land or to help with the movement. He opted for the movement.

Akio had spent the night in a room in the kitchen building, the room Machiko had intended for him. He slept little, instead obsessing about his future. Without the temple, he would have no social standing. But it was selfish to think that way. It was the thinking he had fought when competing with Seiji to become Tomeo's assistant. It was not Buddha-like.

Then he thought about being a priest. If he left the temple, he could not spread the spiritual lessons of the Buddha. All he had studied, he would not be able to teach. But spiritual thoughts weren't really helping people. What Machiko was going to do was what was truly needed.

He also remembered a discussion he had with Machiko. They discussed the joy charitable giving created, joy without obligations or guilt. A liberation from selfishness. The giver and the receiver not transacting, but caring. Joy Machiko told Akio that she first witnessed when the orphans helped each other at the orphanage.

In Akio's mind, it all came down to whether he could disrespect the organization that had taken him in as an orphan. He had to weigh that against the good he would be doing as part of the movement. He finally decided that he could not repay the temple for his entire life. He would do more good as part of Machiko's movement. The future was more important.

That morning, Akio confidently walked to Machiko's house to join her for breakfast. He did not need an invitation. When he arrived, she sat in her living room overlooking the pond. It was a glorious morning.

They both sat there for a while. Machiko could sense what Akio had decided. He was too relaxed to be delivering bad news.

"We are partners in crime," she finally said with a smile.

"Yes, when it is a crime to do good," Akio responded with a chuckle.

Machiko was pleased, and she knew the decision had not come easily.

Sitting there, they saw two farmers leading horses down the road. Machiko had hired them to help transport the food to Nara. Once the horses were rigged to a cart, Fumito loaded it with food, and Machiko, Akio, and the two farmers left for Nara.

After an hour, they crossed the hill from which Nara was visible, and after another half hour, they reached the city's outskirts. The noise and smell of the factories were unchanged, unrelenting. Between and now in front of the factories, the makeshift dwellings had grown into little villages. Unbathed children ran and played in the open spaces. The only adults around had empty stares. They were solitary and did not interact with any bystanders.

"Let's set up close to the dwellings," Machiko said. Once they did, no one came. It was a surprise. They did not anticipate this.

"They are not used to this," Akio said. "They don't know what to make of us. They think it's strange that we're giving away things. Everything has to be earned these days."

Akio spoke to people to convince them to come. Eventually, they did, slowly and one by one. Despite their reluctance, they took some food. They were hungry. They took the food without acknowledgment, looking down while stretching out their arms and wondering if this was real, preferring not to take food from strangers. They were embarrassed about their circumstances.

New circumstances were part of the new economy that no one understood or knew how to handle. That was why they did not express gratitude. It was all too strange for them.

It was not the reaction Akio, Machiko, or the two helpers expected.

On the way back to Tomo, the four of them were quiet, still trying to understand the crowd's reaction. The people they met were so disillusioned that they did not see the goodness being offered to them.

To break the awkwardness, Machiko started singing a song. Akio and the two helpers joined in. They had formed a camaraderie of sorts. The singing relaxed them. When they arrived back in Tomo, Fumito was waiting for them. The farmers took the horses from the cart and left with them. Akio went to his room. The day had made him less sure about his decision, but he wrote a letter to Tomeo. In it, he said he had no choice but to leave the temple. It was his calling. Tomeo should see it as a desire originating from the charity they had shown him when he was an orphan. With the letter, he crossed the Rubicon and would never be able to return to the temple.

After leaving the letter at the foot of one of the statues in the temple gate, where it was sure to be found, he roamed the streets of Nara to sign up volunteers. It was much harder than the first time. People needed their jobs and could not afford to get into trouble. None of the few volunteers he found were willing to travel to Tomo from Nara. They agreed to distribute food in Nara, but could not take the time to travel to Tomo. Machiko would have to continue hiring help for that, at least for now.

Machiko went to Akeno that day to see Zakari, who was running the farm in her absence. She needed more money for the movement. Zakari shook his head.

"Construction of Tomo has depleted us. We can't keep on doing this and run the farm." He went to a cabinet, took out most of the money, and gave it to Machiko. "This is all we have to spare. We will have some more coming in with the harvest in the fall, but we need that if we are going to complete the minimum repairs on the equipment." It was frustrating to Machiko, so she left early the next day to join Akio in a distribution run to Nara. She did not want to think about Zakari's issues.

It took some time, but eventually, the crowd in Nara started to appreciate what they were doing. They sensed that Akio's and the group's intentions were pure. They began expressing their gratitude while eating food, but shared some terrible stories. One of the women told them that she had malaria and was not able to work. They met a boy about twelve years old who had broken his hand unloading a cart at one of the factories. His family was now not able to make ends meet. A woman had lost her husband, and the factory where she finally found a job laid her off. A farmer who had lost his farm was still looking for a job in Nara. Moreover, they heard stories of people who were sick at home. People had to collect food for them.

"I am glad I came today," Machiko said to Akio on their way back to Tomo. "It took my mind off things and reminded me of what we are doing, but we only have enough money for the next few months. I need to figure out a solution."

It was not on top of Akio's mind. Since he left his letter, he became concerned that that might not have been a good idea. "I may have done something stupid," Akio confessed. "I wrote a letter to Tomeo explaining that I am leaving the temple. It probably tipped them off that the movement is starting again. I am sorry, but I thought I owed them that at the very least."

"It should not be so hard to do this," Machiko said and started singing, as was by now their well-established tradition on the way back to Nara.

10. The Message

The movement continued, and after several weeks, with a lot of effort, they built up a group of thirty volunteers. Machiko asked everyone to come to Tomo on a Sunday. It was time for some inspiration.

"Stop worrying," she told Akio when he fretted about the meeting potentially attracting attention. "We stayed out of their sights."

They gathered in the barn built for that purpose. Machiko and Akio took their time to greet everyone.

Akio did what he usually did when he greeted strangers. He played the game in his mind that any of the older men could be his father. It still pained him.

Machiko finally went to the front of the room, and when the chatter quieted, she addressed the gathering.

"Thank you all for coming. It is time for us to reflect on the reason for our mission. Have you noticed what a happy group we are? Every time we go to Nara, we come back happier. Have you wondered why that is? Have you wondered why it is so fulfilling to be part of this?"

She paused, looking around at the many eyes trained on her.

"It is in our nature to help each other. We have done it for generations in the farming communities. It is natural that we need to find a new way in our new society. At first, we all prayed at a temple or shrine. I did. Akio did. But it was not enough. We were given our souls to pray, but it is not enough. We were given our bodies to act. To undertake. To produce. To help."

She looked into as many eyes in the crowd as she could.

"By acting, we are doing what the creators wanted us to do. The creators sent us spirits to help. We can seek their help and encouragement, but then we must act. We worship our creators best by doing. That is why we feel so good when we go to Nara and why we need to continue our cause."

She paused again.

"If there is anything this new age has taught us, it is that organization is needed. Small acts of kindness are great, but they are not enough. We need to organize to help, and if our organization grows, we will have an impact. Just think of all the people we can feed. I mean you, how many you can feed. Then, think about how this organization could grow if only some of the people we help join us. We become a movement of action, not prayer."

The room remained quiet even after Machiko was done. Akio was impressed. Machiko had said what he had been feeling. Action was a kind of worship, one more needed than spirituality.

He slowly went to the front of the room. He thanked Machiko for her inspiration and the volunteers for their commitment and courage. Then, he discussed the details of the next food delivery and asked everyone to line up so that each could be given a task and a three-hour slot once a week to help. The event finished without an incident. The movement continued to grow.

At the food deliveries that followed, they started to pick up sick, homeless people, bringing them back to Tomo. The rooms in the kitchen building next to Akio's room began to fill with patients. Tomo became a small hospital of sorts for the needy.

One day, Akio asked Machiko to speak to one of the patients.

"When I am well, I want to help the way you are," he said. Machiko noticed the smile on Akio's face. She smiled as well, understanding why Akio had chosen him. He proved her vision. "You get better first," Machiko said. Machiko noticed some patients who had been brought back on the food cart, unable to walk, were better and trying to walk again.

"It is a great success," Akio said to Machiko. "We have cured at least a dozen people by now."

"Yes, but I am afraid it is also coming at a tremendous cost," Machiko responded. "We have used almost all the money Zakari gave me."

Machiko decided she needed to get Toshiro's advice about her financial problems. She went to Nara the next day. It was the middle of the day, and she visited Toshiro at work. On her way there, Machiko walked by the temple. She tried to rush by without being seen. It was awkward, but they had avoided any adverse actions so far, and she did not want to take any chances.

Toshiro had established an office park for his many ventures. There were about a dozen two-story buildings surrounded by a wall. Two guards were stationed at the gate. Machiko asked them for directions, and they pointed her to a building in the middle of the complex. She entered the building, went upstairs, and ran into Toshiro's son, who was carrying a load of papers. He showed Machiko the way to Toshiro's office.

"It is so good to see you," Toshiro said with a big smile when Machiko entered. He asked the people in his office to leave.

"I have heard a lot about your movement." It surprised and scared Machiko a little; she hoped it had all been kept quiet.

"You are like the US gunship that recently arrived in Edo harbor—causing all sorts of concerns, asking people to take sides. The emperor likes it, but the shogun does not. Some like your movement, and some don't."

Toshiro chuckled, having amused himself. It was meant to calm Machiko, but she did not like diversions. She had come with a purpose.

"You are always so well-informed," Machiko said.

"I hear your new house is much smaller than your parents'. Perhaps not overly indulgent?" Toshiro smiled gently. "They would be proud of you."

"I came here to speak to you about my finances. I can't sustain the movement even if I take most of the money from the farm. I already stopped Zakari from expanding the farm."

"And stopped modernizing. We have noticed."

"I have to confess, I have ignored the farm. Zakari is running it. My father told me not to trust others to run the farm, but I did not know what else to do. I need money for the movement. Its success comes with a burden." Machiko hung her head.

Mackiko knew what she probably had to do, but wanted to hear it from Toshiro. He always advised her parents, and if he recommended it, they would approve.

"You have to sell the farm. It is the only way," Toshiro said as Machiko hoped he might. "Your father was right. Samurai have tried for a long time to be absentee farmers. It does not work. You must choose to run the farm or run your movement."

Thoughts of Machiko's parents and how they had dedicated their lives to the farm raced through Machiko's head, but she was relieved that Toshiro supported what she had concluded.

"Also, if you decide on the movement, you must figure out how to make it sustainable. Even the proceeds from the farm sale will eventually run out. You have started with volunteers, which is good, but you will need donors."

With that, Toshiro reached into the drawer at his desk and gave Machiko a pouch with gold coins.

"It is what I can do," he said. "We are moving to a society where doing several things may not be possible. Just like you can't run a farm and the movement, others will find it difficult to devote time to help you. Those people will be happy to help through donations instead." Toshiro said.

Toshiro's mood changed. He noticed in himself a new feeling. He was doing something that was not transactional. His usual guard of giving only for receiving something of equal or greater value was broken. This was different. It was liberating. Giving felt good.

He had to tell Machiko.

"You see, I am not able to become one of your volunteers. I can only help this way, and I wish to contribute. It makes me happy. For a country where everything is starting to be about transactions, it is nice to do something that is not one."

Machiko knew what he was talking about. It was the liberation she felt when she started the movement. She took the pouch and smiled.

Toshiro smiled back. Then, he became more serious.

"You need to find others like me. But you have to be careful. To persuade people to donate, you will need to describe the need and the poverty that has been created for the people who are left behind. It will focus people on the dark side of our economic development in the cities. They will not like that. The powers that be are already starting to talk about you again."

"I appreciate that. You are right, as always. Thank you, you have been so good to my family."

Machiko paused for a moment.

"If I could impose on you for one more thing."

Machiko waited until Toshiro nodded with encouragement.

"How would I sell the farm?" Machiko said. "It will be a large purchase for anyone."

"Agreed. Few will be able to afford it. But I can do that for you. I know the other wealthy farmers in the area and others who could provide part of the funds. We would, of course, take a commission for the sale."

Machiko thanked Toshiro again, but said she had to think about the sale. It would not come easily to her.

11. The Gunship

Tomeo was headed down the beautifully manicured gardens of the temple to Seiji's office for their weekly meeting. He stopped to admire a particular mulberry tree, one of his favorites. Then, he entered Seiji's office. Seiji was busy with some papers, but stopped. He got up and sat next to Tomeo in front of a screen door that had been opened to allow for a beautiful view of the gardens. The temple faced threats and Seiji's position with it. He wanted to be closer to Tomeo again and took time to talk to him in a more comfortable setting.

"You heard about the US gunship?" Seiji asked.

"Of course, the US wants trade. We have resisted their influence long enough. For all these centuries, we have only let Chinese culture in, but we may not be able to resist this anymore."

"Well, Emperor Meiji is young and ambitious. He wants to modernize. I think he may open up."

"The emperor asserting himself. Maybe it is time."

"No. You don't understand. This is not good for us. The emperor is close to the Shintos."

"I would be if they made me a god," Tomeo joked.

"This is serious; they are taking our power," Seiji screeched.

He was right, as usual. The Shinto religion was gaining power. Even Kiyoshi, at his Shinto shrine, had noticed how the senior priests were conspiring with enthusiasm. It was finally their time, and they knew it. He had observed them hurrying across the temple grounds with an unusual determination in their steps. Their faces not seeking harmony, but a future. Their gait was less natural, and their minds were racing. They were close to the emperor, and the Buddhists were not. This was what Seiji was referring to.

"You mean our influence is in jeopardy?" Tomeo asked, expressing some concern.

"Yes. The shogun is resisting the emperor. He does not want change, and we are seen as aligned with the shogun. What is worse, the emperor wants to get rid of the samurai. Their expensive lifestyles are draining resources, and they are not of use anymore."

"Of course, the gunship. We don't have a modern army. We have spent our resources on the pensions for the samurai instead."

"Precisely."

"I have gone to Edo several times to forge new alliances, but it is difficult. These things take time. I will go again later this week."

"You should meet with the seniors at the Shinto temple."

"Yes, I have tried that, but they know what I am up to. I did meet with the daimyo, and at least he is on our side."

"Not sure that is good if he is not siding with the emperor. We may have to distance ourselves, right?" Tomeo said, looking at Seiji sideways.

"Yes, but I don't want to lose our allies until we have new ones. At any rate, he told me he could not afford any unrest. He can't afford it given the circumstances."

"You mean Machiko?"

"Yes, we must try to stop her before it gets out of hand."

"But you will…"

"Protect Akio, yes. Don't worry. And the authorities don't know why. They think it is because he was one of us."

"We may have to try something different with her. Take a different approach. I haven't figured it out yet, but I will. I also have to figure out something for the emperor."

Seiji was unusually worried. Tomeo almost felt sorry for him.

"You could help him with what he wants. Arrange for a modern army," Tomeo said.

"That would be a first."

"These are times for firsts."

"And how would I do that?"

"Talk to Toshiro. He knows the new industrial complex and how to get things done, and this time, insist that he stop Machiko any way he can."

12. Second Audience

Machiko's movement grew at a surprising rate. Every week, more volunteers arrived. They no longer needed to hire farmers for assistance. Volunteers went to Nara every day except during the weekly gatherings in Tomo. The gatherings became quite large. Over a hundred people now attended regularly. They could barely fit in the barn.

A routine was established for the gatherings. First, they met informally and spoke with one another. Machiko would make her rounds. Then she would say some words, and Akio would assign tasks. Some were asked to cook food, some to assist in the hospital, and some to help deliver food to Nara, among other tasks. Assigning tasks was part of the ceremony; as Machiko had said, actions were a form of worship, so assigning tasks was important. A meal always signified the end.

Machiko ended up asking Toshiro to explore selling the farm. It was the only way. When she told Toshiro, he sent his son to see Zakari to go over the books and determine a value. Once they determined a reasonable price, Machiko told Toshiro to find a buyer. She trusted him.

It was all going well until a monk approached Akio while distributing food in Nara. He had a message from Seiji. Seiji wanted to see Machiko and said he would visit Tomo next Sunday morning. When Akio told Machiko, she could not believe it. "What could Seiji possibly want? What can he achieve by coming here?"

"He will have an angle; he always does," Akio responded with a serious tone—one she remembered well from the first time she'd met him.

"Do you still hold a grudge against him?"

"I don't think so. I did for a long time, even after I became Tomeo's assistant. His unrelenting effort to outmaneuver Tomeo bothered me. I was not sure if I was to use my Buddhist training to avoid it or fight it. In the end, I saw Tomeo making peace with Seiji, so I gave up, but I don't trust him."

"I always admired that about you—your discipline, I mean, trying to apply Buddhist training to such a situation."

"Thank you, but I use it less now. The movement is what liberated me. Since I've been part of it, I've put all that behind me. But with Seiji coming here, it is unfortunately coming back."

A visit from the head of the most important Buddhist temple in Nara, the religious center of Japan, was an honor. If it were not for the Shinto priests in Edo, with their allegiance to the emperor, Seiji would be one of Japan's most important religious figures. Seiji's decision to come to Machiko instead of requesting that she come to him was unusual. Machiko had her house cleaned and prepared for the visit as she wondered what Seiji could want.

On the morning of Seiji's arrival, Machiko dressed in her best kimono. It was a hand-me-down from her mother. It was dark green pure silk decorated with silk reeds you could find on the edge of a pond. The silk had come from the silk farm they had started; her mother had it spun into cloth and a kimono made out of it in Nara. It was like the fancy ones Machiko had often seen during her time in Nara - one of the few luxuries her mother had allowed herself.

Machiko sat in her house overlooking the pond. She was watching some volunteers come over the hill from Nara for the gathering when she saw a grouping of twelve monks, including Seiji. He was arriving early.

Machiko got up and went to the gate to greet him. Machiko stood straight, her arms to her side, with her back slightly leaning forward. Hers was the only posture that was tense. It was how one could always tell who would do the greeting, but Machiko was also worried about the meeting.

When Seiji stood in front of her straight, she bowed slowly, just pivoting her hips. She uttered some words of greeting, barely audible. Seiji then bowed back, but not as low as Machiko. It was the way. Machiko bowed one more time.

Then, they briefly walked around the grounds. Seiji commented that he heard about what she had built. Eventually, they retreated into Machiko's house, where Fumito served them tea.

As he sat in Machiko's house, Seiji was overcome with jealousy. As a monk, he was trained to notice and avoid such emotions, but could not help himself. Machiko's house was the perfect Buddhist retreat—the water in front, the stream to the west, the road to the east, and the mountain in the back. It was perfectly serene. The only imperfection was that the house had started to look a little worn, and there were baskets full of clothes everywhere— clothes that needed washing before being distributed in Nara.

Seiji saw more volunteers coming over the hill on the road. He collected himself.

"This looks like a Zen Buddhist monastery, only with no monks."

"You give it too much honor."

"It is good to see you, Machiko."

"I am honored that you would come. How are things at the temple?"

"The temple is fine, but Nara is not. There is discontent, and you are making things more difficult."

"I don't mean to."

"Your rhetoric is catching on. People quote what you say in Nara. They claim you say that society is not providing, and that your movement, therefore, must. They say you are selling the farm to fund this."

As usual, Seiji was well-informed.

"I am trying to sustain the movement as best I can."

"They say you demand action and scorn prayer—is that true?"

"Honorable Seiji," Machiko said, "Japan is changing. We are filling a void that has emerged as people move around in our new economy. A void that has been growing despite prayers. It cannot be ignored."

"You want to tell me what is needed in the new Japan?" Seiji said, angered.

"Of course not," was all Machiko could say.

"Akio seems to be doing well. I did not know he had it in him." Seiji said with sarcasm. He was angry. Akio had beaten him when he became Tomeo's assistant, and now that he had outsmarted Tomeo and become the head of the temple, Akio left. He would never be his boss.

"We appreciate you noticing. Given the right opportunity, goodwill thrives," Machiko said.

Seiji noticed the suggestion that the temple had not provided the right opportunity for Akio and was not doing what it should. Insulted, he rose abruptly. "I guess that sums it up. I have urgent business to attend to in Nara," he said. Machiko did not know what to say or do. She rose and bowed. She knew Seiji had not said what he had come to say.

"Should we discuss this further?" She asked respectfully, but it made no difference.

Seiji left, clearly irritated.

On his walk back to Nara, Seiji tried to calm himself down.

"Don't let emotions carry you away," he told himself, but it was little use. He was losing power, and one of his initiatives had just failed.

Seiji had come to have Machiko join the temple, with whatever conditions she came up with. The temple would get credit for doing good, and they could avoid any word of discontent in Nara getting to the emperor; on the contrary, they might be seen as progressive and as helping the new Japan. Tomeo had suggested that he should be the one to speak with Machiko about this, but Seiji had not fully let go of his competitive feelings about Tomeo, and he did not wish to empower him. So Seiji had gone himself, but he had allowed his emotions to get the better of him. Ultimately, he failed in his mission.

Machiko was equally upset. After Tomeo left, she hurried to the Shinto shrine they had established where the stream entered the pond. She quickly purified herself at the water basin. She took the ladle, dunked it, filling it to the rim instead of leaving some room, and then spilled more water than she used on her hand. She did not care. She quickly threw the ladle back and rushed to the presence of the kami, clapping her hands so quickly that it all seemed irreverent. Her mind was still racing from the meeting with Seiji. She was afraid she had enraged him and was unsure how that would end. It was not good. No thoughts came to her as she was praying to the kami. All she could do was ask the kami for harmony to save her movement.

She went to see Akio and told him about the incident, rambling as she did when she was nervous. He tried to calm her down.

"Don't worry. We are partners in crime, remember?" he said, giving Machiko a reassuring look. It at least caused Machiko to smile.

Then he urged her to accelerate the sale of the farm. If Seiji knew about that, he might try to find a way to stop it. "He is closer to Toshiro than you think," Akio warned. "Are you sure you can trust Toshiro?"

13. The Response

Seiji did not sit still. Even though he tried to avoid such meetings, he arranged a special meeting with the daimyo. If Machiko did not align with him, he would gain favors by opposing her.

The daimyo agreed with Seiji, urging that something needed to be done about Machiko. He continued to be concerned with avoiding social unrest in Nara. Other regions of Japan had recently seen major demonstrations and unrest, and he could not afford any. They agreed that Machiko should be arrested and imprisoned.

Machiko was performing one of her services when Teijo appeared with four other officers at Tomo. He'd been told to make an example of her and had timed it so that hundreds of people would witness her arrest. It was a risky move. Five men would not be able to control the mass of people present.

Tensions rose in the gathering as soon as they arrived. Everyone knew about Machiko's first arrest. It had been a matter of frequent discussion. Those in the crowd who were there felt guilty about not having voiced any opposition back then, and those who were not there thought they would have.

Teijo and his officers moved slowly through the crowd; they had to break formation and move forward one by one. The crowd barely made enough room for them to pass; it was a form of resistance. Teijo made eye contact with some in the crowd, but his officers did not. They were afraid.

When Teijo finally got close to Machiko, Akio stood in front of her, as he had done before. He again thought that he should be arrested, not Machiko. Machiko smiled and asked Akio to stand aside.

"This is Mara's army," she said, referring to the army that the god of the underworld had unsuccessfully summoned to scare the Buddha.

"We have come to bring you to Nara," Teijo said quietly, trying to avoid provoking a riot.

"My fellow volunteers," Machiko said loudly, addressing the crowd. "Our movement will endure, but only if we don't pick a fight we can't win. Let me go to Nara to clear this up." Then she turned to Teijo and smiled at him in a way everyone could see.

Teijo was surprised and, at first, just stood there. He admired Machiko, but he had his duties.

"Well, what are we doing?" Machiko finally had to say.

That caused Teijo to command his officers to surround Machiko and start a procession through the crowd. He could not believe that Machiko did not make it more difficult for him. Why was she not resisting? Did she not appreciate what was happening?

He escorted Machiko down the road that led out of Tomo. They had purposefully not brought any horses. He did not want to create a symbol of confinement by putting Machiko on a horse. They slowly walked back to Nara.

Machiko was expecting what she'd received the last time: a talking-to by senior officers. But when they arrived at the police station, no one was there. They put her in a prison cell—a dark, solemn room in the back of the station, so barren that it demeaned anyone who was thrown there, particularly Machiko, who had always taken refuge in pleasant surroundings.

Machiko, for the first time, was alone, truly alone. She had no one to speak to, not even the guards. They gave her food hurriedly, the way one feeds farm animals, without any interaction. Despite the deprivation, however, the idleness bothered Machiko the most. After two days, Machiko concluded this was very different from her first arrest.

On the fourth day, a senior officer came to the cell to tell her that she was under arrest for organizing meetings she had been told not to organize and for starting a religious movement, which was a more serious crime. Religious movements were the least tolerated opposition. They disturbed the purity of Japan.

As she sat in her cell, she became frightened. The authorities might be going after her volunteers. They might arrest them. They might also confiscate her property. Her parents had labored all their lives and had always stayed on good terms with the authorities. Now, she was risking everything. She began to contemplate what she might say to mend things. However, as the days passed, she realized there would be no opportunity to mend things with the authorities. She gave up contemplating what she might say. The authorities had put her out of commission and did not need her cooperation. The world closed in on Machiko. She lost hope and her purpose.

14. Kiyoshi

Unbeknownst to Machiko, she was losing her farm, not by confiscation, but by sale. Toshiro found a buyer. The main issue was that prisoners had no rights, so after conferring with lawyers, Toshiro figured out that Kiyoshi could agree to the sale. The only obstacle that remained was Seiji.

"You can't sell the farm," Seiji told Toshiro when they met in Seiji's office.

"I told Mashiko I would handle this for her," Toshiro said.

"You are taking the wrong side," Seiji warned.

"So be it," Toshiro responded. It was his bushido business ethic speaking. It was the way he conducted business. He promised to sell the farm, and he was going to do it. Still, when Kiyoshi came to sign the necessary papers, Toshiro gave him a stern warning.

"Stay out of the matters your mother started, or they will come after the fortune you are about to receive."

Kiyoshi signed the documents for the sale but did not heed Toshiro's advice. He asked to see the daimyo. He considered bribing Seiji to convince the daimyo to release his mother, but did not trust Seiji to keep his word. A bribe or "payment" to the daimyo would cost more but be less risky. The only concern was that the daimyo might get upset and arrest Kiyoshi. It was a delicate matter.

"We have come to a fortune and paid our taxes," Kiyoshi said when he had his audience.

He was seated on the floor in front of an elevated platform where the daimyo sat. In reverence, he did not make eye contact with him.

"The circumstances in Nara are dire," Kiyoshi continued. "We feel that taxes are not enough to address them. There are larger needs than current taxes can address."

Of course, the daimyo agreed but did not show it.

Kiyoshi took a chest with gold coins he had brought and put it in front of the daimyo, stretching out both arms and bowing as he did so. The gold coins chimed as he put the chest down. It was a lot of money.

"Accept this as an additional tax payment," Kiyoshi said. "We are trying to do good and think this is the best way."

The daimyo smiled cynically and straightened out. Kiyoshi sensed that the daimyo knew what this was about and that he was not objecting, at least not yet. After a sufficient pause, Kiyoshi continued.

"I must also inform you that it is being talked about that the Buddhist temple instigated my mother's arrest. Being a Shinto priest, I humbly suggest that the Shinto shrine would not have disturbed the balance that way."

Kiyoshi knew the emperor was about to announce that Shintoism would become the state religion. Buddhism was falling out of favor. He suspected the daimyo knew. Pointing out that his mother's arrest, condoned by the daimyo, was instigated by the Buddhists was a smart move.

The daimyo did not respond. It was best for him not to. He waved his assistant to escort Kiyoshi out. Kiyoshi bowed while walking backward out of the room. Since he had not been arrested, he suspected he had achieved his objective.

It came as a great surprise to Machiko when she was released. No ceremony, no discussion. An officer unlocked the cell and told her she was free to go. Machiko did not know what to make of it, nor was she sure what she should do next. She considered going to Toshiro to ask for advice, but her primary concern was the movement, so she walked back to Tomo to find out what had happened to the volunteers.

During the walk, she dreaded what she might find. Would she learn that the volunteers had been arrested? What would she do then? Might they have seized her property? Could they forbid her from entering Tomo? Would Akio or Fumito even be there?

However, upon her arrival, she saw Akio and Fumito moving pots from the carts into the kitchen to be cleaned. Akio had just returned with some volunteers from Nara. She gasped in disbelief. The movement was alive. She ran towards Akio and embraced him. Machiko was so surprised that everything was fine that she broke out in laughter and joy; she could not speak.

Akio was not surprised to see Machiko. Kiyoshi had told him what he had done.

"After they took you, we heard nothing. We just continued as normal. Then your son, Kiyoshi, arrived. He said he would be taking care of things, and did he ever," Akio explained.

"Kiyoshi? He is here?"

"We were as surprised as you are when he arrived. He is staying at your house."

"We will catch up more later," Machiko said and ran to her house.

She hugged Kiyoshi, who was full of smiles and proud of what he had done. "How is it that you are here?" she asked.

"Toshiro asked me to come. Someone had to protect you," he said. "It will all work out."

"Don't be so sure," Machiko said.

"I spoke to the daimyo," Kiyoshi said.

"You did what?' Machiko said. Her family had never been granted an audience.

"How can he refuse to meet a Shinto priest in times like these?" Kiyoshi said with a grin. "We are gaining power. The emperor will declare us the state religion."

Machiko was proud of Kiyoshi. He was not a Shinto priest overcome by ceremonies but a smart operator.

"If you want the movement to be safe," Kiyoshi continued, "I think you now need to align it with Shintoism. I am not telling you this because I am a Shinto priest, but because it would solve all your issues. They will leave you alone. You could become a new sect aligned with Shintoism. It would give you the cover you need."

"I will think about it. It is hard to make any decisions right now."

Kiyoshi left to give Machiko time to rest. But it was not like her to rest during the day, and she was too excited. Machiko saw a pile of letters that had arrived while she was gone. She started to go through them to see if there were any important ones. To her surprise, there was one from Tomeo. She opened it right away.

Tomeo wrote that he would like to see Machiko and Akio soon. Clearly, he knew that she was going to be released. The letter said it was an urgent matter. Tomeo was officially not in charge of the temple; Seiji was. But with Seiji sidelined by the daimyo, perhaps Tomeo had reasserted himself. If it was about the movement, it was strange that he had asked to see Akio and her. Akio had always been absolved of his involvement.

Machiko lost her joy. She became concerned again about what might happen and went to see Akio. They debated whether they should give this some time.

"What if they arrest me again?" Machiko said.

"It would be unusual for Tomeo to get directly involved in something like that. Like Seiji, he would do things indirectly. He also frankly has always looked out for me. It would not make sense for him to ask for me if he will have you arrested—at least not right then and there."

"Maybe you are right. He said it was urgent. Let's see what he wants after our gathering tomorrow. I can't wait to see the volunteers again."

The gathering was a joyous occasion on a glorious sunny day. Hundreds of followers gathered in Tomo. The barn and the veranda around it were filled to capacity. Everyone was eager to hear Machiko speak. She kept her remarks to a minimum.

"Our movement has grown, and it is strong. Because of you, we exist—Akio and I are now less important. You have made this possible. Your determination, spirit, and actions make a difference."

She paused and looked at Akio and then at Kiyoshi.

"We should recognize that the kami spirits in Tomo aided us. We are Shinto, even if we had to overcome its traditions and reluctance to change. But our survival also depends on Buddhist discipline. We cannot be deterred, even if we must fend off Mara's army trying to intimidate us. We must stay the course."

Kiyoshi smiled. This time, he thought his mother was the smart operator, agreeing to align with Shintoism.

Then, as was the tradition of Machiko's movement, tasks were assigned, and they celebrated with a meal. Machiko, Akio, and Kiyoshi mingled with the crowd. There was a lot of laughing, and the volunteers even sang some of the songs they usually sang at the end of a food delivery. Machiko thought how different it was from their first gathering of shy, scared volunteers.

15. Tomeo's Audience

The next morning, Machiko and Akio left for Nara. They wanted to avoid raising any concerns and left early. During the walk, they rehearsed responses to what Tomeo might say about the movement.

"If they accuse us of starting a religion, we must tell them that we are Shinto—we have no choice. If they accuse us of causing unrest, we must tell them we are only concerned with actions, not speeches that stir emotions. If they accuse us of criticizing the system, let's tell them that we want to help the new system with new forms of charity," Machiko told Akio emphatically.

When they arrived at the temple and asked to see Tomeo, an apprentice monk tending to him came to escort them to Tomeo's quarters. That was unusual; audiences were held in official rooms, not sleeping quarters. When they entered the room, they understood why. Tomeo was very ill. He was lying in his bed in the corner - alone, as though forgotten.

He waved them in, happy to have visitors, and asked them to sit on two chairs in front of his bed.

Tomeo spoke softly and with a dry mouth. "As you can see, I am not well." He pushed himself up on his pillow and produced a smile. "It is good of you to come."

"Of course," Akio responded.

"You both should be proud of what you have done." He turned to Machiko. "Machiko, your vision and perseverance are admirable. I want to apologize for what the temple has put you through. We were afraid, threatened by changes, and too focused on our survival. We ignored the real needs of people. It was easy for us; our religion focuses on contemplation. You recognized that action was needed. Charity is an important part of any religion, and we ignored it."

"I thank you, honorable Tomeo. You give us too much credit." Machiko said, but before she could think of something kind to add, Tomeo spoke again.

"Our opposition is over. The Shintos are in charge for the time being. They are the national religion. Please accept my apology for what we have done. Your movement is safe from us. If I said much more, I would be pretending that we have influence that we don't."

"So, do you think the authorities will leave us alone?" Machiko asked, wanting to get that reassurance.

"Yes, I think so," Tomeo said with the little energy he had. Then he looked at Akio.

"I would like to spend some time alone with Akio," he said, smiling at him.

Akio was not surprised. He had been Tomeo's assistant. They had a long history. Machiko respected that. She left the room, thanking Tomeo again.

Once they were alone, Tomeo continued. "Akio, I do not have much time to live." Tomeo looked him straight in the eyes. "My biggest regret is that while I always looked out for you, I never told you the truth. Our Buddhist traditions have not adapted, and these traditions can cause hardship. They don't allow us to have children. I couldn't bring myself to admit it, even to you. Akio, I am your father."

Akio was shocked. What he had been wondering about all his life was right before him. Finally, he knew. Tears welled in his eyes. He gasped for air and did not know what to say.

"I was too focused on maintaining my status—just like the temple was with Machiko's movement. I am sorry. I am sorry for the hardship I caused you. I know it pained you not to have or know your parents. Your mother was a good woman, kind and faithful. She died when you were young, and I saw that you were brought to the temple. I always used my influence to look after you. I made you my assistant. I kept the authorities away from you. But none of this is the same as letting you know you are of my blood. I am sorry for hiding it all these years."

"I—I don't know what to say," Akio said, trying to conceal his tears. His relief was palpable, almost beyond words. The moment he had always coveted was here. "I am glad I know. I have been wondering all my life, and have been so lonely. Now I know."

Then Akio thought about Tomeo dying. He started to feel anger inside him. Tomeo was only saying this now because he was safe. There was no more time for a relationship or for him to be a father. Moreover, Akio had thought that Tomeo and the temple had been incredibly kind all these years. They had taken him out of charity, not out of a sense of paternal obligation. He had even considered not joining Machiko because of the indebtedness he felt he had for all they had done for him. Tomeo had only been concerned about his status, nothing else.

Nevertheless, it is difficult to be angry at a dying man. Akio also did not want to share his feelings. Tomeo was not entitled to them. He had not been a father, and Akio did not want to allow him to be one at this late stage. He summoned his inner strength, wiped away the tears from his cheeks, and subdued his anger. He went to Tomeo's bed, hugged him, and said, "Thank you. I am at peace."

He did not linger. It would have given Tomeo too much credit. More importantly, Akio feared what he might say if his anger returned. So he opened the door and gave Tomeo one last look. Tomeo made a last nod, unspoken questions on his face, knowing he was returning to his loneliness. Akio left the room.

Machiko could tell that Akio was upset. It was the first time she saw him without his glasses. He had taken them off when he became emotional. His eyes were red and watery.

"What happened?" She asked. "Is he dying?"

"Well, he is the one," Akio said.

"The one? What do you mean?" Machiko asked, frowning.

"He is my father. He could not admit it all these years, but now I know."

"I don't know what to say," Machiko said, just as shocked as Akio was.

"I know. Oh yes, all his life, he looked out for me. He was actually around, just like a father. But he could not admit it, even to me. Everything he did for me, which I thought was out of kindness and charity, was out of paternal obligation and guilt for valuing his status at the temple over the truth. Over me." Akio paused.

Akio signaled that they should leave. Walking across the temple grounds, they could not help but notice how beautiful it was. The trees were lush with new leaves, the moss by the walkways was soaked with recent rain, and flowers were blooming in a kaleidoscope of colors. They had forgotten how well arranged it was; the geometry of the shrubs, the layers of grass, flowers, shrubs, and trees was exquisite.

Then, they realized that there was something entirely different about the temple grounds. They were empty. There were no people honoring the statue of Amida. No one was waving incense at themselves at the censer. Smoke was rising with no one to take it in. The temple had an unnatural calmness, the kind that does not belong. Machiko and Akio rushed through the eerie silence without talking.

It was only when they were outside the temple grounds that Akio continued to talk about his encounter.

"Even the one achievement I was proud of, though I never wanted to admit it—becoming his assistant—was fake."

"He never learned compassion. None of them did. I am so sorry," Machiko said.

"I am glad I am not part of it anymore," Akio said angrily, though he felt a strange guilt in accusing his father.

"I am glad I am now part of something good that focuses on doing good, not maintaining status."

"You are stronger than they are, you know. You always have been."

"Strangely, trying not to be too proud of becoming Tomeo's assistant now makes it easier. I care less."

"It is the internal struggle that matters in the end," Machiko said.

"I thought you were aligning with Shinto, not Buddhist thoughts," Akio teased.

"The last thing you can accuse us of is creating harmony," Machiko responded.

She briefly looked at Akio. He put his glasses back on. Then, they both stared at the ground as they walked silently, the way friends can.

16. Frogs Leaping

When they returned to Tomo, Akio went to the kitchen to help. He wanted to clear his mind, at least for a little while. Machiko went to her house. She was still in disbelief over what had happened to Akio. She thought about it to try to make sense of it. She could not.

Machiko went through her letters to start to think about something else. One of them was from Toshiro. She opened it carefully. It contained a bill of sale for the farm and a share certificate for Machiko's ownership in the trading business. There was also a note that the company would soon be able to pay dividends out of its earnings. Machiko smiled as she realized that her personal holdings had also transitioned to the new Japanese economy. With the sale of the farm and the success of the trading business, she'd become a passive shareholder who had time to do good and totally dedicate herself to the movement. Her parents' investment in the trading house had set her up to succeed in the new economy.

She thought about her movement. The one thing she could learn from what Tomeo and Seiji had done was that they were so concerned with their status that they had allowed Buddhist teachings to be ignored. Pride was their enemy. She needed to make sure that her movement stayed humble. They needed to focus on actions, not let their successes blind them. They needed to ensure that their mission was always about helping, never about proving anyone wrong or being better than them. She had to admit that that had been her mistake when she'd fought with Seiji on his visit. Her pride had gotten the better of her. In the future, she would be more careful.

Machiko was interrupted by a subtle knock on the sliding door to her house. She was not expecting anyone, and guests would usually be announced. When she opened the door, she was shocked to see Teijo. She thought Kiyoshi had taken care of things.

Teijo was not wearing his uniform, and he was alone. Was he going to interfere again somehow? Was he there to deliver a harsh message?

"I am not here in an official capacity," he said, which put Machiko's mind at ease. But why was he there?

Machiko invited Teijo in.

"Can I offer you some tea?" Machiko asked, pointing to the table with a view of the pond. Teijo shook his head slightly and sat down. Machiko was impressed by how straight and disciplined he sat at the table. He must have learned that from his samurai father or years in the police force.

"I came to see how I can support your movement," Teijo said.

He did not say "join" but said "support." Machiko noticed. But then, how could he join? He would lose his position.

"We would welcome your support in whatever way you can give it," Machiko said.

"I may be most helpful if it is unknown," Teijo said.

"Understood, and so it shall be," Machiko assured him.

"I will figure out where I can help. I want you to know that I admire what you are doing."

"Thank you for that, but more importantly, thank you for being willing to help. I assure you, it will make you feel good."

Teijo got up. Machiko was surprised at how short the meeting was. It was to the point. She hurriedly rose as well. Teijo straightened out like Machiko knew he would and bowed. Machiko did the same, bowing deeper than he to show her respect. Then Teijo left as quickly as he had come.

Machiko sat down by the sliding door overlooking the pond. It was as beautiful as ever. She overheard volunteers singing on the road as they returned from Nara. She remembered when she had overheard her parents' worries about the farm and their wealth— growing and keeping it; now, she listened to singing - pure joy. The movement was growing.

She noticed ripples on the water's surface in the pond. The frogs had jumped in on their own. She marveled at the ripples, glittering swells that added a dynamic beauty.

"It is better with the ripples," she said. "Much better."

Afterword

The real-life inspiration for this fictional piece is Nakayama Miki, who lived in the Nara region from 1798 to 1887 and started the Tenrikyo movement by selling her parents' farm. The movement is one of the many sects of Shintoism, but one focused on actions. It has over three million followers—one of the largest religious movements founded by a woman.

During the reign of Emperor Meiji (1867–1912), vast changes were made to the traditions of Japanese society. The samurai class came to an end, and merchants were taxed. The state organized an education and welfare system. Laws were enacted to protect the working class.

After World War II, religious freedoms were enacted in the Japanese constitution, and the recognition of Shintoism as Japan's state religion ended.

Part III

Moksha

The Federal Republic of Nepal, circa 2000 AD

1. Arrival in Nepal

The autopilot disengaged for landing, and the airplane made a little jolt, waking Gatik. He'd long since lost count of the times he'd woken up on an airplane, but he gasped all the same.

Disha put her hand on top of his on the armrest. "Are you all right?"

"Yes," Gatik said, taking a deep breath and blowing it out hard. "Recurring nightmare. You'd think it would stop upsetting me so much at some point."

"Dreams do that; they matter," Disha said.

Gatik and Disha were together at college in New York. They met there. He was studying computer science, though he was unsure if he should keep that major. Disha, on the other hand, knew what she wanted. She was pre-law.

They had dated for three years. Disha was unsure if the relationship would be the one. She avoided doing things in relationships with the sole goal of cementing them. To her, they needed to come naturally. She was coming to Nepal because it was interesting, though Gatik had asked her.

Disha grew up in Chicago, where her parents had immigrated from India. She liked New York. She was unsure which law school she would get into and where that might take her, though she felt she might choose a lesser school if required.

Gatik grew up in Nepal. His parents sent him to college in the US. They never considered that he might not return, but Gatik was thinking just that. In the past, he felt that his desire to get away came from his adolescent drive for separation, but now he was unsure. He had issues with his father, which he was still trying to understand.

Gatik's father was a prominent politician and businessman in Nepal—an early hero of the revolution that had deposed the king and established a democracy. It would be easy for Gatik to have a successful career in Nepal, probably a more successful one than he would ever have in the US. However, Gatik resisted this. The trip was another test of whether he ever wanted to return.

"What was the dream about?" Disha asked.

"I have it a lot. I am taking a multiple-choice test, and there is no right answer. I go up to the professor, and he just looks at me. No reaction. But I am sure there is no right answer. Then, I decide to just randomly choose an answer. But I can't. I can't write." Gatik said. He chuckled to make light of it.

"I often have the one where you keep forgetting to attend a class all year," Disha said. "Horrible."

Disha held his hand only for a second more. Gatik liked to deal with things himself. She knew that.

The plane broke through the clouds, and Gatik reached over Disha to point out the window. They could see the mountains and the city below. Disha was eager to see the neighborhood where Gatik grew up, but the airplane was approaching from a different side of town. Kathmandu looked strange to Disha. It mainly had low-rise buildings, a sea of them. Some buildings or landmarks usually stood out in cities Disha had flown over, but not here. The buildings had the same height and blended together. In the foreground, you could make out white, yellow, or even light green buildings, but they all blended into beige in the background. Of course, if you looked straight down out of the plane, you could see streets filled with people, cars, and motorcycles, but they disappeared between the buildings if you looked further out.

Disha tried to make out some temples. She knew temples, spectacular ones, existed in Kathmandu. There was even talk of building one of the largest statues of Vishnu on the city's outskirts.

She could not see any. She sat back, frustrated. Gatik told her not to worry. They would visit temples even in the little time they had in Kathmandu.

Disha and Gatik were Hindu. They had both gone through the Hindu rituals when growing up, but had learned little of the doctrine. "Religious doctrine is holding us back," Gatik's father used to say, "it reinforces the establishment." Disha's parents were also not particularly religious. They only undertook essential rituals. Disha wanted to draw on Hindu doctrine for her law school admissions essays, but couldn't. She did not know any. She came up with the idea of visiting an ashram during the trip to Nepal. Gatik gladly made the arrangements. He wanted to learn more as well.

"The airport has been updated since I was here last," Gatik said as they went through it. "The party in charge always wants to impress with public works," he scoffed.

He looked around the crowd as though he was expecting to recognize someone, but then he remembered that he had not been in Nepal for a long time and that the chances of seeing someone at the airport were small.

They hadn't checked any bags, so it didn't take them long to make their way through. They would be in Nepal for only a week: just enough time for Gatik to see his parents and for them to visit the ashram. Gatik's parents were disappointed with how quick the visit was. That was Gatik's idea.

Once they left the airport building, they were immersed in the typical mass confusion of Kathmandu. Disha was surprised at how different everyone looked. She saw Nepali businesspeople rushing for their cars, tourists trying to take everything in, families happy to be reunited with loved ones, and people just hanging out. Clusters of men with torn, old, dirty clothes that blended with the unlandscaped dirt patches they were standing on were doing nothing. Disha assumed they reflected the economic hardship still borne by many in Nepal.

Disha and Gatik stood out even from the tourists. Disha wore typical American travel clothes, jeans, a T-shirt, and sneakers, with her hair mostly hidden under a cap, but Gatik wore a button-down Oxford shirt and khakis. He cared about his appearance back home.

"Bira," Gatik suddenly yelled, and a woman with sunglasses standing next to a new white SUV in the parking lot produced a broad smile. "That is my sister," he said to Disha and picked up his pace. He had not told Disha that what he looked forward to most on the trip was seeing his sister.

Bira looked nothing like Gatik. She was slender, had delicate lines, and was taller than he was. She looked like she belonged in a city. Gatik, on the other hand, was muscular with short, heavy legs. His mother often thought he probably took after one of his father's village ancestors. He looked like he belonged in the fields.

Bira wore one of those dresses with long slits on the sides that looked like an oversized shirt and a matching sweater. It was not particularly cold, but the sweater relaxed the sophisticated look. Disha felt comparatively underdressed.

"It is lonely here without you," Bira said with a smile that showed off her brilliant straight teeth. Then she flung her long black hair to the side and hugged her brother.

"It is great to see you," Gatik said as he let go of Bira and introduced Disha.

"It is so nice to meet you, Bira," Disha said, "You look so beautiful. I am afraid we Americans don't know how to dress."

"Nonsense, American wear is all the rage here," Bira said.

Gatik did not like it when Disha denigrated her country and gave her a disapproving look. "Americans are different and should own it," he told her before.

They got into Bira's car and started driving to the hotel. As they drove down the entry to the airport, Disha again saw small groups of men standing idly by the side of the road. They looked at the passing cars. Were they hoping for someone to stop? Why were

Bira and Gatik oblivious to them? Disha wanted to ask Bira and Gatik about them, but thought it might be inappropriate.

"I hope your mother does not mind us staying in a hotel," Disha said instead. That also was Gatik's idea, and Disha felt bad about it.

"Probably less than you going to an ashram. She feels that Gatik knows the Hindu customs and rituals. What else is there?" Bira said with a grin and looked at Gatik to see if she could get a reaction before concentrating on driving again.

"Religion is about traditions for mom, not concepts. Aren't you ever curious what all those Hindu stories really meant?" Gatik asked Bira. "We are."

Disha smiled at Bira through the review mirror. Then she looked outside and saw more poverty and chaotic traffic. A stream of small cars and mopeds was endlessly weaving through the narrow streets, avoiding each other and people if they dared to enter the streets. With no traffic lights, the only rule seemed to be to avoid hitting anything. Disha was too tired to continue watching.

She caught herself staring at Bira's necklace. It was a small gold chain with a gold ring at the end. Disha was sure it was Western, the type of necklace you could buy in one of the fancy stores in Chicago. Disha's parents had only given her Indian jewelry, which she never wore.

"Gatik always liked his principles," Bira said when she saw Disha looking at her. "But an ashram?"

"Disha is the one who is pre-law," Gatik said to defend himself.

"Computer science has more rules," Disha retorted. "Do you know that on our first date, all Gatik could talk about was some documentary he had seen about some dialectic? What was it?"

"Dialectical materialism, how to approach reality," Gatik said, "And I was nervous."

Disha was teasing. She liked Gatik's preoccupations with knowing things. It was something they had in common. They both liked to study things at college, even things that were not assigned. They had talked about it. They concluded that it was not about the power of knowledge. It was the joy of discovering a constant in a world of confusion. However, they were embarrassed about that and never repeated it to anyone.

Bira smiled at Gatik. "Mom is happy that you're here for Dashain."

Then Bira turned to Disha. "It is our most important festival. We celebrate the slaying of the buffalo demon Mahisasura by the goddess Durga. On the eighth day, they slaughter buffalo and goats in Durbar Square in the center of Kathmandu. The blood is then sprinkled on objects of work—even on planes at the airport. It can be quite gruesome. I hope you don't mind."

"I look forward to learning about the traditions here," Disha responded.

"We will have dinner at our parents' home on the ninth day of the festival. It is one of the few times a year I see them. You are not skipping that, are you?" Bira said, turning to Gatik.

"We will be there," Gatik replied. "It is why we came this time of year."

Bira told Gatik that their father had recently been appointed to the governing board of the country's sovereign wealth fund. It was a pivotal position that oversaw many of the government's holdings. Bira said that she had always been treated differently at school and work, given that their father was a hero of the revolution. But now, with his important position, she received special treatment wherever she went. "They really admire him here."

It did not take long for Gatik and Disha to experience that royal treatment firsthand. The owner of the hotel where they were staying ushered them to the best room. The room overlooked Kathmandu with mountains in the distance. Immovable, timeless mountains that set a boundary for the chaos below. Gatik opened the windows to let it all in.

2. Civil War—Thirty Years Earlier

Two shots were fired at the same time, and the guards on the left and right of the gate to the military barracks fell to the ground. The Maoist militants had split in half to storm the barracks—one hiding on each side of the road, the best shot in each group aiming for the guard on their side. They timed the shots to be simultaneous and then stormed the gate. One guard held his stomach wound, trying to contain the blood. He was in shock, not making any noise. He stared at the group that reached him in such disbelief at what had just happened that they felt sorry for him. It could be them one day. They ran past quickly, hoping they would not remember what they saw.

The other group found their guard, the one they were responsible for killing, lying on the ground, screaming in pain. Their immediate reaction was more one of fear and panic. They did not want the other soldiers in the barracks to be alerted to where they were or what was happening. One of the men in the group quickly shot the guard again, looking away as he pulled the trigger. The guard fell back and stopped screaming. Then they ran past the gate, but unlike the other group, with enthusiasm, not regret.

So far, everything was going according to plan. It was Prashant's plan. He was an army-trained police officer, free from suspicion, collaborating with the underground Maoists. He'd wanted to lead the attack but had a rival in Chitavake.

Chitavake was only twenty, from one of the small villages close to the barracks. At first, the Maoist seniors in the village were skeptical of him. He was ambitious, and some feared he might be using the movement for his advancement. But after the army rounded up all the men in his village and lectured them about respecting the king and resisting the evils of the Maoists, Chitavake continued to attend the rebels' meetings. The senior Maoists slowly became convinced that he had the right motivations.

The Maoist group that organized the attack met regularly in a makeshift shed in a field at night. They had covered up the walls with blankets so that the flashlights they were using would not be seen. Chitavake had reported spying on the army barracks at one of those meetings.

"There are thirty soldiers and five officers at the barracks, but after they train in the mornings, they go on expeditions—like when they raided my village. They leave about ten soldiers and a couple of officers behind. Usually, they don't come back until after eight o'clock."

"We have enough men to attack the soldiers they leave behind," Prashant interrupted. "I have a plan."

The Maoist seniors were impressed. They felt they needed to do something to fight back. They had been part of the Jana Andolan movement of protests, but it was time for an insurgency. Attacks on army barracks or police stations would raise their profile. But the seniors did not want to participate in the actual attack. They knew the parents of many of the soldiers in the barracks.

"It is one thing to talk about killing a man, but quite another to do it," one of the senior leaders said, realizing that he could not bring himself to end another's life. They were going to get the younger men to do it, but they had reservations even about that. "The men have never killed. They need to be motivated. We need to get Chitavake to motivate them. He speaks so passionately about our cause," another senior leader observed. So Chitavake was chosen to lead the group, but they followed Prashant's plan.

They started by training in the mountains for a week. It was awkward; all the men knew each other. They could not quite get themselves to file in line and do army-like drills. Instead, they gathered in the mornings, ate breakfast, and listened to Chitavake give speeches about how the people should rule Nepal. It was not such a straightforward argument, as the king was deemed an incarnation of the god Vishnu. Chitavake avoided that topic, focusing instead on establishing a multiparty democracy. He reminded them that their suppression at the hands of the army defending the king was funded by the taxes they paid.

They spent most of the day hunting. It enabled target practice without raising suspicion, built camaraderie, and provided them with food. They sat around a campfire in the evenings and inevitably spoke about army raids. Some had stories of being beaten in front of their children.

Remembering those stories made it easier to storm the barracks. As they were doing so, they all tried to recall them.

Chitavake separated from his group. He ran ahead. He was still uneasy about his rival, Prashant, and wanted to continue to prove his leadership. He reached the officers' hall they were meant to storm well before the others. When he opened the door, he found two officers. One got up from behind a table full of papers, trying to assert some authority where he had none. The other stood at the window, perplexed that Chitavake had gotten in. He had looked out the window, trying to figure out what was happening. Neither officer had a gun. They had forgotten the training they received when they were juniors.

Chitavake stopped for a second. This was it, the moment he had contemplated for so long. A jolt of excitement came over him. It all happened so fast. He could not believe he was facing the officers, who were staring straight at him in terror and disbelief.

The officers did not move, hoping to calm down Chitavake. Time seemed to slow. None of them spoke.

The officer at the table sensed Chitavake's hesitation. He figured that Chitavake might be reluctant to shoot. He looked at the officer at the window, then back at Chitavake, and tried to move slightly towards him.

"I have to act," Chitavake thought. "They chose me, not Prashant. There is no turning back now." He aimed at the officer standing by the table. The officer stopped moving. Then Chitavake looked away, squinted, and pulled the trigger. He could not look even after the shot and instead turned his gun on the officer by the window. Out of the corner of his eyes, he saw the first officer lying still on the ground. Chitavake was in charge—he had proven he could do it, and only one officer was left to contend with.

"I am part of your movement, and I have a son," the officer pleaded. "Don't you remember me?"

Chitavake faltered but did not want to listen to the officer. "I have to prove myself," he told himself to regain composure.

Just then, the rest of the rebels entered the room. They stopped and stared, perplexed as Chitavake had been. This was Chitavake's opportunity to prove his resolve and show leadership. "No one can doubt me if I kill both officers single-handedly," he thought.

This time, he looked straight at the officer as he pulled the trigger. The officer's intense stare shifted away as the bullet found its mark. Then, the eyes locked on Chitavake again. Chitavake expected his victim's eyes to shift from fear and pleading to anger and accusation, but they did not. They were blank like the mere body part they were—devoid of all humanity. Chitavake could not bear to look any further. He ran out of the officers' hall.

The men who had tried to storm the soldiers' hall had not been as successful as Chitavake. They'd received gunfire from the windows as soon as they got close to the building. All they could do was fire back, and judging from the commotion, they thought they might have hit some soldiers, but they could not be sure.

Chitavake ordered everyone to retreat. They had achieved what they had come for—at least he had. They ran back through the gate and into the woods, regrouping briefly. None of them had been hurt, but there was no celebration.

Prashant gave Chitavake an accusatory look as he left. He knew the second officer and did not think Chitavake should have shot him.

Of course, the army did not waste time. They organized raids of local villages to find them, but no one gave them away. They limited their actions to participating in mass demonstrations of the second Jana Andolan movement. In the crowd of a demonstration, they did not stand out.

The demonstrations and general unrest continued for months but eventually succeeded. The movement ended in the Maoist Party being able to appoint the prime minister. At that point, the group believed they were safe. Even when the Maoist prime minister resigned within a year over not being able to fire the army chief, they were convinced that no one would go back to the past.

Chitavake remained in the Maoist Party throughout all this time, but he never killed again. The look in the eyes of the second officer haunted him. Fortunately, he had already proved himself in the eyes of the party. He became a prominent member of the Maoist Party—an early hero.

Chitavake never spoke of that night at the army barracks. When he married Hitu, he told her—but no one else—that he had killed. He did not tell her any details. There were also some other things about those early days that he kept a secret.

When Chitavake and Hitu had two children, Gatik and Bira, they agreed never to tell them anything about their father's rise to power.

3. Dinner at Home

Gatik slept only briefly at the hotel before it was time for them to go to his parents' house for dinner. He had not brought any special clothes for it, but Disha put on a dress. She was excited to meet Gatik's parents.

It was a little awkward for Gatik to bring Disha along for the trip. Even he knew the relationship did not warrant a parental visit. It was his way of introducing some balance of power. His father could not preside over the Dashain dinner like he otherwise would.

Disha was mesmerized again by the busy streets of Nepal as they made their way to Gatik's parents' house. She stared at some of the lost souls on the side of the street. None stared back. This time, she noticed how pedestrians managed to cross streets without traffic lights. They entered the street very slowly, allowing traffic to curve around them. It was scary, but it made sense.

When they got to Gatik's house, Disha was impressed. The house was intimidating: an imposing U-shaped two-story mansion in apparently the best neighborhood of Kathmandu. Each house on the street seemed to rival the one next to it. Disha did not expect that there would be such wealth in Nepal, but of course, there had to be.

A security guard waved them in from a small makeshift gatehouse at the entry to a large courtyard in front of the house. The gatehouse was not there the last time Gatik came to visit. He liked that Disha was impressed by it — better than the opposite, he thought.

A uniformed housekeeper opened the door to the house and led them to the living room, where Gatik's parents were sitting on two of three white couches. It was a little awkward since they must have heard the commotion of Gatik and Disha arriving, but they decided to remain seated until they came in.

The room was empty—no art, no distinctive furniture. The white of the coaches even blended in with the white of the walls. Disha was sure that it was not a minimalist thing. There was nothing artsy about it. It was more that nothing had been committed to. No effort had been made to personalize the home.

Hitu, Gatik's mother, was the first to get up. She was short like Gatik, with beautiful, long black hair that she tied in a knot. She had given up fighting off middle-age weight during the ups and downs of her life, but she had not given up her warmth. If anything, instead of becoming bitter as she got older, she softened into appreciating kindness above all. She dressed well but wore no jewelry.

She hugged Gatik quickly without saying a word. She seemed uncomfortable. Disha at first thought that it might be because of her being there, but then Hitu greeted her with the same broad, soft smile that she had seen Bira produce at the airport.

"We are so happy to meet you, Disha," Hitu said.

Chitavake, Gatik's father, was a tall, slender man dressed in a suit without a tie. When he got up, he towered over everyone. He had a full head of gray hair, which Disha thought was unusual for his age. Chitavake pulled back his shoulders and stood even taller as he shook Gatik's hand. He greeted Gatik formally. Disha wondered if this was a Nepali father/son custom, but quickly decided it could not be.

"Father," Gatik said, nodding slightly while he shook his father's hand. He took refuge in completing the greeting the way his father had initiated it. He avoided a hug.

Chitavake quickly turned towards Disha with a discerning and slightly mercurial look.

"I hear you are going to be a lawyer," Chitavake said.

"Hopefully!" Disha responded. She said it like she had to stand up to him.

"They need a lot of those in the US," Chitavake said. Disha could not tell if it was a way for Chitavake to seem worldly or to come back at her.

"It is an important profession," Disha responded, this time with a disarming tone.

"What interests you about being a lawyer?" Chitavake asked. It was a fair question.

"I like the rule of law. Laws that make sense, or at least should. They help us live together. Learning the purpose behind them. That interests me." Disha responded.

"I see," Chitavake said.

"Would you mind representing both sides? I mean, advocating if your client is wrong," Hitu asked.

"It is the process. That is how it is done, isn't it?" Disha responded.

"Not entirely morally satisfying, though," Gatik said quietly as though he was saying it only to Disha and in a way that did not require a response. Disha did not mind; they often spoke about such things.

"Gatik is the one working really hard; computer science is brutal," Disha said to shift the focus to him. Usually, Gatik would have said something self-denigrating or humorous in response. He said nothing.

"Computer science is useful, but it could be a lot easier for you here," Chitavake said, looking at Gatik. "Now that we are in charge again, things are moving forward. You could run one of the businesses I started when the party was out of power." He realized it was too early to bring up the subject, but it was all he could think of.

"Moving forward?" Gatik responded, slightly angered, the way only a family member could. "The classes are still divided. Little is moving forward." Then he looked around the living room. It was a way to avoid eye contact with his father and simultaneously comment on his wealth. Gatik did not have an issue with his parents' wealth per se; he disagreed that the Maoist Party was achieving what it stood for - equalizing wealth. Gatik immediately regretted his tone —this was no way to start a visit. He could have said all this later.

"The security guard is new?" Gatik said to change the subject.

"Yes, I have been getting threats," Chitavake said, looking at Hitu. He, too, promised himself he would be more subtle for the remainder of the visit. That was the only way he could persuade Gatik to return to Nepal. It was becoming embarrassing for him at work that his son was considering not returning.

"Threats," Gatik asked. "What threats?"

"Nothing to worry about," Chitvake said.

"Awful letters, and specific ..." Hitu added.

"Yes, specific to me. So what. Just a crazy person," Chitavake said, waving it off.

"Shanti, Shanti, Shanti," Hitu responded. It was her personal mantra, which she learned at a young age; it was directed at purifying the body and mind and relieving suffering. Gatik heard it all the time when he was growing up.

Then there was silence. Gatik suspected the threats had to do with politics. Violence had always been part of it.

Disha wanted to break the awkward silence —how unfair for it to fall to her again. She said how glad she was to see where Gatik grew up and then reluctantly asked about the only thing that she had read about Nepal in the US papers—the recent massacre of the king and his immediate family.

"Is it true that the crown prince was blamed as the sole perpetrator for the massacre of the royal family, and then his brother assumed control?"

"I believe it is more complicated than that. Still, the US supported the new king and even contributed to his army. They could have done more. As much as they hate communism, they did not really mind it here."

"So, how did the king finally lose control?"

"In 2005, he declared a state of emergency and assumed total control. It was the step backward we needed to galvanize our movement. We started the second Jana Andolan, which eventually undid him. Sometimes, you need the opposition to do something strong and foolish. But Gatik is right. The movement is not over. There is more to be done."

Chitavake looked at Gatik, trying to reconcile, but Gatik looked away. It was Hitu who broke the silence that time, asking everyone to go to the dining room for dinner.

"I have been looking forward to Nepalese cooking," Disha said as they sat in the dining room. "Gatik has been telling me about the dumplings, your momos." She also wanted to experience the customs that Gatik told her his mother insisted on keeping. The oldest person at the table always ate first; one had to leave something on the plate, or more food would be put on it, and one was not to say please or thank you. That would imply that the behavior was unexpected, which could be perceived as an insult.

Then, there was the rule that nonbelievers and menstruating women were not allowed in the kitchen; it would cause the food to be jiuto or impure. Disha was glad that, instead of inquiring about these circumstances with guests, the custom had evolved to allow only family members and staff in the kitchen.

They mainly spoke about Gatik and Disha's plans in Nepal. They would see Durbar Square, with its temples and palaces, in the center of town the next morning. Gatik's mother urged them to see the Garden of Dreams. It was one of the few gardens showcasing Nepal's verdant and diverse flora, as well as some non-native plants. Gatik and Disha had little interest in this—they could see gardens at home.

On the way back to the hotel, Gatik confessed to Disha. "I don't know what comes over me. I hate it when my father takes the high road and talks about the country."

"Parents can do that," was all Disha said. Gatik was sure his anger was not the result of usual father-son issues - if one can ever be sure of that.

"The government spends more money on education and tries to create opportunities, but the elite still have private schools and rule the country," Gatik continued. "Of course, I went to one of those schools," he finished apologetically.

"So did I in Chicago. Nothing wrong with that," Disha said.

The next morning, they woke to priests ringing bells at a nearby temple and the noise of crowds gathering. "Sorry about this," Gatik said.

"I like it," Disha said, to Gatik's surprise. "A good way to start our day of sightseeing. Or my day of sightseeing." Disha was referring to the fact that they were going to see the sights for her. Gatik had seen them before, though he was hoping to learn something from the guides.

It was still early, and Disha opened a book about Himalayan folklore she had been reading on the airplane. She was trying to immerse herself in the culture as much as possible. She was reading the story of Saunu and Birmu, two brothers.

Birmu was jealous of Saunu and told him that his wife, Kunjavati, had tended the cattle in the village incorrectly, and he was best off to kill her. However, before he could, she left to live with her father. A little while later, Birmu caught Saunu poaching deer, and Birmu reported him to the king. About to be arrested, Saunu committed suicide. Then, Birmu approached Kunjavati, but she knew his treachery. She retreated to a forest to give birth to two sons she had with Saunu before he died. The two sons ended up killing Birmu's sons. One of Kunjavati's sons then died, mistakenly believed to be part of an approaching army, when he tried to visit his family, who did not know him, given that he lived in a forest; the other died in grief. In the end, the family was ruined.

“This story is really dramatic and a bit confusing," Disha said.

"I know," Gatik agreed. "All this back and forth, and everyone dies. I think I remember that it is trying to tell the story about ruin caused by the wicked Birmu," Gatik said.

"I suppose, but in a pretty roundabout way," Disha said.

"Yes, Kunjavati," Gatik joked. "She was the only one who understood the treachery."

Gatik took out one of the books he was reading.

"Another philosophy book," Disha said.

"Don't mind if I do," Gatik responded.

"Ready to enter your cave," Disha said. It was a joke between them. Gatik once told her how he thought that "the mind wanders in a cave without exhaustion, hunger, or pain." It was his poor attempt to describe how much he enjoyed philosophy, and Disha never let him forget it.

"Very funny," Gatik said.

When it was time to start sightseeing, like most tourists, they started with Durbar Square, which Gatik explained meant "place of palaces." The oldest palace was Hanuman Dhoka. It spread over five acres and dated back to the mid-sixteenth century. Gatik did not care for the monarchs who lived there—his father had at least managed to persuade him of that when he was growing up. The guide reminded them that the monarchs had been deemed living Hindu gods, so the Durbar Square palaces were more like temples.

They went to Kumari Ghar, a temple where a living goddess, the Kumari, resided to that day—a young girl deemed to be the manifestation of the divine female energy. She was considered the incarnation of the goddess until her first menstruation, after which the spirit was believed to leave her body and reside within another.

"What is it with menstruation in this country?" Disha whispered to Gatik, who chuckled.

Next, they saw Pashupatinath Temple, a Hindu temple built in the fifth century, destroyed by Mongol invaders in the 14th century, and rebuilt in the nineteenth century. The temple was dedicated to Shiva, the contemplative God; this was where Disha's Shaivite family would have worshiped if she had grown up in Kathmandu. Disha's family undertook their rituals at a temple dedicated to Shiva.

Gatik belonged to the Vaishnava sect, primarily worshiping Vishnu, the protector deity. Being of different sects was common, given the many gods. Gatik and Disha were even going to an ashram that was neither a Shaivite nor a Vaishnava one.

Their guide explained that Brahma, Vishnu, and Shiva, the three main gods of Hinduism, were each manifestations of Nirvana Brahman.

"Brahman is a supreme deity that is not comprehensible to the human mind, so it projects itself onto Brahma, Vishnu, and Shiva, whose forms are closer to human forms and comprehensible to us. So, despite popular belief, Hinduism is a one-god religion or at least a religion that has a hierarchy ending in one cosmic being or concept," the guide said.

"A little bit like the trinity of God in Christianity. God the Father, Jesus, and the Holy Spirit," Disha said.

After sightseeing, they had lunch and returned to Gatik's parents' house. Only Hitu was home. "You have to show me your room," Disha suggested. "I want to see where you grew up."

Gatik felt a little uncomfortable. He was used to projecting his mature self. Still, he allowed it. He wanted to see if he could shrug off his childhood and adolescence, even in the room where it happened.

The room was large, with its own bathroom. It looked exactly like the day Gatik left for college in the US.

"They don't change it," Gatik commented. "It is part of their hope that I will return someday—though I would never live here."

Disha walked over to a large bookshelf. She liked seeing this part of Gatik.

"What is this book about?" Disha said, randomly picking a book with a particularly vivid cover.

"It is about the legend of Gurumapa—a terrible story for children. The legend goes that Kesh Chandra lived in Itumbabha, a courtyard in Kathmandu, with a man-eating creature named

Gurumapa. Kesh Chandra promised Gurumapa he could take away children when they were bad. To stop Gurumapa, the locals in Itumbabha promised him a feast every year if he moved out of the courtyard to live in a field. To this day, every year, they leave food for Gurumapa in that field."

Gatik had a disturbed look on his face. He had said it was a terrible story for children, but he seemed more upset about it than he should be.

"Did you hate the story when you were young?" Disha asked.

"The story really scares children; I am not sure why they tell it," Gatik continued.

"More traditions, " Disha murmured, looking around Gatik's room.

Even though Nepal had never been a British colony, it had adopted a British-style school system, right down to the extracurricular activities. The awards on the wall were from debate tournaments Gatik had won.

"You must have been good," Disha said. Gatik produced a smile.

Disha pointed at a painting next to the awards on the wall. It was of a scorpion and a turtle. "What is this about?"

"Another story—this one I really like. The scorpion is a poor swimmer, so he asks a turtle to carry him on its back across a river. The turtle is reluctant, afraid that the scorpion might sting him. The scorpion explains that he would drown if he stung the turtle while crossing the river. Hearing this, the turtle agrees to take the scorpion across the river. While the turtle crosses the river, the scorpion stings him. As he dies, the turtle asks the scorpion why he did it. The scorpion, about to drown himself, replies, 'Because it is my nature.'"

Gatik smiled. "Nepalese like this story because it reminds them that actions taken don't always make sense. But I think they have it wrong. I like the story because the scorpion sticks to who he is, even if it costs him his life."

"Interesting. You should take it with you," Disha said.

"It would upset my parents," Gatik said. "But I have an idea: we should play Bagh-Chai. It is a Nepalese board game, similar to checkers." He wanted the exploration of his childhood to stop. He pulled a couple of drawers of his dresser and found the game.

"Let's play this with my mother. We can show you. The rules are pretty simple. One player has four tigers, and one player has twenty goats. The tigers jump over the goats to capture them, and the goats try to block the tigers' legal moves."

"Bagh-Chai," Hitu yelled when they came downstairs. "I have not played it in years."

While setting up the game, Hitu asked Disha if she had seen Gatik's debate awards.

"Yes, pretty impressive," Disha said.

"He always hated that they told him what side to argue, and when he won a round, he usually had to argue the other side in the next," Hitu said, smiling at Gatik.

Gatik moved around uncomfortably.

"I suppose one has to in debate tournaments," Disha said, "just like being a lawyer."

Hitu and Gatik grinned. "Well said," Gatik commented.

When the game started, they moved pieces, sometimes frantically, sometimes with much thought. It was not clear who was winning until the end. There was a lot of back and forth. Soon, all three laughed together.

"I am glad you both came," Hitu said as she reached to squeeze her son's arm. "I have not had so much fun in a long time."

Gatik smiled at her. "I am glad I came," he said.

They played until they heard a commotion in the courtyard: Chitavake's motorcade. Once the gate to the courtyard closed behind them, he rushed inside.

"Is all that security really necessary?" Disha asked Gatik.

"There have been incidents, but mostly in large crowds, not at homes, and they are rarer now. Still, I don't know if my father will ever feel safe in public. And now the letters, apparently, are pretty specific, addressed to him, about things he supposedly did."

Over dinner, Chitavake aloofly asked about their day. Gatik and Disha matter-of-factly responded, telling him what they had been up to.

"Sounds like you are enjoying yourself. What are your plans tomorrow?" Chitavake asked.

"Tomorrow, we are going to Swami Mahindra's ashram," Gatik responded.

"Is that really necessary?" Hitu asked.

Gatik's father interrupted. "I know Swami Mahindra, and she is a great choice. I have taken some foreign dignitaries there. They liked her."

"Disha and I want to learn about the doctrines of Hinduism. We know the traditions. We want to know the doctrines." Gatik explained to his mother.

"Well, you should ask her about karma and dharma," Chitavake said with a bit of sarcasm.

When Gatik was growing up, his father referred to it as "the dangerous formula." First, you persuade people that their status in life has to do with misdeeds in their prior lives—karma. Second, you preach that acceptance of one's status and selflessness is required to gain a higher status in another life—dharma. Presto, you preclude any social change. Everyone has to accept what they have. The king is a god, and the caste system must persist.

Gatik explained this to Disha.

"But there are different types of karma," Disha protested. "Some you can deflect. It is not just black and white. You can fix bad karma."

"I have never heard this," Hitu said to Chitavake, who shrugged.

"Wish we could deflect some of the threatening letters," Hitu said under her breath. "Shanti, Shanti, Shanti." It was a new disapproving tone Hitu had taken on lately. It was born out of frustration. Chitavake decided to ignore it. "Hitu should be happy with what success has brought us, even if there are some costs," Chitavake would tell himself.

"Even so," Gatik said, "The ability to deflect some karma only softens the impact of the formula. It still works to discourage change, only maybe to a lesser extent. The concept stands. Dharma and karma preclude change."

"Something we can agree on," Chitavake observed, glad that Gatik was not fighting him on this.

Talk soon turned to the Dashain festival and the ritual slaying of the bulls in a few days.

"It is gruesome, Disha, but I hope you will join us?" Hitu said.

"We can get you into the dignitary stand. Some people want to meet you, Gatik," Chitavake added.

"I would like to go if you are okay with it," Gatik said to Disha, who nodded. He then turned back to his father. "But I don't feel comfortable in the dignitary stand. We will be part of the crowd."

Before Chitavake could press his case, Hitu said, "I think that makes sense. It is safer that way, anyway. I always worry about all those dignitaries and large crowds."

4. Ashram

The next morning, Gatik and Disha went to the ashram on a small, quiet hill in the southern part of Kathmandu. Several buildings were organized around a large central courtyard filled with gravel. The gravel was sparse in places, revealing the dirt below. There was no landscaping or statuary. The rectangular organization and barren cleanliness away from Kathmandu gave it a sanctuary-like aura.

Gatik and Disha were greeted by a young apprentice who guided them to their room—clean and simple, overlooking the courtyard, with a dresser and two beds. There was nothing for comfort.

"I am glad we came," Disha said. "We will learn something, no matter where it leads." She wasn't sure of that, but Gatik had agreed to come, and she wanted to thank him.

It was not as though Gatik minded coming. When he was young, in his Nepali coming-of-age ceremony, his bratabandha, he had been given a personal mantra:

Om Bhur Bhuvah Svaha Tat Savitur Varenyam
Bhargo Devasya Dhimahi Dhiyo Yo Nah
Prachodayat.

We meditate on the most auspicious, radiant light of
the Divine, which illuminates our intellects.

It encouraged him to pursue Hindu knowledge. To this day, the mantra swirled around in Gatik's head. Sometimes, he would forget about it for weeks, but it always returned. Always there, always in his mind.

Gatik and Disha heard people making their way down the hallway, speaking French and laughing loudly.

"That must be part of our class. Serenity has not set in."
Gatik said with a chuckle.

"I like to see you in a serene state," Disha joked.

They then walked across the courtyard to a small, indistinct
building with one big room. The room had twenty chairs arranged in
a circle. Gatik found the faint smell of curry in the room distasteful
for a religious place. He could not figure out where it was coming
from, but he said nothing to Disha, even though he was surprised at
how much it bothered him.

Inesh, a middle-aged, short teacher with gold-rimmed round
glasses, welcomed them.

"Welcome, welcome," he said to each participant as they
entered the room. He then rushed to sit behind a small table that held
some books. He did it enthusiastically, suggesting that what he was
doing was of great importance. Almost as if he were about to change
everyone's life. Gatik and Disha smiled at each other.

He asked everyone to introduce themselves. All the
participants were foreigners. The Frenchmen Disha and Gatik heard
in the corridor were college students on a trek who had come mainly
for the cultural experience of being at an ashram. Then there was a
woman from Indiana who was interested in becoming Hindu, a
couple from Argentina who were interested in Hinduism but had no
interest in converting, and a Hindu couple from the UK, Tony and
Elisabeth. It did not matter that Disha, Gatik, Tony, and Elisabeth
were the only practicing Hindus. "We welcome everyone," Inesh
said. "There have never been initiation ceremonies or requirements
for being Hindu. You can take as much or as little as you like."

Inesh settled in. "What is special about this class is that we
shall focus on Hindu principles. A famous swami once observed that
most Hindus understand their rituals, but few understand their
religion. Here, we will focus on the religion. Rituals and customs
vary by country, and we will not discuss them."

He paused as though offering students an opportunity to object or leave. Gatik and Disha were happy. It was why they chose the ashram. They were in the right place.

Inesh continued. "So this morning, we will start with the sacred texts of Hinduism. In the afternoon, we will talk about chakras and yoga. Tomorrow, you will each have time alone with Swami Mahindra. You should prepare a question for that. Something you really want to understand. The swami only answers questions, but we will talk about that later."

Then he picked up a big book from the table before him and said it contained the ancient Vedas. "Most Hindus, even those who try to understand the religion, can't claim to understand the ancient Vedas. They are hard to comprehend. I will start with the Nasadiya Veda. It is about the creation of the universe, a fitting place to start, don't you think?" Inesh winked and then read:

Then was not non-existent nor existent: there was no realm of air, no sky beyond it. What covered in, and where? And what gave shelter? Was water there, unfathomed depth of water?

Death was not then, nor was there aught immortal: no sign was there, the day's and night's divider. That One Thing, breathless, breathed by its own nature: apart from it was nothing whatsoever.

He tilted the book down, looked at the class through his round gold glasses, and said he would skip some verses and get to the end.

The Gods are later than this world's production. Who knows then whence it first came into being?

Inesh put the book back on the table. "It is beautiful, simple, and full of questions. In not giving answers, the Veda says there are no answers, only questions. I like it, but like many ancient Vedas, it can frustrate you. That is why we don't emphasize them."

So far, so good, Gatik thought, and briefly looked at Disha, who was thinking about the Veda.

Inesh put on a mischievous smile.

"There is one Veda I can't resist telling you about. The Veda concerns Manu. He is performing religious rituals on the banks of a river when a little fish appears and promises to protect him from an impending flood if Manu protects him until he is big enough to fend for himself. Manu puts the fish in a jar, then in a tank, and finally, when the fish is fully grown, into the ocean. The fish then asks Manu to build a boat and to be in it with the sages and food on a particular day. On that day, a deluge comes and floods everything. The fish pulls the boat to the Himalayas. Once in safety, the fish reveals himself as Brahma, the creator god."

Inesh grinned. "Yes, it is like Noah's ark, except that sages instead of animals are rescued. The story in both forms describes the rewards of faith and trust in God."

Disha smiled at Gatik. She thought about the comment about the trinity of gods in Hinduism and Christianity that they heard about during their sightseeing tour.

"Another similarity," she whispered to Gatik.

"I think the Vedas are just too vague," Gatik interrupted. He said it to Inesh and the class, even though he was not sure he was meant to make comments.

"Go ahead," Inesh said. He liked class participation.

"I read a few, and it is just so hard to figure out what they stand for," Gatik said. "I get the Manu story, but why does it have to be so indirect?"

"They are vague," Inesh said. "But I had to mention them at least. Have you read the newer Vedas, the Upanishads? They are easier to make sense of."

Gatik nodded.

"Great. Let's start with one I am sure you are familiar with," Inesh responded.

"I want to talk about the Katha Upanishad. So, for those who don't know it, Vajashravas gave away all his possessions to gain religious merit. His son, Nachiketa, was young but had studied the scriptures. He challenged his father and told him that giving away useless cows would not gain him merit. He needed to give away something he really cared about. He insisted that only giving away things one cared about deeply could provide real merit and a path to enlightenment."

Inesh looked at the class.

"So you know what Nachiketa challenged his father to do? He challenged his father to condemn him to death to gain merit. His father at first refused. Nachiketa kept on insisting until his father got angry and finally did it. He condemned his own son to death. When Nachiketa entered the realm of death, the underworld king, Yama, was not there. Nachiketa had to wait for three days until Yama spoke to him. Yama apologized for this and said he would give him three wishes in return.

"Nachiketa made his first wish to appease his father's anger, and his second wish was to learn sacrifices that would allow him to end up in heaven and not with Yama. Both were granted.

"However, Yama was reluctant to grant Nachiketa his third wish. Nachiketa wanted to know if people still exist after they die. Yama offered Nachiketa sons who would live for a hundred years and wealth on earth. Nachiketa called these temporary pleasures and insisted on his third wish. Yama finally admitted that the all-knowing self is never born and never dies."

Inesh paused for a minute, looking around the circle.

"There are a lot of elements here. Merit for the afterlife, reconciliation with the father, the temporary nature of things on earth, and the reluctance of the god of the underworld to admit that there is life after death. We could spend a lot of time on each. Each deserves a lesson. But we don't have that much time, so I want to pick up on the most important element, the all-knowing self that never dies. It is a core principle of Hinduism."

Tony chimed in this time.

"Yes, but the way I always thought about it is that Nachiketa realizes that if he knows that there is an afterlife, it creates a juxtaposition for the current life. The current life is less important. That is why Nachiketa was so smart to focus on that."

"Well said," Inesh said. "You are right; the Katha teaches us that if we know that our self never dies, it radically changes the context of our lives."

"So the belief in that makes all the difference," Tony said, happy that Inesh agreed.

"Still pretty abstract," Gatik said.

"Yes, it is abstract but important," Inesh said, picking up another book before him.

"The Self comes up over and over again in the Upanishads. Here it is in the Brihadaranyaka Upanishads:

This Self is the honey of all beings, and all beings
are the honey of this Self. Likewise this bright,
immortal person in this Self, and that bright
immortal person, the Self. He indeed is the same as
that Self, that Immortal, that Brahman, that All.

Gatik gave Disha a bewildered look. This was not shaping up to be what they wanted from the class.

Inesh continued from his second book after flipping some pages:

Which Self is within all?

He who overcomes hunger and thirst, sorrow,
passion, old age, and death.

Inesh put the book down and explained.

"The Upanishad describes a self or a soul separate from the body. It describes how the self or soul is impacted by one's physical life on earth. The goal is to liberate the self by not having the physical life impact it."

At that point, the woman from Argentina asked, "Is that what the men, the sadhus, we see on the streets do?"

"In a way. By the way, they can be women. We call them sadhvi. They renounce their worldly struggle, known as moksha. They focus their lives on meditation and contemplation of Brahman and renounce the material world. They are in the fourth stage of their lives after completing the other three: studying, being a parent, and undertaking pilgrimages. So, yes, they are trying to do that, but I want to be clear: no one is suggesting that you should do that. You may still have stages to go through. The Upanishads suggest that we realize that the physical world won't impact our souls if we don't let it. The way to do that is to be selfless. That is all."

That made more sense to Disha and Gatik, but was still too abstract for them.

At that point, one of the French students became a little agitated and spoke out. "That is what I don't understand. If I ignore the physical, become selfless, and have no desires, I cease to exist."

One of the other French students agreed. "Selflessness must be a goal, not a destination. It may be good to strive to be more selfless, but it is impossible to be completely selfless."

Disha whispered, "I agree" to Gatik and wondered what Inesh would say.

Inesh flat-out rejected both of these views. "Think of it this way. Suppose you want food, you want power, et cetera. Is it possible that your soul is the same whether you have satisfied those desires or not? You are the same person whether you have sated your hunger or not, whether you have become powerful or not. That is what the concept is about. Realizing that the self, the soul, does not need to be impacted if you don't let it. It is not about not eating or not striving."

"Moksha is a separation. It is moving on that allows one to focus on what is important," Tony insisted. "That is what I was taught."

"A focus on the relevant," Elisabeth added.

"I agree with that," Inesh said.

"I like this," Gatik whispered to Disha.

"Me too." Disha said, "But we knew this, and I think most things should impact our souls; why ignore them? Better to resolve them."

"You may be right," Gatik said.

The group then started discussing the concept among themselves. Inesh lost control of the class but was pleased with the level of engagement. After a while, he called the session to an end and urged everyone to take a break.

The class went to the courtyard to mingle. Gatik introduced himself to Elizabeth and Tony. They seemed the most similar to Disha and him. When Elizabeth discovered that Gatik was from Kathmandu, she asked what sights to see, and Gatik obliged.

In the meantime, the woman from Indiana introduced herself to Disha.

"I will try to read some of the Upanishads. They seem interesting, at least in part," the woman said.

"I am looking forward to meeting the swami. I want to hear what she has to say," Disha said.

The couple from Argentina stayed by themselves. They had taken yoga classes and were mostly looking forward to learning about the connection between yoga and Hinduism.

When they returned to the classroom, Inesh had taped up a poster outlining the human body with seven circles going up the spine.

"Science and religion meet," Gatik whispered to Disha, who grinned.

"So," Inesh began. "Before our break, we learned that the self needs to be separated from desires, yes? These circles represent the seven chakras. They are the sources of desires that demand fulfillment."

He pointed at the poster. "First is the Muladhara, the base or root chakra at the base of the spinal cord. It is fulfilled through killing and eating. Second, the Svadhisthana, the ovaries, and the prostate represent the carnal. Third, the Manipura, the naval area, which centers on power and influence."

Inesh explained that humans share the first three chakras with animals.

"As we move up further, we enter the purely human chakras."

He pointed toward the top of the poster.

"The fourth is the Anahata, the heart; it centers on compassion and altruism—Fifth, the Vishuddha, the throat, represents spirituality. Sixth is the Ajna, the third eye, where intuition and understanding are housed. Lastly, the seventh, the Sahasrara, is the top of the head, which concerns cosmic consciousness.

Inesh explained that the chakras represent a hierarchy of needs. It was a more detailed illustration of the needs they had talked about before the break—a hierarchy to move up in.

"The chakras allow us to identify and categorize desires. When we feel an impulse or recognize a desire, we can pinpoint where it comes from and release the self from it. Then we can move up the hierarchy."

"That may be helpful," Disha whispered to Gatik.

"Something concrete," Gatik responded. "But no rules."

Inesh then turned to yoga. He explained that there is a misperception about yoga in the West. "Yoga comprises physical and mental exercises used to attain the righteous path. To separate the self from desires, we must identify these desires and their source— the chakras—and release them. Some exercises can help us do that. That is where yoga comes in. There are many types of yoga. For example, Bhakti Yoga has exercises to help in the devotion to a deity; Jnana Yoga has exercises to help rational inquiry with distinguishing between the real and unreal, and Raja Yoga has exercises to fight spiritual ignorance through concentration."

Gatik looked around the group, fearing the evident confusion could result in another chaotic dialogue. Before that could happen, Inesh continued:

"Let me give you an example. Suppose you are doing things that are not right in order to get ahead in your job. Krama Yoga has an exercise to help. The mental exercise it would prescribe is for you to try to ignore the fruit of your actions. It tells you to ignore any potential advancement or money you could earn. Doing that makes you more likely to act righteously at work."

Inesh looked at the class. "Figure out what you want to work on, and yoga will have an exercise."

When questions inevitably arose regarding yoga classes in the West, Inesh did not want to answer them—he had said he would not comment on customs in Nepal or elsewhere.

"Not bad," Gatik said to Disha. "No one has ever put this all together for me."

"I agree," Disha responded. "But, as you said, no rules."

It was not a particularly long lecture. Inesh reminded everyone they would have a personal session with Swami Mahindra the next day.

"Remember, you have to ask a question. Swamis guide you to an answer. They don't lecture; they answer questions. Also, make it a good one. Swami Mahindra prefers you ask only one question so you focus on something important."

Gatik and Disha sat with the couple from Argentina at dinner that evening. The couple had found the day fascinating. They liked what they had learned about yoga; it was a surprise. They also felt like they had achieved their goal of immersing themselves in a foreign culture in a way not usually done by tourists.

Disha was not sure that was right. Much of the culture of Nepal she was witnessing seemed to revolve around rituals, not the things they had learned about that day. But she did not say this. She would save those thoughts for her question for Swami Mahindra.

They began discussing recent events in Nepal. The Argentinian couple was surprised to learn that the Maoists had recently come to power. They wanted to know if the elections had been truly free. Gatik assured them that they were and they had been.

"And no one did anything about it?"

"Why should they? The US provided an insignificant amount to try to oppose the Maoists, but no one really cared," Gatik responded. "And why should they? It was the will of the people."

Before returning to their room, Gatik and Disha also spoke to Elisabeth and Tony, who asked about the Dashain festival.

"Strange how they sacrifice animals as part of a national Hindu ritual," Elisabeth said.

"There is a lot of controversy over that," Gatik responded.

"I feel a little guilty about watching it, but how can you not when you are here?" Tony interjected.

"Perhaps we should go together?" Disha offered, and Tony and Elisabeth gladly accepted.

When Gatik and Disha retreated into their room, they spoke briefly about the day's events, but they both had reading to do for school.

"Time to feed the upper chakra," Disha joked.

Disha was reading *Marbury v. Madison*, an early case in which the US Supreme Court decided that the judiciary could review actions by the executive branch. Essentially, the court gave power to itself, which Disha objected to. There was something wrong with that. She put her book down.

"What book are you reading?" Disha asked Gatik.

"It is about a mathematician called Gödel." Gatik knew Disha might not be interested, but could not resist going on. "He developed theorems that mathematics is an incomplete set of principles."

Disha, of course, knew Gatik would not want to leave it at that.

"Dare I ask?" she said with an appreciative smile. She did, after all, love this side of Gatik.

"Not sure I understand it. His first theorem says that any formal system, like math, contains statements that cannot be proven within the system, making the system incomplete," Gatik responded.

"Pretty dense," Disha said.

"Yes, and I have not even gotten to his second theorem. It says that any system cannot prove its own consistency; doing so would require a perspective from outside the system, making it incomplete."

"Well, if you can't find consistency in math, where can you find it?" Disha said.

"Pretty confusing," Gatik responded.

5. Chitavake

Chitavake did not go to work the next day since he was attending the Dashain festival. He spent the early morning hours sitting in the living room, thinking about his life. It was unusual. Chitavake was a man of action, not contemplation.

Why does Gatik resist joining me? His life could be so much easier here. He is so principled. He should take advantage of the best opportunity offered to him. That is what I would do. But not him. I wish I had raised him differently.

Then, his concerns turned to fear.

Maybe he is not a fool. Maybe he has figured out some things. Perhaps he knows about my past. I doubt it. Not even Hitu knows the whole story.

Chitavake provided Gatik and Bira with all they could ever want. They'd had an upbringing without worry, with a good education, and without tragedy—a better upbringing than his own.

Could they not see that? I worked hard for them. I worked my way up in the party. Defeating the king, a god. The movement gave me opportunities, but pursuing them was hard work.

Then Chitavake thought about his relationship with Hitu. She had taken the ebbs and flows of his career well. After the Maoist party came to power, it lost it again. He had become a businessman. Then, when the party reconstituted itself, it regained power. Now, he was an important man, but his wife was no happier.

Why was she distant? Indifferent. She is like Bira and Gatik. Disrespectful really.

Hitu cared about him as a person. When he was depressed, she had supported him. She comforted him when he woke up from a nightmare in the middle of the night. He was still haunted by the look in the eyes of the second officer whom he had killed.

But why did she not show pride in what he had achieved? Did she suspect something?

Hoping to distract himself, Chitavake went outside and watched kites flying in the sky. It was October, and kite flying, Nepal's national sport, was at its height. The winds were strong. The aim of a kite flying contest was to knock the other kites out of the sky. He and his friends played it in their youth, but he did not like the adversarial nature of the game.

"It just creates animosity. Why fight when you don't have to?" he used to say, and the other kids would make fun of him.

"I avoided confrontation from a young age," Chitavake thought. He tried to take some pride in that, pride in the pragmatism that had ruled his life.

I always got things done. That is what counts.

He looked around his garden and up at the gleaming white facade of his large house. He had come so far from the village he grew up in.

As he was taking pride in his accomplishments, Hitu came home full of energy.

"Gatik and Disha will stay with us the night before and after the Dashain dinner," she said excitedly when she saw Chitavake. "I think Disha persuaded Gatik. I have a lot to do."

Chitavake was happy they were coming. It was a good sign. Was Gatik reconnecting?

Hitu went into the kitchen to work on her shopping list. The dinner had taken on a new importance, and she wanted to make a variety of dishes that her son liked.

Chitavake remained in the backyard for a few more moments. He saw one of the kites knock down another. He shrugged his shoulders. "What a waste."

Then he went inside to put on a tie. He struggled, having only recently learned how to tie it. As a Maoist, he never wore one. He asked Hitu to help.

"Hurry; the motorcade is already outside to take us to Durbar Square," he said when Hitu also struggled.

"I don't like these events," Hitu said.

They had never gone before. It was a Hindu custom, and the Maoist party had fought the custom. Hitu hated the slaying of animals. Chitavake insisted they go. Now that the Maoists were in charge, their senior politicians were expected to be there.

6. Swami Mahindra

While Chitavake and Hitu spoke about the dinner, Gatik headed to the building at the ashram across the courtyard. As he made his way, he could see the kites in the sky. He had never flown kites; debate had been his thing until he became disenchanted with arguing both sides.

In the room, all the chairs had been moved to one side. Swami Mahindra was sitting on a big pillow in front of the room, and a smaller pillow was placed at a suitable distance. Gatik sat on it awkwardly, shifting around and forcing a smile.

Swami Mahindra wore a simple white robe, not what Gatik had imagined. She introduced herself without trying to assume any authority. She said that she knew Gatik's father and quickly got started. "I am here to answer your question," she said.

Gatik started to formulate his question.

"I am not particularly religious. My girlfriend Disha is, to some extent, and I want to be, but I can't quite figure out how. It seems too abstract to me. There are no rights and wrongs, no concrete rules about how to lead a life.

"I don't believe that you are not spiritual; I understand you have resisted the easy road with your father. That independence and determination must come from somewhere." Swami Mahindra smiled and continued. "Your question is, of course, a good one, maybe even one of the most important. How spiritual should one become? Do you know the Brahmavar Upanishad?"

"Yes, I heard it from my mother many times."

The Upanishad started with a great monster enclosing all the waters of the universe. As a result, there was a drought. A man called Indra had a box full of lightning bolts, and he figured out that he could use them to defeat the monster. When he did, he made the waters flow again. With this power, he became a hero. So he hired the master builder Tekton to build him a palace worthy of this status. However, whenever Indra inspected it, he said it was not big enough.

Tekton finally went to Brahma, the creator god, and complained that his entire life was going to be consumed with building Indra's palace since Indra was never satisfied.

Brahma said he would fix it. He woke Vishnu, who took the form of a blue-skinned boy and went to the palace. Indra was intrigued and invited the boy in. The boy told him he had heard that Indra was building a palace unlike any Indra before him had ever built. Indra, in astonishment, asked, 'Indras before me? I thought I was the only one.' The boy noticed an army of ants on the palace floor, pointed to them, and said, 'Former Indras, all of them.'

"What do you think the Upanishad is about?" Swami Mahindra asked.

"The palace was a fleeting undertaking. Indra ended up building it and released Tekton. Then, he decided that since the material world was fleeting, he should become a yogi and meditate at the feet of Vishnu. Right?" Gatik said.

"Correct, but the best part is the last. Indra's wife, Indrani, was upset about Indra's decision. She wanted her husband back. So she went to a priest, who promised to solve that problem. The priest told Indra that he had penned a sacred text some time ago, and in it, the position of the philosopher king, a manifestation of Brahma, was for him, Indra. Indra understood. He became a compassionate husband and king."

Swami Mahindra paused.

"I did not know that part," Gatik admitted.

"It is the most important part, and it is often ignored. The story's point is that Indra should not go to extremes, whether building palaces or practicing meditation. The Upanishad teaches us that making compromises in our lives is acceptable. We should neither be the selfish material Indra who drives Tekton crazy nor the meditating yogi at the foot of Vishnu who neglects his wife and family. Find your balance; continue the path of your spirituality. There is no need to go to extremes."

"No need to go all out," Gatik confirmed.

"Right," Swami Mahindra said.

"I understand, but in the end, isn't compromising like that a way of avoiding an answer? A cop out, when one does not want to decide which of two choices is better."

Swami Mahindra's face dropped. She had not answered his question satisfactorily. Gatik moved uncomfortably on his pillow. He concluded he was not going to get a better answer from Swami Mahindra for his question.

"I know I was supposed to ask only one question, but I have another one," Gatik said.

"Go ahead," Swami Mahindra responded. She was hoping to help Gatik better on his second question.

"One issue has held me and, frankly, my father back from Hinduism. I wonder if you could shed some light on it."

"What is it?"

"Hinduism's reluctance to change, to adapt. The caste system. Dharma and karma perpetuate it. You know, all that."

"What is your question?" Swami Mahindra knew what Gatik was talking about, but took refuge in the rules of dialogue with a swami to gain some time.

"Here is my question. How can I believe in something that has caused so much misery?"

"You don't know if it caused misery. Did you ever think that maybe people were more content back then?"

Swami Mahindra had no defenses for "the dangerous formula," so she tried an easy way out.

"People might have been more content knowing their life was their dharma," she said.

"That is the point, though," Gatik retorted, unsatisfied. He started slowly getting up from his pillow with respect, but also with determination. "That is what I am struggling with. The vagueness and the insistence on the status quo."

He left the room while Swami Mahindra was struggling. What could she have said? He was eager to become more spiritual, but his objections remained unanswered.

Disha was sitting outside waiting for her time with Swami Mahindra. She could tell that Gatik was not happy. "Are you okay? What happened? I can skip my session."

"We can talk later. Go see her."

"Are you sure?" Disha asked.

"Yes, maybe you can get something out of her."

So Disha entered the room. Swami Mahindra was still in thought. Disha approached softly, wondering if Swami Mahindra was upset about what just happened with Gatik. Disha sat on the pillow in front of the swami.

Swami Mahindra straightened out. "What question do you have?"

Disha's primary concern was with traditions. Hinduism followed them. Followed rituals. Why were these rituals so important, yet different in different countries?

"If traditions are different in different countries and change, can they prove to be wrong?" she asked.

"You have a good perspective," Swami Mahindra said with a smile. She could tell that Gatik and Disha were much alike.

"Yes, they can be wrong. For example, I was frustrated that we had capital punishment in Nepal for a long time. How could that be? We are a Hindu country that used to be ruled by a king who was an incarnation of Vishnu. Recently, we got rid of it," Swami Mahindra said.

"So traditions could prove wrong!" Disha insisted.

"I suppose, though I hope core values don't."

Swami Mahindra raised her hand before Disha could say what she thought she might.

"I realize this is not a satisfying answer. To retreat to some core that may not change, but that is all I can say."

Swami Mahindra was a little afraid she was failing with Disha as well.

"I do have a second question," Disha said apologetically before Swami Mahindra could nuance her answer.

"Go ahead," she said. She had allowed Gatik that privilege and was again hoping to do better on the second question.

"Why did you become a swami? With all due respect, if things change, how can you be dogmatic if you know that some things may prove wrong?"

Swami Mahindra had not gotten that question before. She looked at Disha earnestly and answered slowly. "I considered three paths. One path was to be a mother living in everyday struggles. It involves selflessly sacrificing oneself so that one's children do well. You must have a good sense of community for that. A second path is to be a leader in your community. It involves selflessly moving society in the right direction. You must be charitable to do it well. A third path is to be a spiritual leader. It involves selflessly guiding souls to higher states. You can do well or poorly in any of these paths. No path is superior. I decided I could do the best job in the last path."

It was not the answer Disha expected.

"On that point, I would like to see Gatik again," Swami Mahindra said. "I don't think I have done a good job guiding him."

The meeting ended. Disha did not like Swami Mahindra's response to her first question, but she loved Swami Mahindra's answer about the three paths of life. They all had an element of selflessness, and they had learned that to be a core value.

When she caught up with Gatik, they briefly discussed their meetings.

"Maybe Hinduism survives because it is vague," Disha said. "Maybe we are chasing a ghost."

"Or maybe we are demanding too much," Gatik responded.

7. Durbar Square

When Disha and Gatik arrived at Durbar Square for the Dashain Festival, they were surprised by the significant police presence. It took them a while to go from where the taxi dropped them off to where they could see the bulls. The bulls were tied to stakes in the center of the square, inside a wide circle. They were to be dragged around that circle after they were killed. Spectators, now lined up a safe distance outside the circle, would then be allowed to collect some of the bulls' blood.

A stand for political dignitaries stood at one end of the square. Gatik wanted to be far away from it so his presence would not be awkward for his parents.

"Still feel guilty about being a spectator to the sacrifice?" Gatik asked Tony when they met up with him and Elizabeth.

"A little, but if it is for the right intentions . . ." Tony tried to make light of the question by playing to religious overtones.

As the officials filled the stand, Elisabeth asked who Gatik's father was. Gatik reluctantly pointed him out. It was easy; he was the tallest one on the stand. Elisabeth sensed that she should not ask any further questions.

"How was your meeting with Mahindra?" Elizabeth asked Disha instead.

"She told me why she became a swami. She said you must be selfless and consider what you are good at. You should only be a swami if you think you would be good at it. A surprising answer. She did not claim superior knowledge or anything of the kind. Humble and selfless. I liked it."

"My meeting was not that interesting. I asked her about how Hinduism develops new thoughts. Like how they can abandon the caste system or take a position on abortion. She did not have a good answer."

"I think that is generally an issue, you know. Gatik and I had hoped for more." Disha said.

"It is why we came to the ashram," Gatik interjected.

"Well, Mahindra wants to see you again, Gatik," Disha said.

"She does?" Gatik was surprised.

"She said she did not do a good job with you and wants to see you again."

"Great," Gatik said and focused on the festival.

"It is about to start," he said.

They saw one of the heads of a local temple step up to a bull with a saber.

"I think it is getting serious," Tony said.

Then, the priest put the saber under the throat of the bull. Gatik wanted to see the priest's eyes. Would he mind? Would he have a hard time doing what he was about to do? Unfortunately, the priest was too far away. Still, with the grandiose gesture with which he slit the throat of the bull, it seemed he did not mind.

The ox immediately fell to the ground. The priest had to jump out of the way to avoid being buried by it. The sound of the bull falling was something the crowd would not forget. It was a surprisingly loud, deep, hollow sound coming from a now limp, malleable object. Blood spewed out of the ox's throat and seemingly every other crevice.

The crowd wanted to commiserate, but that would negate the sacred nature of what just happened. Instead, they cheered. However, they cheered as though they were telling a lie - reluctantly, half-heartedly.

Disha was glad it was over. She regretted coming, as did Tony and Elizabeth.

The bull was then dragged in a circle, and the crowd started cheering more earnestly. Why not celebrate what could not be changed? Spectators began to collect blood from the bull in the containers they brought.

As that was happening, a commotion started around the dignitary stand. Gatik could not make out what it was. There was a lot of noise and screaming, first from the spectators, then from those on the stand. The screaming was one of fear, perhaps even in some cases, of pain. It was loud and grew to come from every direction. Police officers from all over the square began rushing to the stand. The crowd tried to head the other way to escape the square. A general panic ensued.

Gatik was sure something serious had happened. However, he could not figure out what it was. Some spectators appeared to have rushed the stand.

"Stay here. I will go and see if my parents are OK," Gatik yelled back at Disha as he started pushing his way against the crowd toward the stand. It was dangerous against the panicked crowd. Several times, Gatik was almost knocked over.

As he was pushing forward, he worried about his parents. Did something happen to them? What? "If the next person I pass wears orange, nothing will have happened to them," Gatik thought. It was the superstitious game he played when uncertain, uncontrollable things happened in his life.

The next person was not wearing orange.

"If the next person I pass wears blue, it will still be OK."

The next person was wearing blue, but did he see it in the corner of his eyes and cheat?

Gatik kept on playing that game until he got to the stand. Police officers barred his entry. However, he could see that the stand was empty. All the dignitaries, including his parents, were gone. The only thing left behind was blood. There was blood everywhere. Gatik had never seen so much blood. The entire stand and all the seats were almost completely drenched. In some places it was smeared, and in others it was in deep puddles.

"Let me through; my parents were there," Gatik pleaded with the officers, but they would not.

"What happened?" he asked, but the officers did not know. "You have to clear the area," they insisted.

Gatik had no choice but to go back to Disha. Tony and Elisabeth had left with the crowd.

"Are your parents alright? What happened?" Disha asked.

"I don't know. There was a lot of blood. I have never seen so much blood. The police would not let me through. They could not tell me anything." Gatik said.

Disha tried to comfort him, but Gatik ignored it. "We have to make our way back to my parents' house," he said.

That took a long time. The streets were full of people escaping the festival. Some ad hoc demonstrations sprang up, encouraged by what happened at the square.

Gatik started playing that game again.

"If the next car is white," and so on. It was a superstitious, silly game. He knew that. He had realized that long ago, but he could not stop.

"If the next car is red.."

They finally arrived at Gatik's parents' house and saw a police car stationed in front of the gates to the courtyard. Was this a good or bad sign?

Once they got through, they found Hitu in the living room with blood on her dress, clearly shaken. "I am fine. We are fine," she said in a broken voice. "Shanti, Shanti, Shanti." Gatik hugged her.

"Where is Dad?" he asked.

"He is in the study. He is fine," Hitu responded.

"It was scary. These spectators ran towards the stand and threw blood on us. We did not know what was happening or how bad it might get. You should have seen the faces of the attackers. They were so angry. They were shouting about how the blood should cleanse the government. Weird stuff. Such angry faces. Shanti, Shanti, Shanti."

"I am glad you are all right. Horrible. Absolutely horrible," Gatik said. It was his time to be shocked.

"How could they do this?"

"I can't imagine what you must have gone through," Disha added.

They heard Chitavake in his study yelling at someone on the phone at the top of his voice.

"This is a disaster," he screamed. "This never happened when the others were in charge."

After a while, he came to the living room.

"I am sorry about this," he said. "The police tell me it was opposition radicals. Two of them were apprehended."

Then the phone rang, and he went into his study again.

Disha and Gatik sat quietly with Hitu. She clasped her hands together and loosened them again and again, nervously shaking her head. "It has always been like this. Always some violence on both sides. At times, it was worse, a lot worse. People died. Ambushes, bombings, shootings; it was terrible. I had hoped it was over."

Chitavake returned, and Hitu gave him one of those accusing looks that are hard to respond to. Gatik, sitting next to Hitu, also looked up at him with the same look. They were upset.

Chitavake had been trying to hide how shaken he was by the incident, but he was tired and gave up. He had never felt so exhausted. Once again, his family was not behind him. Gatik had never respected him for his struggle. His wife did not support his cause. He could not stand it anymore. Why could they not appreciate what he was trying to do? Why were they blaming him?

He sat down next to Gatik, looking at the floor. The phone rang again, but this time, he ignored it.

"I have to try another approach with Gatik," he thought, or lose him forever.

"In a way, the perpetrators were right," Chitvake started. "When they threw their containers of blood, they shouted that all should see the blood we had on our hands. They had no way of knowing, but it is true in my case. I do have blood on my hands."

Chitavake was ready to confess. Hitu shook her head, looking at him, trying to stop him. They had agreed not to tell the children. But Chitavake would not, could not stop. He looked at his hands and continued. "These hands have killed."

Then he looked Gatik straight in the eyes. "Thirty years ago, I killed two army officers at point-blank range. I led an attack on an army barracks, found them in a building, and shot them. I have lived with this ever since. I killed. I did."

"That is enough," Hitu said firmly. "Enough!"

Chitavake continued his plea. "I am sorry I never told you. I didn't want you to grow up knowing what I had done. I was afraid, but also concerned for you."

Gatik put his arm around his father. He was overcome with compassion for him. How could he not be?

"Maybe this is the way to reconnect with Gatik; it seems to be working," Chitavake thought.

They sat there for a while, looking at the floor. Chitavake thought about other things he could share. But he decided against it. Gatik couldn't handle that. Hitu probably couldn't. He still had not told her.

Chitvake and Gatik finally looked at each other briefly, and Gatik decided he needed some time alone. There was a lot to make sense of. He told Disha that they should go for a walk. He was concerned about her. She did not need to witness all this. She was not part of the family.

They passed the police car and the guard as they left and walked into the open streets of Kathmandu. Disha wanted to comfort Gatik, but he had rejected that before, and she felt it was not her place to say anything. These were deep family matters. They walked for a while down a quieter street of the neighborhood before Gatik opened up.

"I can't believe it. Now he tells us."

"It is good that it is out," Disha said.

"Is it? Maybe I preferred not knowing. I suppose I should not be surprised."

Thoughts continued to race through his head. How was he going to handle this? What relationship would he have with his father, knowing this about him? What would they say when they saw each other next?

Disha had thoughts of her own. She was thinking about her relationship with Gatik. She did not need to be part of this. They had not committed to each other. Should she walk away? She loved Gatik, but this was a serious matter that was not easily resolved. There was so much drama, so much baggage.

"Your father confessed, and it was long ago," Disha finally said.

"It is not that easy, is it?" Gatik said, almost accusing Disha.

"You are tough," Disha said.

"You think he should just be forgiven?" Gatik asked. He had thought about it. Killings happened, but something about his father doing it bothered him.

"Not what I mean. You are tough and can handle it," Disha said. "Give it time."

When they finally returned home, Bira had arrived.

She was in the study with Chitavake. She was yelling at him.

"You finally tell us. Don't you think we suspected this?" Bira yelled.

Chitavake responded in a soft voice, too soft to make out.

"It is not what you did; it is the hiding and the pride for the good of the country, no regret…" They could make out Bira yelling.

Hitu retreated into the garden, afraid that her family was coming undone.

Gatik and Disha went to Gatik's room. They could not listen anymore. They had agreed to stay the night. Any change from that would have been interpreted as a sign of disapproval. Bira stayed as well, primarily out of concern that the streets were unsafe given the demonstrations.

The next morning, they all gathered for breakfast.

"I have arranged for you to see Officer Rai," Chitavake said matter-of-factly when he entered the room. He had regained his composure. "You remember him. He was at our house for dinner a few times when you were growing up."

Bira had asked her father if there was someone they could talk to to gain some perspective. Chitavake thought of Officer Rai.

"I called him. He has time for you today. He is the best person I can think of to help you think through this, Bira. He knows what it was like. He is a good man. Gatik and Disha, you can, of course, go as well."

It was the first that Gatik heard about this; he felt railroaded. Disha also did not belong in such a discussion, but he could not leave her alone with his parents.

"We will go," Gatik said reluctantly.

"OK, that is settled then," Hitu said. "Now, tonight is the Dashain dinner. I don't want to talk about this. It all happened a long time ago. You will have your talk with Officer Rai. Let's enjoy the dinner. That is our tradition, a time to celebrate as a family."

No one said anything. Gatik nodded lightly, not sure if he should agree. Disha was relieved that it was not her place to react. Bira stared at her mother and reluctantly produced a nod. Chitavake blew out a sigh of relief; he did not want to talk about the past anymore.

Bira drove them to police headquarters. No one talked on the drive over. It was the type of silence that, if broken, would almost feel irreverent to the gravity of the situation or the people going through it.

When they arrived, to their surprise, they were ushered to the top floor of the building, where only the most senior officers sat. Officer Rai had been recently promoted. Usually, he would not have come to work on the day of the Dashain dinner, but he had agreed to lead the investigation into the Durbar Square incident.

Officer Rai was sitting behind a desk full of files and papers. He had a sign with "Officer Prashant Rai" on the front of his desk. It was a desk sign from when he did not have his own office. It was unnecessary, but it demanded respect.

He rose to greet them with a big smile. "Bira, Gatik. It has been a long time. You must have been five or ten when I saw you last. It is nice to see you. It is also nice to meet you, Disha. Welcome."

"We appreciate you taking the time," Bira responded and paused. Then she smiled awkwardly and said, "You know why we are here, don't you?"

"Officially, no, but unofficially, yes." Officer Rai knew that —theoretically, at least—Chitavake could still be prosecuted for his actions. "Our country had a difficult recent past. Many of us don't know how to deal with it. We are not set up to deal with change."

"True," Bira said. "We are hoping you can share some specifics with us so we can better understand what happened."

"I think the specifics are clear. There were killings on both sides. Your father sent you here because we were both part of the struggle on both sides. Your father was in the Maoist movement; I was in the police force."

The room became quiet. Bira, Gatik, and Disha could not help but wonder if Officer Rai had also killed. To break the silence, Gatik said, "You mean opposite sides, not on both sides. You were on opposite sides." It was the only thing he could think of right then and there.

"Yes, of course." Officer Rai said, a little shocked, too shocked for just a wording slip. Gatik noticed it.

"The problem is that most of us on both sides—and I do mean on both sides—don't know how to resolve the struggle with the past. The only way to end a struggle with the past is forgiveness. That is our only option, forgiveness."

"An interesting perspective, especially coming from a police officer. I mean, from someone who enforces the laws, pursues the misdeeds of the past," Bira said, slightly perturbed. "But we came here to get some details and perspective on why it happened the way it did. Why did my father have to kill? Can you tell us that?"

"It was an incredibly tense time. Things escalated. Neither side needed to kill, but both sides did. That is the truth. The Maoists did not have a way to force change without causing disruption. They felt their uprisings were the only way for them to be heard. At times, with some extreme factions, it got out of hand. The royalists saw the uprisings as illegal—treasonous, really. The movement was a threat to our king and god. So their extremists also did terrible things."

"So you fought on opposite sides, yet you are friends with my father?" Bira asked.

"Yes," Officer Rai said. "It is not easy, but parties at odds must reconcile. It is the only way to break the cycle of retribution. That is what happened at Durbar Square—retribution. It will keep happening, but less and less. It has already subsided, to a certain extent; no one was seriously injured in this incident. Eventually, we will find peace."

"But you already have made peace, I mean. You became a good friend of my father early on, years ago, a long time ago, when you came to our house." Gatik said.

"Yes," Officer Rai responded, a little taken aback. He was not sure where Gatik was headed. There was another pause. Gatik could not put his finger on it, but something was off about Officer Rai and his relationship with his father. Why were they such good friends if they were on opposite sides? He did not trust him.

"Well, you have given us a lot to think about," Gatik said, giving up. He looked at Bira.

"But I wanted to gain a fuller perspective. Is that it? Killing had to occur?" Bira asked, a little frustrated.

Officer Rai looked at her and opened his hands in despair.

"I am afraid there is not much more I can say."

Bira got up. "Well, thank you," she said.

As she, Gatik, and Disha were leaving, Officer Rai stopped them.

"You remember my son, Sajit?"

"Yes, of course," Gatik said with a smile.

"He is having his bratabandha tomorrow; you should all come," Officer Rai said. He was glad to have found something to soften the tone at the end of their meeting.

"I remember him when he was quite young," Gatik said. "Will Kumar be there?" Kumar was Officer Rai's adopted son. He was much older than Sajit. Kumar had gone to school with Gatik. They were friends.

"Of course," Officer Rai responded.

"Your parents are coming as well," Officer Rai continued. "Despite all that has happened."

"A bratabandha is a Nepalese coming-of-age ceremony for boys," Gatik explained to Disha. He turned to Officer Rai. "We look forward to it."

8. Dashain Dinner

At the Dashain dinner that evening, everyone was on their best behavior, as Hitu had requested.

"No serious discussions," Hitu reminded everyone. Normally, she would have welcomed such discussions, but she was afraid it would end like the evening before.

"Fine with me," Chitavake said, though he was unsure what they would talk about.

"We can speak about Gatik's debate days," Bira said, teasing Gatik. "How he liked to dress in a suit."

"Or about your many boyfriends," Gatik teased back.

Hitu liked the lighter tone, even though it was contrived. She pulled out a photo album of a family vacation to the US.

"Who would have thought Gatik might end up there?" she said as she leafed through it briefly. "Look at these," she said to Bira and Gatik.

"I want to see," Disha said.

Gatik sat back, unsure he wanted to participate in a further display of his childhood in front of Disha.

"He looks so young," Disha said.

"Don't let that fool you," Bira responded. "He was never young."

Disha saw the usual tourist photos, including Gatik and Bira in front of the Statue of Liberty, as well as other sights, along with photos of them in hotel swimming pools.

Then there was a picture of a dinner. "Gatik with a tie, cute," Disha said. "He did like to dress up," Hitu commented.

"Do I have to endure this?" Gatik said.

"I think that is why he liked debate," Bira said.

"You liked your dresses," Gatik defended himself.

Hitu finally turned to Disha. "Have you had enough of us yet?"

"Oh, no. I am happy I came," Disha said.

She regretted the words as soon as they were out of her mouth. She was becoming complicit in the strange charade Hitu insisted on. How could they all continue to pretend that nothing was wrong? Yes, they all hoped they could move forward. But this was not dealing with what had happened; it was a total disregard for it.

Gatik understood what Disha must be feeling. He saw it on her face. It was contorted - not subconsciously but intentionally. Everyone noticed it, and the room became quiet. Gatik asked if Disha and he could be excused. They went to the living room.

"I know what you must be thinking," Gatik said.

"I need to get away. I need a break," Disha said. Gatik became concerned that he might be losing Disha. He held her arm.

"I understand," Gatik said.

"We could go back to the hotel. My parents won't like it, but . . ." he said when Disha interrupted him with, "Yes, please. Let's do that. Let's please do that."

Gatik agreed. He also needed to get away. He went to tell Hitu.

"No! Why?" Is there something we have done wrong?" Hitu said when Gatik told her.

Gatik said nothing but pleaded with his eyes for her to let it go.

"I understand," Chitavake said. "You need time. It is natural. Remember that you do many things when you fight for a cause. We made the country better. No one has to make such choices anymore."

There it was again, the greatness of the country. The argument that never seemed quite right. But Gatik let it go.

Gatik and Disha took Chitavake's chauffeured car to the hotel; it was the only option available late at night during Dashain. Almost no taxis were on the road. As they left the house, they noticed that the police car was no longer stationed outside. Were things normalizing already?

"I am sorry, Gatik. I know this is about you and your family. It does not involve me, but I felt so uncomfortable," Disha said on their drive to the hotel.

"No, I am sorry you had to experience all this. I would not have come if I had any inkling, and I certainly wouldn't have exposed you to it. I am sorry."

Gatik waited until Disha made eye contact to see if she was OK.

When they got back to the hotel, they went to their room and skipped their usual evening reading for school. As they lay in bed, Gatik raised the topic again. He could not avoid it.

"I have been thinking. The fact that this happened thirty years ago does not mean anything. Time makes us feel better, but it does not dilute guilt. The only way to forgive is to remember that he was a soldier. Soldiers do things."

"Yes, they do," Disha said.

She had also thought about that aspect, but concluded that it was not applicable. She did not want to upset Gatik, but he had raised the subject.

"Soldiers obey orders," she said. "But have you thought about the difference between soldiers and leaders? Leaders devise plans and give orders. No one ordered your father, did they?" Disha immediately regretted it. She shouldn't make it tougher for Gatik.

"You are right, of course," Gatik sighed.

9. Rama

The next morning, Gatik decided to go for a run. "I need to clear my head," he told Disha.

Gatik liked running. It gave him a sense of freedom. He even liked the sweat once it started pearling up and soaking the front of his T-shirt. It usually came before the runner's high, which Gatik refused to believe in. Gatik instead preferred to believe that it was pure joy produced by free fluid movement, not some common physical or chemical reaction.

Gatik started down one of the major avenues. First slowly and then at his regular pace. He did not think much of the police buses amid the sea of traffic. As he settled into a rhythm, he ran to the Garden of Dreams. Perhaps he could find a reprieve there.

Kathamdhu was settling into its routine of chaos with cars hurtling and people dodging in every direction. Gatik realized that the crowded streets were not ideal for running. He diverted onto one of the side streets in a quieter neighborhood.

As he approached the end of one of the streets, where it rejoined with a major avenue, he saw a crowd gathering to watch something. As he got closer, he could see they were watching a demonstration.

The demonstration was about the rural healthcare system. The demonstrators appeared to be university students. They shouted slogans with raised fists: "Health for all! Health for Nepal!"

Gatik read their banners and watched them for a while.

Some demonstrators stood out. One was wearing an orange headband and jumped and shouted so vehemently that sweat had soaked his headband and was now dropping from his forehead. He was spitting out saliva as he was shouting. He did not seem to care. Another wore a cut-off shirt he had painted with slogans. He became so tense that he looked like a ball of muscle about to explode. They were all young university students passionate about their cause.

Gatik noticed that besides their banners, the demonstrators carried signs of Rama. According to the well-known story, the deity Rama's wife, Sita, was abducted by his father, the king. Rama remained peaceful and virtuous, but tried to get Sita back. When he had to cross an ocean to recapture Sita, he prayed to Varuna, the ocean god, for three days to let him cross. It did not work. Deciding that Varuna only respected violence, Rama started shooting arrows to burn up the water. Varuna appeared and apologized for being unable to part the ocean for him. Instead, he urged Rama to build a bridge.

"They must be trying to say that they don't want violence. If it erupts, it will be the police's fault." Gatik thought. Rama stood for non-violence.

Gatik saw the police putting up a line. They did not want the demonstration to get to the prime minister's residence.

"Not good," Gatik thought.

The demonstrators stopped well short of the police line. A few started shouting at the police, but others pulled them back. They tried to focus the demonstration on the crowd that was watching.

Gatik wanted to continue watching, but had to leave. He had a busy day ahead: Sajit's bratabandha, the appointment with Swami Mahindra, and the flight back to the US that afternoon.

As he ran back down the side street, he looked back a few times. He felt newly unsettled—something beyond the distress over his father's past. The image of the two demonstrators kept popping into his head. They were risking everything. They were risking their futures for their cause. They could be blacklisted or worse. They could go to jail. And it was not for themselves. They were doing it to get healthcare for others.

"I have never risked anything for a cause," Gatik thought. "But my father has, hasn't he?"

Then he thought about what his father had achieved. His father did not end up like those demonstrators might.

Gatik stopped in the middle of the street, hands on his knees, panting. He exhaled loudly and slumped.

"That is it," he said out loud. "How could I have missed this?" He beat his thighs with his hands repeatedly. When he caught his breath, he continued, "My father always came out on top! No matter what."

He straightened out and resumed his run with a new understanding powering him.

When he got back to the hotel room, Disha was packing.

"I saw a demonstration, people advocating for better rural healthcare," Gatik told her.

"Were they from the countryside?" Disha asked.

"No, university students, advocating for others," Gatik said.

"Was it violent?"

"Not yet. But the police formed a line to confront them. It looked like it could take a turn for the worse at any moment."

"So they were risking arrest?"

"Yes, and all for their cause, for the good of others. They had nothing to gain. Truly selfless."

10. Chitavake and Prashant

Chitvake was somber as he was being driven to meet Officer Rai for breakfast that morning. He asked him to meet for breakfast when he arranged the meeting for his children.

It was an inconvenience for Officer Rai. He was busy at work. They had just apprehended another perpetrator of the incident at Durbar Square. His son's bratabandha was also that day. Still, he did not want to refuse Chitavake.

They met at a restaurant frequented by the political establishment. It had become popular, even for breakfast, and Chitavake was well-known there. He greeted several guests as he walked in. Officer Rai came in late, apologizing.

"Chitavake, I am sorry. As you can imagine, we are busy right now."

They were friends, but Chitavake was the senior official at the time. Prashant was used to respecting that, though at times, when Chitavake was just a businessman, he had been the more powerful.

"It is good to see you, Prashant. Thanks for taking the time. And thank you for seeing my children."

"You have wonderful children. They care about you."

Prashant did not want to tell Chitavake that he had noticed how they had inquired into the past to figure out if they should really care for him. They seemed skeptical.

"Did you tell them anything I should know about?"

"No. We spoke about reconciliation and forgiveness. I did not tell them I was part of the group with you at the army barracks. They understood me to be a police officer on the other side."

Chitavake lowered his voice. "So nothing slipped out? Nothing about how close we were early on? Given how they reacted to what they've learned so far, they couldn't handle it."

Chitavake and Prashant were the closest of friends during the Jana Andolan uprising. They got to know each other when they trained in the mountains for the attack on the army barracks. After

Chitavake killed the officers at the barracks, it felt natural for him to turn to Prashant to figure out how to deal with it.

"They deserved it, right?" he asked Prashant when they met in the forest after the attack.

"Of course," Prashant said, even though he had his reservations about why Chitavake had killed the second officer, who he knew was a Maoist collaborator. Chitavake suspected this but was glad that Prashant never raised it.

When the Maoists finally came to power, Chitavake and Prashant noticed that they were not true believers. They noticed each other talking more about how this might benefit them rather than how it might benefit the country. However, at first, nothing much happened. The Maoist Party went through four prime ministers, each lasting less than two years, and then the Independent Party appointed a prime minister. It shocked Chitavake and Prashant. What was even more upsetting was when the old NC party gained control less than a year later.

At that time, Chitavake and Prashant devised their plan. They would help each other by being on the opposing side. Prashant would leave the Maoist movement and side fully with the NC Party. That was easy. He was a police officer, and his involvement in the Maoist movement had been kept secret. Chitvake, on the other hand, would remain with the Maoist Party and become even more active. That way, if the Maoist Party was in control, Chitavake would help Prashant, and if the NC Party was in control, Prashant would help Chitavake.

Over the following years, control shifted between the two parties, and their arrangement benefited both. When the NC Party was in charge, Prashant used his influence to help Chitavake in his business ventures. When the Maoist Party was in charge, Chitavake ensured Prashant's career advanced in the police force.

Chitavake never told Hitu about this arrangement. He never told anyone.

"They must never find out," Chitavake repeated.

"If we want real relationships with our children, Chitavake, we must base them on the truth. I know a lot is at stake, but we may have to risk our relationships to gain real ones," Prashant urged. He had done that with Kumar, his adopted son. He told Kumar that his father was killed during the Jana Andolan uprising and that he was part of the attack.

"You always were a little soft," Chitvake responded. "They would not understand all that happened," Chitavake said sternly. "Only fathers can understand the pressure to succeed."

Tea was served, and it became a convenient interruption. When the server left, Chitavake changed the subject. "How is it going with the Durbar Square perpetrators?" he asked.

"We think we apprehended the last one. You probably noticed we pulled the police car away from your house."

"What will happen to them?"

"I don't know. We are meeting with the prosecutors' office this morning. No one was seriously hurt, and their intentions were pure. Intentions matter to the prosecutors. They care about intentions almost more than actions."

Chitavake considered the prosecutors fools, but did not say so. Moreover, the circumstances wore on him enough that he no longer wanted harsh treatment for the perpetrators.

"I hope this gets resolved quickly so we can move on," he said instead.

"What about the security guard at your house?" Prashant asked. "Don't you think you can do away with him now?"

"The letters were pretty specific," Chitavake said. "I am not sure this is over."

"Up to you," Prashant responded. Then, his face lit up.

"I hope to see you at Sajit's bratabandha later today; it should be good," Prashant said enthusiastically.

"I will try to make it," Chitavake said and got up to leave.

Prashant stayed to greet some of the other guests at the restaurant, while Chitvake made his way to the door. He found his driver around the corner from the restaurant. However, when the driver got out to open the door for him, Chitavake told him he would walk home. He was not going to the office given the bratabandha later that day. The driver was surprised. It was a long walk, but Chitavake wanted time alone.

"Is it safe?" the driver asked.

"I am not afraid of crazies," Chitavake said and walked off.

11. Sajit's Bratabandha

Gatik and Disha rushed to Sajit's bratabandha. The ceremony was held in a courtyard Prashant had booked for the event. Gatik knew it well. It was a beautiful square surrounded by a red brick wall with an elaborate water fountain. It was the place used by all the influential families.

"Sajit went to the same school I did. He was a star on the track team, and his brother Kumar did debate with me," Gatik said to Disha as they arrived.

"Did you have your bratabandha here?" Disha asked Gatik.

"I did," Gatik said with a proud smile. He had gotten his mantra then. The one about religious inquiry that he kept a secret, as he was supposed to.

Most of the women wore orange saris. Disha put on an orange scarf. Gatik wore his usual button-down shirt and khakis. He did not bring a blazer for the trip.

A Hindu priest sitting next to the fountain started the ceremony by lighting a small fire. A second priest chanted Vedic verses that no one understood. Sajit sat in a chair near the priest, making offerings and trying to avoid looking at the guests while they were slowly drifting in. He was wearing a yellow headband with porcupine needles.

"The porcupine needles are to ward off evil spirits. Next, they are going to shave his head. It signifies a transition, a new start," Gatik explained. He was getting a little excited about showing all this to Disha. The guests were similarly exhilarated and stared at Sajit. You could overhear them making comments about their bratabandhas. Sajit forced occasional smiles at his parents as they started shaving his head. He hated it, but he knew not to let that show. His parents watched anxiously to ensure Sajit would not embarrass himself or them. He was doing a good job.

They shaved all of Sajit's head except for a tiny patch at the back. After they finished, Sajit put on a bright orange outfit, and the priest used yellow paste to put a tilaka on his forehead. It had vertical lines standing for the lotus feet of Vishnu. Sajit's family was Vaishnavi.

Sajit looked like a monk. A thin white cotton string was finally put around his shoulder.

"That's the janai. It signifies his manhood," Gatik explained.

Disha could not help but think that part of Sajit proving his manhood was him taking all of this with the right demeanor. He looked so strange and uncomfortable after his transformation.

Sajit then sat in front of one of the priests. After a few chants, the priest put a big blanket over his and Sajit's heads.

"This is where he is given instructions on how to be a man in society," Gatik said. "It is done under the blanket so no one can hear what is said."

"And he is given his mantra, right?" Disha said.

"Right," Gatik said, a little surprised that Disha had picked that up somewhere.

"Which mantra do you think Sajit is being given?" Disha asked.

"I don't know. Maybe the Gayatri Mantra.

ॐ भूर्भुवः स्वः तत्सवितुर्वरेण्यं भर्गो देवस्य धीमहि धियो यो नः प्रचोदयात्," Gatik responded reciting it in Sanskrit.

"We meditate on the most auspicious, radiant light of the Divine, which illuminates our intellects," Disha said to Gatik's astonished face.

"Pretty common at my sect back home," she explained.

Gatik smiled. "I guess you don't need me to explain things."

He did not admit that that was his mantra, nor did Disha. Those were the rules.

The crowd quieted down and moved a little closer. Even though they could not hear what Sajit was being told under the blanket, it was always interesting to imagine what was said. When it was done, Gatik joked: "Not a long lecture about manhood, is it?"

Gatik was enjoying himself. The bathrabanda was a much-needed reprieve.

"If you say so," Disha responded.

"Now comes the fun part," Gatik continued.

The crowd moved around Sajit. His parents were allowed to join him. They proudly stood next to him.

Sajit was given a stick with a pouch hanging from it filled with rice. He then paraded around the crowd with the stick over his shoulder as though he were on a journey. Sajit and his father finally carried a big bowl around the crowd. Women made offerings by throwing rice or, in the case of Hitu, large denomination bills into it.

Hitu came over to join Gatik and Disha and encouraged Disha to join.

"Go ahead, Disha," Hitu said. "Women are supposed to tease him."

Sajit seemed to enjoy this part. He smiled when he saw Gatik, but then focused on receiving offerings.

The next time Gatik and Disha saw Sajit, he had changed into an English suit and a Nepali topi, the local traditional hat. He wore a large ornament around his neck. A priest put a red bindi on his forehead.

"He looks like a man now," Disha said.

Sajit was beaming. He sat down in a chair in the center of the celebration. Relatives walked up to him and added more paint to his bindi. Gatik and Disha went to congratulate him.

"I am so glad you came," Sajit said.

"We wouldn't miss it," Gatik responded. "Congratulations! You are a man now."

Gatik and Disha turned away to let other guests congratulate Sajit. They listened to the musicians as they started playing dance music, and Hitu joined them again. She told them that Chitavake intended to make it, but probably got held up. Gatik shrugged as if he'd expected nothing else.

"He is just so busy," Hitu said.

"I am going to find Kumar, Sajit's brother," Gatik said and walked away.

Disha was a little taken aback, but by now, she had gotten to like Hitu and did not mind spending more time with her. They watched Gatik walk away and listened to the music.

Gatik walked around the courtyard for a while, but could not find Kumar. He decided to ask Prashant.

"Thank you for inviting us, and again for speaking to us. I loved seeing Sajit; he is so grown up now. I have not seen Kumar. Do you know where he is?"

"I don't know where he is. We tried several times to call him, but we couldn't reach him," Prashant said.

Prashant looked worried but tried to play the proud, beaming parent instead.

"Is there anything I can do?" Gatik asked.

"No, he is probably stuck in traffic, maybe behind one of those demonstrations," Prashant said.

"You will be returning to the US today, right?" Prashant asked.

"Yes, this afternoon."

"Has the trip clarified things for you?" Prashant asked. "Did your father convince you to come back?"

"Honestly, I still have unresolved questions," Gatik said, a little frustrated.

"Anything I can help with?"

"I don't think this is the place. You should be enjoying the bratabandha."

"No, please go ahead. I don't think we will get another chance to chat," Prashant insisted.

"Well, if you're sure you don't mind," Gaitk said, hesitating a little.

"I want to help," Prashant said.

"The thing is, I always thought that my father was a soldier, and soldiers do all sorts of things, most of which you can't blame them for. But then I was reminded that he was a leader of the Maoist movement, an early hero. He decided what needed to be done to change the country, to better the country—a selfless actor for the greater good. The definition of a hero, right?"

"Yes?" Prashant responded.

"Well, that's the thing. I'm not sure he was. I was never sure how much of a Maoist he really was when I was growing up. You have to admit there's something strange about a true communist becoming so wealthy and running big companies. No matter what was going on over the years, somehow, my father benefited. It's taken me years to figure it out, but that's what always bothered me when he spoke about doing things for the country."

Prashant did not like where this was going. He knew Gatik was right. The arrangement he had made with Chitavake showed how little they both cared about their parties. But he said nothing.

Gatik continued. "Then, when we were in crisis over what he did for the Maoist movement thirty years ago after the incident at Durbar Square, he sent us to you. He sent us to an ex-army officer and NC Party member. You were the person he trusted most with his children. You are one of his best friends."

"I told you that we have reconciled," Prashant said, hoping to stop Gatik's train of thought.

"I am sorry," Gatik said, "but you have been friends for a long time. See, I don't think it was reconciliation. I think it was indifference. My father was never a true believer in the Maoist Party. That is how he became such a close friend of yours."

"Even if that were the case, what does it matter?" Prashant said.

"Oh, it matters. You may be a hero if you kill because you believe it is the only way to serve the greater good. But if you do it without being a believer, you do it for yourself. That, that is unforgivable. It is simply unforgivable. It's murder."

Whether Gatik knew about their arrangement or not, Prashant could see that he knew enough. He did not say anything. He started thinking thoughts similar to the ones Chitavake had a while back.

What relationship will I have with Sajit if he figures things out? Kumar had and now fought him at every chance.

The world became quiet for Gatik as he finally made sense of it all. He considered Prashant's silence to be an indication of him being right. He had nothing more to ask him and started to leave. He turned back as he was walking.

"Thank you for inviting us. Sajit is a great kid."

Then he told Disha he'd meet her at the airport and hurried to his appointment with Swami Mahindra.

12. The Second Mahindra Meeting

Gatik ran up the stairs to the reception desk when he arrived at the ashram. He had little time. "You will meet the swami where you met her before," the apprentice at the reception told him, and Gatik hurried across the courtyard. He waited a minute in front of the door, took a deep breath, and went in.

Swami Mahindra was eating. That was the smell that bothered Gatik when they entered the hall on their first day at the ashram. It still bothered him. It did not belong in a religious place, but he said nothing. He had more important concerns, and he was running out of time.

Swami Mahindra put the food aside, got up from her pillow, and walked toward Gatik. "Thank you for coming. Let's take a walk in the courtyard."

"I appreciate your invitation," Gatik responded, following the swami outside, finally catching his breath. "It is always an honor to speak to you."

"I did not do a good job answering your questions," Swami Mahindra said, stopping Gatik. She looked at the ground for a minute and then straight at Gatik. Gatik was not sure where this could lead.

"I was too defensive about Hinduism. You are correct: our religion is focused on customs and is resistant to change. Religions are not perfect." Swami Mahindra paused.

"Please don't get me wrong," Gatik said, interrupting her, "I think religion helps us. I just wish Hinduism had more rules, rights, and wrongs and was not so vague. Disha feels the same way," Gatik said.

"Well, I am asking you to accept religion despite what you don't like about it. Don't dispose of it just because it is not perfect for you," the swami said with conviction.

"I understand, but mixing and matching what you like seems ambiguous and arbitrary. You know, it negates the guidance one wants. Can I choose certain parts and not others? Should I choose what I like and not what I don't?" Gatik asked.

"I believe individuals will get lost if they search for truth on their own. They need context and help. They need guardrails. But I am biased. I am supposed to provide those. You, Gatik, want to challenge your faith before you follow it. You ask questions and don't easily accept answers."

Gatik was astonished at the candor of the swami.

"For you, the challenge will be to accept and build on some truths. Instead of the whole, focus on the parts that work for you."

Swami Mahindra started walking again.

"This sounds a little like Descartes. Give me a point I can place my lever on, and I can lift the world and all that," Gatik said, not meaning to make light of the swami's comments. It was just a striking similarity.

"I suppose, though I never really understood that. I think this is different," Swami Mahindra said. "Look, there are aspects of Hinduism you like that you find helpful, right?"

"Yes."

"Well, start with that, and consider this a journey."

Gatik stopped walking this time and pushed some pebbles on the ground into a tiny pile with his feet.

"I have a lot of respect for the faith. I just," Gatik said and stopped talking. He stood still for a minute. Swami Mahindra looked at him kindly, ready to accept whatever he was about to say. Gatik dropped his shoulders and stared at Swami Mahindra. He exhibited an intensity and calmness that signified he was about to say something important to him.

"I have recently learned that beliefs are important. You must believe in something to provide purpose, or you are just out for yourself. Your actions become selfish. You must believe in the greater good and anchor your actions in that. I want to focus on that. It is important."

"I will not ask about what happened, but I am glad," Swami Mahindra said. "Start with that. Just don't tell anyone I told you Hinduism wasn't perfect."

They both laughed.

13. A Final Homecoming

There was one more thing Gatik wanted to do before he left for the airport. He wanted to go to his room at his parents' house and properly move on. He was unlikely to return for a long time and wanted a transition. It was going to be a private moving-on ceremony. He wanted to sit on his bed, the bed he had lain on so often, thinking about things when he was growing up, and say goodbye to his youth.

When he arrived at his parents' house, he waved to the security guard and entered the front door. As soon as he did, he could hear noises coming from his parents' bedroom. That was strange. A heated conversation was taking place in the bedroom. Was he supposed to ignore it? Was it private? How could he? It was loud and agitated. Something was wrong.

Gatik went upstairs to figure out what was happening, stopping in front of the bedroom door to listen.

"You didn't have to do it," he heard a man, not his father, shout in an agitated way. "You bastard,"

Then he heard his father say, "Calm down." Chitavake was scared. One could hear it in his voice.

Gatik knocked. "Is everything OK?"

There was silence.

"That is only Gatik," he heard his father say. You remember him." He was still trying to calm the other person down.

"Come in," the other person commanded.

Gatik entered and saw Kumar, Prashant's older son, pointing a gun at him.

"Come in," Kumar commanded.

"What is going on?" Gatik said, now trying to calm things down.

"Close the door behind you," Kumar said and pointed the gun back at Chitavake.

"You might as well hear this," Kumar then said. It relaxed Chitavake a little. There were things to talk about. This could prolong things and calm them down. He also knew that Prashant respected Gatik.

"Hear what?" Gatik said.

"You tell him," Kumar commanded Chitavake.

"Kumar, like you, asked about things from long ago. You see, his father was an officer at the army barracks that a group of us stormed."

"Tell him the whole story," Kumar said, now sobbing. He looked like he was ready to do something he might regret. "Tell him the whole story," he screamed.

"Well, his father supposedly was a collaborator with us, even though he was an officer at the army barracks. In all the confusion, he was shot."

"Shot, shot, shot by whom! Tell him, or I swear, I will finish this right now."

"OK, OK. I will tell him. My part of the plan was to storm the officers' quarters, and yes, Kumar's father was there, and yes, I shot him."

Chitavake turned to Kumar. "Have you had enough?"

Kumar was agitated even more by this. "Enough?"

He turned to Gatik. "He shot my father, even though my father was a collaborator with them. He shot him even though he was on their side. He shot him even though he did not have to."

"What does it matter what side he was on?" Chitavake said.

"It matters," Kumar screamed. "It matters, it is all that matters!"

Kumar turned to Gatik.

"He does not even get it. It is not the act; it is the intention behind it. Who does such a thing? Who kills the person on their side?" Kumar said to Gatik and lowered his shoulders. The gun went a little limp in his hand, but not limp enough.

"Someone who does not have a side," Gatik said. "That is who does such a thing."

Chitavake perked up. He thought the dialogue could calm Kumar down, even though it was about his shortcomings.

"Someone who has no beliefs does this," Gatik said.

Gatik looked at his father while he accused him, but Chitavake did not care. He just wanted to get out of the situation.

Then Gatik looked at Kumar. "If he lowers the gun, it will be over," he thought, playing his mind game. But was this superstition or reality? Kumar lowered the gun slightly.

"Doing this won't solve anything," Gatik said. "Doing something to my father will have no impact. It won't further anything. It will kill someone who has no purpose. All it will do is hurt you and ruin your life, Kumar."

Kumar raised the gun again.

"He is so evil," Kumar said.

"No, he is not. To be evil, you must have a cause."

Gatik turned to his father and looked straight at him again.

"He has no cause."

Chitavake was becoming more hopeful that the situation might be resolved.

"If you leave now, I will forget all about this," Chitavake said. "I swear."

"He doesn't want all this to get out," Gatik said. "Trust me, he doesn't."

Kumar lowered his gun again, but then he raised it.

"You did not have to do it," he said now, fully sobbing, but he said it in a way as though he had changed his mind.

Then he lowered his gun, looked at Gatik, and said nothing. He dropped his shoulders and stared at the ground. He was thinking.

"It won't solve anything," Gatik reiterated softly.

Kumar did not look at them. He stared at the ground, but then he started moving slowly toward the door.

"You did not have to do it," he said dejectedly, leaving the room.

Gatik and Chitavake stood in the bedroom for a while, still in shock.

"Don't follow him," Chitavake said. "You don't know what he will do."

Chitavake said it with the pretense that he knew how to deal with these situations, and Gatik did not. Gatik noticed it. There was no compassion or remorse.

"How did he get in here anyway?" Gatik asked.

"The guard let him in. We know him. He is Prashant's son. He has been here many times." Chitavake said. "We had no idea he was the one who wrote the letters."

Chitavake paused and shook his head.

"I told Prashant not to adopt him."

"You fault him for that?"

"Things happen. Prashant never really understood that."

Gatik shook his head this time and wanted to say something, but Chitavake waved his hand to stop him. He stretched his neck to listen to see if Kumar was still around. It was quiet in the house. They waited for a while longer.

"I think we are safe now," Chitavake finally said.

Then, before Gatik could say anything, he continued.

"And let's not tell anyone about this. Can you promise me that?"

It was the type of solution Gatik knew his father would choose. He lowered his head, said nothing, and started to leave the room.

"Can you promise me that?" Chitavake insisted again, but Gatik left. He went to his bedroom and sat on his bed.

"What a strange person my father is," Gatik thought. "Unprincipled. Only concerned about the future. Strange how I never really figured that out before."

He stared at the painting of the scorpion and the turtle hanging on the wall opposite his bed. He got up and took the painting off the wall. He noticed that the wall behind the painting, where it had hung, was a slightly different color. The painting had hung there for a long time. The room looked strange with the spot instead of the painting. He put the painting in a plastic bag to take with him.

"At least the scorpion had character, even if he drowned when he stung the turtle," Gatik said to himself.

He sat on his bed for a while. He needed to lead a different life from his father. That he was sure of.

Gatik took one last look at his room, with its empty spot on the wall. A calmness came over him. It was the calmness from having resolved why he was never comfortable returning to Nepal. More importantly, it was the joy he so often discussed with Disha—the joy of knowing, in this case, what he wanted and what he stood for.

He left for the airport.

When he got through security at the airport, he found Disha at the gate for their flight.

"How was Mahindra?" Disha asked.

"Beliefs matter," Gatik said. "That is what I concluded. Imperfect beliefs are better than none."

Disha smiled and took his hand, and they sat quietly until the flight began boarding.

"I am glad you had a bratabandha," Disha said.

"It certainly is an interesting journey," Gatik responded, thinking of his mantra.

"I just wish my father had not forgotten his mantra, whatever it was. When we get home, I will tell you his entire story."

Soon after takeoff, Gatik noticed the plane stabilizing. He tucked the plastic bag with the painting of the scorpion under the seat in front of him, recited his mantra, and fell asleep. He had no nightmares.

Afterword

In 1990, the Jana Andolan movement created a multiparty system in Nepal, but the country continued to struggle, and an insurrection followed.

In 2008, the King of Nepal abdicated and the Communist Party of Nepal came to power. Ten prime ministers followed in the next ten years. The Royal Kumari of Kathmandu, a prepubescent girl believed to be the living manifestation of Goddess Durga, commenced an official blessing of the president of Nepal at the annual Indra Jatra festival. She traditionally had blessed the king of Nepal, considered an incarnation of God Vishnu.

All incidents, dialogue, and characters in *Moksha* are fictional and are not to be construed as real; any resemblance to actual persons, living or dead, events, or locales is entirely coincidental.